LOST
GRAVES

BOOKS BY S.A. DUNPHY

BOYLE & KENEALLY SERIES

Bring Her Home

LOST GRAVES

S.A. DUNPHY

bookouture

Published by Bookouture in 2022

An imprint of Storyfire Ltd.
Carmelite House
50 Victoria Embankment
London EC4Y 0DZ

www.bookouture.com

ISBN: 978-1-80314-061-2
eBook ISBN: 978-1-80314-060-5

For Emily, who taught me that everything is possible for those who believe.

PROLOGUE
THE BURIAL GROUND

5 November 2018

'The woods are lovely, dark and deep, but I have promises to keep...'

Robert Frost

A small boy stood in the clearing amid the oak and hazel trees and stared at the macabre object his dog had just excavated from the soil of the forest floor, gripping the animal's collar to restrain it from tearing the severed human hand apart.

'Rufus, go and get Da,' the boy said, and instantly the animal, a small brown-and-white creature that looked to be some kind of terrier mix, shot off among the trees.

His young owner took a deep breath and closed his eyes for a moment, listening.

Was he alone? He could hear birdsong: a blackbird somewhere to his left; the distinctive call of a great tit; a song thrush a little further away. The wind whispered through branches all around, and very far off in the distance, someone else's dog barked, the noise carried on the wind.

Satisfied, he opened his eyes again. Whoever had done this was long gone.

The boy was eleven years old and dressed in loose-fitting, earth-coloured clothes, his light-brown hair worn long. Squatting on his haunches, he examined the gruesome find more closely. Most children his age would have been unnerved by such a totem, but this child was not usual. He had seen death before and was painfully aware of the cruelties human beings could inflict upon one another.

He had encountered evil, this boy. And he suspected he was face to face with it again.

There was still quite a lot of flesh on the bones of the hand, but what meat there was appeared mottled and discoloured. The lad assumed the strange item had been there for at least a week, probably longer.

And he was qualified to know.

He and his father had made their living off the land in wild places for so long, the boy barely recalled what it was like to live any other way. Most of the protein they consumed they caught themselves either from traps or through hunting, but quite a few meals were the product of roadkill or accidental deaths they came across.

So being able to gauge how long something was dead was not just an academic conceit – it was a matter of survival. As this thought crossed the lad's mind, he sensed his da's approach. The man made virtually no sound as he moved swiftly through the woods, but his son was aware of him coming nonetheless.

'What is it, Finbar?'

The boy nodded towards the decaying thing at his feet.

'That.'

The man stepped forward and peered down at it. 'Rufus dug it up?'

'I thought he was after a rabbit or something he'd buried.'

The boy's father was a little under six feet tall. Dressed in the same drab, natural hues as his son, he had a shock of dark hair and a thick brow. His face, tanned and lined from exposure to the elements, was handsome and intelligent.

'I wonder if the rest of it is around here someplace.'

Finbar pointed at Rufus, who had come to a stop ten feet away.

'I think we might be about to find out.'

The dog was busily burrowing again. Finbar went to go to him, but his father shook his head. 'Leave him be.'

After about five minutes, the animal stopped and forced its nose down into the hole it had created, coming out with what looked to be a strand of long, dark material clamped between its teeth.

'Let's have a look,' the man said, and they jogged over to the animal, who, with all the strength its little body could muster, was trying to pull whatever it had uncovered from its resting place.

'Drop it, Rufus,' the boy's father said, and the dog complied immediately.

Finbar got onto his knees and tentatively picked up one of the dark filaments protruding from the ground like limp roots.

'It's like fine cord,' the boy said slowly.

The man reached into the hole and gently moved the soil aside.

'Not cordage, Finbar,' he said. 'It's hair.'

The lad looked into the opening in the damp earth and there, gazing back at him from lidless, empty eyes was a skeletal face, the skin stretched across the bones like paper. A small round hole was clearly visible in the centre of the forehead. Whoever this was had been shot with careful precision.

'I don't think this lad belongs with the hand,' the man said. 'Been dead far longer.'

Rufus was already busy in another section of the clearing.

Finbar looked at his father, concern writ large across his young face. 'What is this place, Da?'

'It's a burial ground is what it is,' the man said.

The dog found three more sets of remains in that area of the woods before they called him away. Father and son stood beneath a rowan tree in silence.

'Will we cover them back up and move on?' the boy asked.

The man walked a little way into the trees, looking back towards mounds of disturbed soil, a hand-rolled cigarette dangling from his lower lip.

'I don't think we can,' he said at last, and his voice sounded drained, exhausted.

They had been running for so long, him and the boy. But they couldn't run from this.

'Why not?'

'People know we're here. If someone else finds these, they'll think it was us and then we'll have the police on our trail as well as... as well as the others.'

'What are we going to do then?'

The man took a long pull on his smoke and exhaled through his nose.

'I guess we go into town and we see the Gardaí, Finbar,' he said. 'Let them know what we've come across out here.'

'You always told me never to trust the cops,' the boy said. 'They don't like our people.'

'That lesson still stands,' the man said. 'But here's another for you: you have to pick your battles.'

'Won't they make it hard for us?'

The man picked a piece of tobacco from his tongue and whistled for the dog to follow them.

'I have a feelin' we've only found a small portion of what's here. We have to hope the truth wins out. At least one of the ones Rufus unearthed has been in the ground for more than a year, and we've only been here three days. Common sense says this couldn't have been us.'

'Okay, Da.'

'Let's get it done. Sooner we do, sooner it'll be over and we can be on our way.'

Joe Keenan would live to regret those words.

But by then, he had other things on his mind.

PART ONE

A FOREST

7 November 2018

'In my dream I see before me a forest of crucifixes which gradually turn into trees. At first there appears to be dew or rain dripping from the branches, but as I approach, I realise it is blood.'

John Haigh, The Acid Bath Murderer

1

'We'll get something to eat as soon as we speak to the lead detective,' Jessie Boyle said.

Jessie, forty-five years old, six feet half an inch in height, with short dark hair framing a strong, intelligent face, was standing with her partner, Detective Sergeant Seamus Keneally outside the police station on Sligo Town's main street. Slim but strong, she wore a long woollen overcoat over blue jeans, which today was paired with a Gillian Welch T-shirt.

Seamus was twenty-eight years old and six foot two tall, lean and rangy, dressed in a grey suit over a grey shirt and blue tie, which was slightly askew. Clean-shaven, his auburn hair was worn in a crew cut that, short though it was, somehow managed to seem a little messy and in need of a trim. He was looking at Jessie with an unhappy expression.

Jessie, a criminal behaviourist, and Seamus, a decorated police detective, along with genealogist and tech specialist Terri Kehoe, made up a team formed by the newly appointed Irish Police commissioner Dawn Wilson, tasked to investigate cases of violent crime that standard police procedure had failed to progress.

They were in Sligo to assist on just such a case.

'I don't see how half an hour will make much difference,' Seamus said. 'We've been driving since daybreak and you didn't stop once. If my blood sugar gets low, you know I get cranky.'

'I don't see how your blood sugar can have plummeted,' Jessie said. 'While I drove, you slept! Now stop complaining and let's go and see what's brought us here.'

'I would like it noted for the record that I am complying under sufferance,' Seamus said but followed her into the station.

The detective they had travelled across the country to see was a hard-faced man named Josh Glenn. In his early fifties, the blue shadow of a thick beard was visible about his jawline. Jessie thought he must have to shave a couple of times a day to keep it in check. The man's dark hair was worn long and gelled back from his forehead.

When Jessie and Seamus sat down to talk to him in the station's only meeting room, a spartan space with bare magnolia walls containing only a long table and six straight-backed chairs, he was wearing a leather jacket over a denim shirt and black jeans.

'I don't know why they sent you two,' he said in an accent Jessie thought sounded pretty close to Seamus's rolling Kerry lilt.

'We're just here to help out,' she said. 'I've read the file, but could you run through the facts of the case for me again?'

'There's not much to run through,' Glenn said. 'At five minutes after five on the fifth of November, a man who identified himself as Joseph Keenan, claiming to be a Traveller originally from County Wexford, walked into the police station in Ballinamore, a small town in County Leitrim. He informed the desk sergeant that his dog – he had the animal in an unregistered 1986 Ford Transit van outside – had dug up some human remains in the Derrada Woods, near where he and his son were camping. The van has been impounded as evidence.'

'According to the files I read, the van is modified?'

'Yeah. Quite ingenious really. It's not a big vehicle, but it's been turned into one of those tiny homes, you know like the ones you see on TV shows? I was amazed at how much he's managed to pack into it. Beds, cooking gear, a toilet and shower, a table and sitting area, and under the floor there were storage units *and* some secret compartments, which is where we found his weapons – an old revolver and a shotgun.'

'Were the weapons used in any of the murders?' Jessie asked.

Glenn shuffled in his seat. 'So far, forensics have drawn a blank on that.'

Jessie gave the detective a hard look. 'So that would be a "no" then.'

Glenn shrugged.

'To be clear, this man reported the remains?' Seamus asked.

'Yes. Not in detail – just that his dog had been digging and had unearthed some bones. That was a pretty big understatement.'

'Did he give an exact location?'

'He brought Waters – the officer on duty – out there and showed him. As soon as he had a sense of the scope of what they were dealing with, Waters called us here and a team was sent out. The lads in Leitrim, well, they aren't used to dealing with real crime, if you know what I mean. Leitrim has a tiny population, and the police forces of the two counties were combined a few years back. Most of the heavy lifting gets done here in Sligo.'

'So they mostly deal with cattle and the illegal sale of green diesel,' Seamus said. 'Did you see the scene yourself before forensics took it apart?'

'Yes. I was the first from the Sligo station on site.'

'And? Did his story seem plausible to you?'

'What do you mean?'

'Did it look like a dog had dug up some bones that turned out to be human?'

'I'm not a forensic expert, Seamus. What I saw was a burial ground that had been disturbed. I don't know which animal did it – those woods are full of foxes and badgers and, in recent years, wild boar too. Any of those could have been responsible.'

'I'm curious as to why you've arrested Mr Keenan, seeing as he reported the remains immediately,' Jessie observed. 'You're admitting it looked like an animal dug up the bones, but I can't see why you think Keenan had anything to do with putting them into the ground in the first place.'

'The whole site looks like a burial ground to me – somewhere for the Travellers to put their dead after one of their feuds or faction fights or whatever mayhem they've been up to. I think Joe Keenan was sent to make a body disappear, got there and found the place had become unstable due to too many corpses being placed there over too long a time. You've heard of graveyards where the earth starts to push the coffins back above ground? I reckon that's what was happening here, and he panicked.'

'How soon did forensics arrive?' Jessie wanted to know.

'We cordoned off the area and they got there yesterday morning. They're based out of Dublin, so it always takes time for them to come this far north.'

'And what did they have to say about it all?'

'They went to work and, as we'd figured out already, the whole clearing was a charnel pit. Ten distinct sets of complete human remains were found, along with three sundry limbs that didn't belong to any of them.'

'Do you know the causes of death yet?'

'Various. Three had been shot execution style. Two had their throats cut. After that it's varying degrees of unpleasantness. The pathologist can go into specifics with you at the postmortem. I want to sleep tonight, so I'll pass on it.'

Jessie grimaced. 'A mixed MO,' she said. 'Can you be sure this was all done by one person?'

'Does it matter?' Glenn asked, his voice becoming hard. 'Even if Joe Keenan only did one of them, he deserves to be locked up.'

'And you're sure Joe Keenan is guilty of anything other than being in the wrong place at the wrong time?' Jessie said. 'He did report it. Not exactly the act of a hardened killer.'

'Pure trickery and an attempt to look sympathetic,' Glenn spat back. 'He's very good at playing the sympathy card. All his crowd are.'

'You mean members of the Traveller community?' Jessie asked.

'I mean knackers, yes.'

'I take it you're not a fan of their way of life,' Seamus said.

'I'm sick to death of cleaning up the messes they leave behind,' Glenn seethed. 'We've had more than one feud to deal with in the Sligo/Leitrim area, and the bodies in that clearing could well be the result of a major bust-up that got out of control. I've seen worse, let me tell you.'

'It still doesn't explain why he didn't run,' Jessie said. 'He's a Traveller, and one who still lives nomadically. It makes no sense for him to stay put if he's guilty of what you suggest.'

'It makes perfect sense,' Glenn snorted. 'There were check-points on all approaches to and from Ballinamore that day. Some sheep had been stolen from Quirke's Meadow, and road-blocks were set up to prevent them being taken outside the area. Keenan knew he was hemmed in. So he played the only card he had left – appealing to our pity.'

'Have you established a plan towards identifying any of the remains yet?'

'No. We took DNA samples, fingerprinted any that we could, checked dental records... and nothing. We don't know who any of them are. And that, Ms Boyle, fits the theory that they're Travellers. Those guys don't like leaving records or being on the system anywhere. I'm telling you, that's what we're dealing with here. A feud gone too far.'

'How long had the bodies been in the ground?'

'The oldest for five years, the most recent a month. The others various points in between.'

'And this Joe Keenan person is local?' Seamus asked.

'According to the file, he says he's only been in Leitrim for a matter of days,' Jessie said. 'Have you looked into that?'

'He says a lot of things. Doesn't mean they're true.'

'Have you confirmed when he got here?' Seamus asked. 'That's a simple enough matter surely.'

'We're looking into it,' Glenn said drily. 'Keenan says he's feuding with one of the big Traveller clans, a group called the Dunnes. It makes sense the bodies are a result of that feud.'

'You're dealing with one guy, living off-grid with his young son and a dog,' Jessie said. 'Is your hypothesis that he waged a one-man war against this clan?'

'It's a theory. And the Dunnes are not unknown in this neck of the woods either. They pass through here from time to time. They're a bad lot. Basically a criminal gang.'

'Which surely makes it more likely *they're* behind the bodies,' Seamus said.

'I think you're approaching this in entirely the wrong way, if you don't mind my saying,' Jessie put in.

Glenn looked at her aghast, but if Jessie noticed his expression, she paid it no heed and just kept going.

'You've based your entire case around pinning the deaths on the most convenient suspect. You've made virtually no effort to find out who the dead are and have bought into a theory that has nothing to commend it other than it's easy.'

'How am I supposed to identify the bodies? There's nothing to go on!'

'Have you talked to the pathologist?' Seamus asked. 'The

trails might be cold, but the longer you leave it, the colder they'll get.'

'Finding out who the bodies in the woods were will help you find out who killed them,' Jessie said evenly. 'In my humble opinion, *that's* where your investigation needs to be directed. Joe Keenan is probably a dead end.'

'All I know is that something about that man doesn't sit well with me,' Glenn said, his voice heavy with annoyance.

'Could you tell me what exactly?'

'He's like a... a blank slate, and he just writes whatever story the situation requires on it,' Glenn said. 'I mean, how do we even know his name is Joe Keenan? He doesn't have a passport. He claims to have lost his driver's licence. He has no social security number, no papers for his vehicle and no income that I can discern, not even the dole. The same applies to his son, who hasn't attended school for years, according to what he told his carers. These people are ghosts.'

'It doesn't mean they're guilty ghosts,' Jessie said.

'The whole thing is rotten,' Glenn replied. 'And he's in it up to his neck.'

'On what charges has Mr Keenan been arrested?' Seamus asked.

'Currently for holding firearms illegally and failure to display current tax and insurance on a vehicle that has not passed an NCT. The discs and certificates he did have on display are all counterfeits.'

'No judge is going to give him a custodial sentence for failing to have an insurance disc,' Jessie said.

'No, but the guns could bag him a five-year stretch. And it gives us an excuse to hold him while we continue to process the scene.'

'With a view to conclusively linking him to the murders?'

'With a view to crossing him off our list of suspects, if that makes it more comfortable for you,' Glenn said drolly.

'Who else is on the list?'

'At the moment, it's a short one.'

Jessie tapped her fingers on the table, thinking. 'You're near the border with Northern Ireland here.'

'Leitrim is a border county, yes.'

'Could the bodies be linked to terrorist activity?'

'We are exploring that possibility.'

Jessie nodded. 'And do you suspect Joe Keenan is a member of the continuity IRA or a similar group?'

'We're ruling nothing out at present.'

'I'm not aware of many Travellers who're involved in that kind of political activism,' Seamus said.

'That doesn't mean one can't be though, does it? And Travellers are *certainly* involved in organised crime. The Rathkeale Rovers are just one example.'

Jessie knew he was right about that – the Rathkeale Rovers were a major international crime syndicate made up of Irish Travellers that Interpol had been trying to shut down for more than a decade. They were involved in everything from dealing in ground rhino horn to trafficking in stolen art, and while they were not known to be excessively violent, they were still not a group you'd want to cross.

'Did you check traffic cameras or the passenger manifests of boats arriving here from the UK to see when, exactly, Joe arrived into the country?' she asked. 'He says he's only recently returned from the UK.'

'This isn't the only case on the books,' Glenn said. 'And we're a very small team.'

'Meaning you haven't then?'

'It didn't feel like a priority.'

Jessie nodded. 'So your working theory is that the bodies in the woods are the victims either of a Traveller feud or terrorist activity, and that Joe Keenan, either on his own or in the company of as yet unknown accomplices, is the murderer.'

'That's about it, yeah.'

'But you can't prove that one way or the other.'

'I will.'

'How? You've got a murderer who decided to draw attention to his crimes by presenting himself at a police station and bringing the local Garda to the place he'd buried his victims, thereby giving the authorities all the evidence they needed to lock him up for the rest of his natural life. That doesn't seem plausible either.'

'People do strange things,' Glenn said.

'Has it occurred to you at all that there's a murderer on the loose in the area, and that he may strike again?' Jessie asked. 'You're gambling the safety of the local population on the fact that Joe Keenan is guilty. That seems a deeply foolhardy risk to me.'

Glenn scowled and fiddled with his watch strap.

'I am in deadly earnest,' Jessie pressed. 'What you have is either the work of a single individual who's extremely disturbed and very dangerous, or a group of killers organised enough to hide their activities for an extended period. Neither option is good.'

'I'll take it under advisement,' Glenn said without emotion.

Jessie looked at Seamus, who looked back, both unsure what to say.

'Thanks for your time,' she said eventually – and, not bothering to shake the detective's hand, the pair walked out feeling angry and a little ill. 'Luckily for you, Seamus and I take circumstances like this very seriously. We *will* find out who the bodies are, and we're pretty damn good at catching killers.'

Josh Glenn seemed unmoved by this declaration.

2

Jessie and Seamus met Professor Julia Banks, Ireland's state pathologist, in the medical laboratory in University College Galway at eleven that morning. They stopped so Seamus could grab a sandwich along the way, so he was in a better mood.

The lab was long, painted a vivid white and smelled of chemicals Jessie couldn't identify. Myriad lights of varying wattage and a series of large magnifying glasses had been suspended from the high ceiling on jointed metal arms that could be manoeuvred into whichever position the professor required. The ten bodies and orphaned limbs were arrayed on autopsy tables, a grisly display of the horrors human beings so often inflicted upon one another.

Seamus approached the visit with the same degree of boyish fascination he brought to almost everything he did. While certainly respectful, he peered at the medical equipment as if it were magician's wands and potions. Jessie had the feeling she often experienced with her partner: she was mildly irritated by him, while simultaneously charmed.

For her, being in that room carried a heavy sense of duty.

Jessie wasn't squeamish, and her entire adult life had

involved her working closely with death. Yet somehow, being in such proximity to the remains of living, breathing, laughing people, people whose hopes and dreams had been prematurely ended, always made her feel the weight of her responsibilities acutely. It was almost like these cadavers were singing out to her, begging for atonement.

If Julia Banks heard the song, she seemed unmoved by it. All brusque business, she was a small, broadly built woman with short, grey hair and a wide, smiling face.

'I don't know what you're looking for,' she said. 'I've put everything I know into my report, and that's very little. I can tell you when they died, I have a fair idea *how* they died, but as to who they are and *why* they died, I can't help you.'

Jessie walked from table to table, pausing here and there to look at what was resting upon them.

'I have no idea what I'm looking for either,' she said thoughtfully. 'I suppose I just wanted to have a look at what we're dealing with.'

'Well, feel free to get acquainted.'

Seamus was leaning down and peering at a bundle of what looked like little more than bones.

'I often wonder how you know these all belong to the same person,' he said.

'Are you looking for a lecture on skeletal recognition?'

'Um... no, I'll take a pass on that.'

'In your report you say the victims were all male,' Jessie cut in.

'Yes. All aged between twenty-five and fifty.'

'Were they all of good health? They looked after themselves?'

'Yes. All were in fine fettle before they met their demise.'

'How fine?'

'What do you mean?'

'I'm looking at ways we might identify them. Does it look

like they might have been members of a gym? Could you tell if they'd been taking vitamin supplements? I'm wondering about their economic backgrounds.'

'I would say these people all paid attention to their physical fitness. As to the rest, I can't say for certain. However, if I had to guess, I'd say you're looking at a group of middle-class individuals, or at least people with access to money.'

'Why do you say that?'

'Remains number three showed signs that his nails had been manicured. Remains number seven had a large swathe of skin flayed from his right arm post-mortem. The only reason I can discern for that would be to remove a tattoo which could be an identifier. Ink on that scale is expensive.'

'Did you identify any surgical procedures I might be able to follow up?'

'The majority were in too bad a state of decomposition for me to ascertain that. The two that weren't showed no evidence of any such procedures.'

'Dental records drew a blank too?' Jessie asked.

'Initially. But I did actually have something of a break-through on that front yesterday. I don't know if it will help, but it's the only lead the bodies offer. Here – you'll want to see this.'

She motioned for Jessie to take a position beside her at the computer.

'Remains number ten are those of the most recent body, the one that was killed only a month ago,' she said. 'Now in terms of his dentition, there wasn't a lot we could tell. Most of the teeth were missing.'

'Had they been removed on purpose?' Jessie asked.

'In a manner of speaking,' the pathologist said. 'They'd been knocked out by force. Probably during a sustained beating. This person was tortured pretty brutally before he was put in the ground. There were a few teeth left though, and on one of them, we found this.'

Julia clicked her mouse and a magnified photograph of a tooth appeared on the monitor.

'Here's one of the remaining teeth. A bicuspid. Notice anything about it?'

Jessie peered at the image. 'You're going to have to help me,' she said.

'It's been capped,' Julia Banks said. 'Some people call it "crowning" the tooth.'

'Isn't that quite common?' Jessie asked.

'It is. The delay on flagging this little nugget of information is that it took me some time to find out exactly what this cap was made of, because it's a little unusual. It's made of a very specific type of porcelain, one that most dentists don't use.'

'Why not?'

'It's expensive,' Julia said, 'so not much in demand. Getting a set would have put this person back about nine thousand euro.'

'If he got his dentistry done here in Ireland,' Jessie said.

'Well, I suppose you can't rule out that he mightn't,' Julia agreed. 'But let's try and be positive, shall we?'

'Can you tell me how long he'd had the crowns in before his death?'

'This one is barely worn at all,' the pathologist said. 'So I would guess he'd only got them very recently.'

'Now that is interesting,' Jessie said, looking at the screen and then across the room at the table that held remains number ten. 'If we can locate the dentists that carry out that procedure, we might just find out who he is.'

'Whoever he was, he lived well, from what I can see,' Julia said. 'But he died hard. Of that I'm very certain.'

'Let's see if we can't put a name to you,' Jessie said to what was left of the body.

It didn't answer.

'While we're here, could you tell us if any of the victims were members of the Travelling community?' Seamus piped up.

Julia Banks gave him a sharp look, and Jessie could see that, despite her recent assurance, this was something the pathologist had, in fact, not thought of.

'Off the top of my head I don't know,' the older woman said, her tone suggesting she was interested in this new puzzle.

'It may be relevant,' Seamus said. 'We're looking at the possibility these people might be victims of a Traveller feud, or perhaps fell foul of organised crime within the Travelling community.'

The pathologist pulled over a computer on a rolling table and punched a few keys.

'The quickest way to find out would be through the genetic coding within the DNA samples taken,' she said. 'Travellers split from the rest of the Irish population sometime in the fifteenth century. So their DNA is distinct, if you know what you're looking for.'

'Wouldn't you have seen that right away?' Jessie asked.

'I'd like to think so,' the pathologist said, her eyes still on the monitor. 'But as you've pointed out, I wasn't looking for it. So maybe not.'

Jessie waited as she continued to click the mouse and scroll through data. A couple of minutes later, she said, 'None of the remains belong to members of the Travelling community. There is, in fact, nothing distinctive in any of their genetic make-up. They're all the type of mixed Europeans you'd expect to see.'

'That's interesting,' Jessie said.

'I would have thought it was the exact opposite of interesting,' Julia retorted.

'It doesn't mean the Traveller clan isn't responsible,' Seamus said.

'No, but it makes it significantly less likely,' Jessie replied.

'So where does that leave us?'

'Nowhere good,' Jessie sighed. 'What I'm seeing looks to be scattergun in its approach. There's no cohesion.'

Seamus shrugged. 'So?'

'We're looking at someone who may be killing indiscriminately. And there's nothing more dangerous than that.'

'Lovely,' Seamus said.

'My thoughts exactly,' Jessie said. 'I think it's time we spoke to the chief suspect.'

3

Ballinamore, in south County Leitrim, claimed to be a town, though Jessie thought it seemed more like a village – and a small one at that.

She supposed such designations must be relative, depending on the county in question.

Like most rural Irish towns, the place consisted of a single broad main street with five tributaries running off it. As she piloted her orange 1973 MGB GT into town, Jessie spotted a small supermarket, a bank, some pubs, a mobile-phone store, a chip shop and a clothes boutique – so she supposed it had everything a body would need. The place was pretty too, there was no denying that, its shopfronts painted a panoply of bright colours, the signs and facades all done in an olde-worlde style.

The street sloped upwards in a shallow gradient, and in the pale light of an autumn afternoon, it was hard not to like the place. Jessie was adept at bearing a grudge against the rural idyll though. Her last stay in the countryside had proven traumatic, and she had no desire to repeat it.

'Why do they insist on sending us to such desolate places?'

she asked her partner as she spotted the small police station and pulled up across the road from it.

'We go where we're needed,' Seamus said, attempting to lighten the mood. 'This one is a puzzler though. I'm not sure what to make of it.'

'I know,' Jessie acknowledged. 'Look, we'll interview the suspect and see what we can learn. Now that Terri is setting up our permanent offices in Cork, we'll have a base of operations located somewhere civilised at least. Even if we aren't likely to see much of it for the next few days.'

Seamus shook his head. 'One city is much the same as any other to me, Jessie,' he said as they crossed the road. 'I'd prefer to work out of a place like this any day of the week.'

They arrived at the door of the police station, and, finding it closed and apparently locked, Jessie pressed the button on an intercom system set into the wall at eye level. There was silence for a few moments, and then the box buzzed into life.

'Who is it please?'

'Boyle and Keneally from the NBCI,' Jessie said.

There was a pause.

'Doyle and who did you say?'

Jessie looked at Seamus without the slightest hint of amusement.

'We have been asked to come here to interview a prisoner. We've had a long drive and we would like to get the job done as quickly as possible. Now open up and let us in please.'

For several long moments it looked as if the door was going to remain closed, then there was a buzzing sound and the tumblers in the lock did their thing, and Seamus pushed the door open.

The single-storeyed building looked as if it had once been a worker's cottage. A reception area had been cordoned off in front of them, and through a glass panel behind that Jessie and Seamus could see a work area with a couple of desks in front of a wall lined with grey filing cabinets. There was no one about, so Seamus called out, 'Hello, the house!'

'This looks like it's going to be a complete waste of time,' Jessie grumbled, but just as she said it, a door at the back of the work room opened and a middle-aged Garda with a very prominent paunch pressing against his blue uniform shirt and a receding hairline came bustling out.

'You're the team from Dublin?' he asked, coming out to the front desk and extending a hand to them both.

'I'm Jessie Boyle – this is Detective Seamus Keneally. Commissioner Wilson asked that we speak with the man you're holding.'

'I'm Frank Waters,' the Garda said, shaking with each of them.

'You've still got the suspect here,' Jessie observed. 'Wouldn't it be more convenient and cost-effective to move him to Castlerea – that's the closest prison, isn't it?'

'He requested to remain with us,' Waters said. 'Says he'll be in danger in a prison envir'nment.'

'Has he a record?' Seamus asked. 'I don't remember seeing mention of it on the paperwork we were given.'

'Not that we know of, but sure he's got no ID nor any kind of papers with him. Like, he could be anyone. Joe Keenan says he's a Traveller. A tinker, like, and I'll grant he does seem to be. Now, I'm often prepared to give a bit of leeway, as them lads tend to live by their own rules. But this fella, he turns up out of nowhere, livin' in the woods like a fuckin' wild man, and then we find a load of bodies? You can't let that go. Traveller or not.'

'What does his being a Traveller have to do with him not wanting to be in the general prison population?' Jessie asked. 'Is it relating to this feud Detective Glenn told us about?'

'Ah, they're always feudin' with one another,' Waters said. 'He's fallen foul of one of the clans, which means his life expectancy will get *very* feckin' short if they get their mitts on him.'

'Which he believes they will if he's moved to Castlerea,' Seamus added.

'Or Mountjoy, or Limerick, or Cork, or any of them,' Waters said. 'There isn't a prison in the country doesn't have a good few Travellers among its inmates. He's right – he probably wouldn't survive for long.'

'If he is responsible for the bodies you found in the woods, he soon won't have any choice,' Seamus observed. 'He can't stay here forever.'

'Let's cross that bridge when we come to it,' Waters said philosophically.

'Can we go and talk to him now?' Jessie asked, the impatience evident in her voice.

'Knock yourselves out,' the uniformed Garda said.

'Thank you.' Jessie gave him a cold smile. 'A cup of tea might make things go easier.'

The fat cop snorted. 'Would ye like some chocolate biscuits with that?'

'I brought some with me,' Jessie said, producing a pack from the voluminous pocket of her long woollen coat. 'Would you show us where he is please?'

4

Jessie asked that Joe Keenan be permitted to leave his cell, and she arranged chairs for them in the work room of the tiny station. Waters begrudgingly brought them tea and all the fixings and then cleared his throat and said he'd wait at the front desk while they talked.

Jessie thanked him and busied herself pouring drinks for them all, applying milk and sugar to the cups as needed, ripping open the plastic wrapping on the packet of chocolate digestives and generally playing the good hostess.

'Help yourself,' she said as she sat down. 'I can't imagine the food is particularly good here.'

Joe, whom she took to be in his late thirties, shrugged, but he took two of the biscuits anyway.

Jessie had interviewed many violent criminals over her career, and there were a number of things she looked out for when encountering one for the first time.

Most made every effort to establish dominance, even the ones who started by trying to lull her into a false sense of security. They would use their height by repeatedly standing to look over her, try to make her uncomfortable by maintaining eye contact beyond where it was reasonable. Some would use erratic changes in the volume of their speech to try and elicit fear.

There was often a sexual element to their conversation too. References would be made to their romantic prowess, former partners they'd had, how well endowed they were. Jessie was aware she was an attractive woman (it wasn't humble to admit such things, but she permitted herself the luxury of accepting that men – and more than a few women – were drawn to her), and that made her a prime target for such psychological assaults.

And serial offenders, particularly serial killers, wanted you to *know* they'd committed their crimes. This was usually a subtle dance, as the majority didn't want to be arrested. But they would find a way to inform the investigator they'd done it. A hint here. A word there. Nothing prosecutable. But always enough to get the message across.

Jessie knew within moments that Joe Keenan was different. She glanced at Seamus and was aware he saw it too. The man in front of them seemed tired rather than full of false bravado. He was obviously unhappy to be in his current situation and carried an air of resignation about him. He took his seat without any fuss or bluster, and while he looked both of them in the eye when they introduced themselves, he did so respectfully.

And when he spoke, he was calm and measured in his speech.

'It's been fish and chips from the takeaway across the street the past couple of nights,' he said. 'Waters there is all right. He's been kind enough. The other fella who works here, Mitchell, he's a bollix, if you pardon my using the word, miss. Doesn't like Travellers and told me as much the first time he was on shift.'

'If you're treated badly at all, let me know,' Jessie said,

passing a card across to him. 'I'm sure Waters will allow you a phone call. Tell him you're ringing your solicitor.'

'He knows I don't have one.' Joe took a pouch of tobacco from the pocket of his shirt and began to roll a cigarette.

'They've offered you a state-appointed one though,' Seamus asked.

'They did, but I don't want one. What feckin' difference would it make? They've decided to stitch me up for them bodies my young lad found, and there's not a thing I can do about it.'

'Mr Keenan, you're very foolish to refuse legal representation,' Jessie said.

'You can call me Joe,' the man said, sticking his smoke into the corner of his mouth and taking a box of safety matches from his jeans. 'And let's agree to disagree on the matter for the moment.'

He's accepting a difference of opinion, Jessie thought. *That's a good sign. He isn't offended that I'm not bowing to his superiority.*

It was another sign that Joe Keenan did not fit the usual profile of a serial killer.

'I'll be returning to it though, so be warned,' Jessie said.

'Fair enough. Now. Who the hell are ye, if you don't mind my asking? You don't look or sound like locals. You're a Dub, but you've lived in England for a bit, by the sound of your accent.' Joe looked at Seamus for a moment. 'And you're from Kerry, if I'm not mistaken.'

'You've got a good ear,' Jessie said. 'I worked for the London Metropolitan Police for almost twenty years, and Seamus is from Cahirsiveen. We're part of a special task force set up by the police commissioner to investigate serious crimes, and we'd like to ask you a few questions.'

'I have nothing to say that I haven't already said,' Joe retorted. 'How is Finbar doing? Me lad? They won't tell me anything about him.'

Jessie glanced at Seamus, who took a notebook from the inside pocket of his jacket and scribbled something in it.

'I'll check up on that and let you know as soon as possible,' she said.

'Me and the lad haven't been parted since he was very small. He's tough and he'll do okay, but *I* need to know he's all right. I'm not as strong as he is.'

An admission of emotional frailty, Jessie thought. *He's telling me he misses his son. A sociopath would see that as a sign of weakness.*

'I promise I'll find out.'

'And Rufus. What happened to him?'

Seamus looked puzzled. 'I thought you only had one child.'

'Rufus is my dog. Well... he's Finbar's really. He's a Jack Russell/bichon frise mix. Smart as a tack. Finbar dotes on him.'

'We'll chase Rufus up too,' Jessie said. 'I'm afraid the fact you have a dog is only mentioned in passing in the paperwork. But I'm sure he's fine.'

'I hope so,' Joe said, and for a moment Jessie saw that he was bereft and close to exhaustion.

He hid it well, and presented as reasonably self-contained, but he was obviously desperately worried about his little family. Maybe that was something they could work with.

He didn't do this, Jessie thought with a prickling of foreboding. *He's innocent. Which means there's no doubt the killer is still out there. And could be planning something else as I sit here.*

'Here's what I'm going to propose,' she said. 'Let's have a chat about what happened in the woods, and when we're finished, I'll find out where your son and your dog are and see if I can't arrange a visit.'

'You can do that? Waters there will let you?'

'I hate to pull rank, but I work for the boss of his boss's boss's boss,' Jessie said. 'I think I can make it happen.'

Joe Keenan took a drag on his cigarette and exhaled smoke in a single plume through his right nostril. 'Okay then. What do you want to know?'

5

'We'd been in England for a couple of years – Finbar, Rufus and me,' Joe said once Jessie had replenished his cup and he'd rolled another smoke. 'But we got wrapped up in something over there, and I thought it might be better to head home for a while.'

'What did you get wrapped up in?' Jessie asked.

'Nothin' illegal. In fact, I ended up helpin' a couple of your lot – cops, like – with a... a difficult situation in some woods near the Scottish border. Saved one of their lives, I did too.'

'Can you tell me what happened?'

'It don't make no difference to what's goin' on right now,' Joe said. 'And I don't have the time nor the energy to get into it.'

'Why did you come home then?' Seamus asked. 'Waters tells us you've some people with a grudge against you.'

Joe sighed and rubbed his hand through his thick dark hair. 'We'd drawn attention to ourselves. They would have got wind of it. Sent people to find us.'

'Who would, Joe?' Seamus asked.

'The Dunnes,' he replied. 'They've got a death call out on me. Me and Finbar.'

'That's like a contract?' Jessie asked.

'There's no money involved,' Seamus said. 'It's an honour thing. Joe, you must have insulted them in some way.'

'Well that's the way they see it anyway.'

'Want to share what happened?' Jessie asked.

'Let's just say we had a disagreement,' he said. 'And they told me that if I ever crossed their paths again, they'd see me dead.'

'Yet here you are back in Ireland.'

'Bein' in the UK didn't make no difference. They still came after me. Might as well be here.'

'They sent people to England to find you?'

'We went as far as Latvia, but they still came after us,' Joe said. 'I got good at hidin', but they sent hunters. Me and Finbar nearly didn't make it a few times.'

'So you came to Leitrim because it isn't crowded?' Seamus asked.

'Lots of open spaces to hide in,' he agreed. 'Places I can see them comin'.'

'When did you arrive in Ballinamore?' Jessie asked.

'Rufus dug up those bodies and the other bits and pieces on our fourth morning here. And I came straight into town and reported it. Is that the behaviour of a guilty man?'

'You drive a modified Ford Transit camper van?' Jessie asked.

'Yes. I did all the work on it myself.'

'Of the remains that were retrieved from the site, two had bullet holes in them,' Seamus said. 'And two firearms were retrieved from a hidden compartment in the Transit: an antique Enfield revolver and a double-barrelled Mauser shotgun. Are these weapons yours, Joe?'

'They are. And before you ask, no, I don't have licences or any of that shite for them. So if you want to have me for that, fair enough. I don't know much about crime detection and the like, but I do know that bullets and the holes they make are kind of a science. I'm damned sure that if you inspect the holes in those bodies, you'll find they weren't made by any of the guns I own.'

'We'll check that – you can be certain we will,' Jessie said.

'Look, here's the bottom line,' Joe Keenan said, sitting forward.

The pain and anxiety in his face was evident. Jessie looked and saw humanity rather than predation. She was sure Seamus did too.

'We got to the Derrada Woods less than a week ago. Those bodies, all of them, were there longer than that. I came across them by accident, and all I can tell you is that's where they were lying before I got there, just where my dog found them. I'm certain you have traffic cameras and what all else that can show exactly when my van, which is easy enough to spot, arrived into Ireland and travelled across the country to arrive in Ballinamore. Won't that prove I didn't bury those bodies in the trees?'

Jessie looked at Seamus and nodded.

'I'm going to make some calls and see if we can't find your boy,' Jessie said.

'I'd surely be grateful,' Joe Keenan said.

'Do me a favour in return then,' Jessie said. 'Tell me what happened in the UK. I know you said it has no bearing on your current situation, but I've learned over a lot of years doing this work that you shouldn't rule anything out.'

Joe nodded and sighed and told her how he and his son had helped an Irish criminologist named David Dunnigan to find a serial killer named Mother Joan in a forest in Northumberland, and how in so-doing the little family found themselves in the middle of a gang war.

By the time he was finished, Jessie needed no further confirmation that this was not the person responsible for the forest burial ground.

6

Jessie and Seamus went out to the front desk, where Waters was scrolling through Facebook on his phone.

'Where's his kid?' Jessie asked the Garda.

'A residential childcare unit out on the Carrick-on-Shannon road.'

'Why hasn't he been allowed a visit?'

'He's being held under suspicion of multiple homicides!' the fat man spluttered. 'We're not runnin' a holiday camp, for feck's sake!'

'You're local,' Seamus said. 'Surely you know when he arrived in town?'

'Look, I'm only the messenger boy in all this,' Waters said ruefully. 'My job is to watch over him.'

'So you've not done any investigating at all?' Jessie asked incredulously.

'The station is usually manned once a week. The only reason I'm here at all is because yer man is being kept here.'

'I'm going to organise for Joe to see his boy,' Jessie said.

Waters shrugged. 'No odds to me. The sarge might have something to say about it though.'

'Well I'll be happy to hear whatever he has to offer,' Jessie said. 'What happened to Joe's dog?'

'Dog warden took it,' Waters said, returning to his scrolling.

'Do you have a number for the pound?'

'Why don't you google it?' Waters drawled without looking up.

'Thanks for your help,' Jessie said, deadpan.

'Animal's probably been destroyed by now anyway,' the cop said nonchalantly as the two investigators went out the door.

Seamus paused and in three steps was back at the desk, leaning down so he was nose to nose with Waters.

'You'd better hope not,' he said. 'If I find out that dog has been put to sleep, I'll see to it that someone rings this office in the middle of the night at least five times a week to report break-ins or intruder alerts in out-of-the-way places, and you'll have to haul your fat arse out of bed to see to them. And you'll *have to*, Frank, because some of them might just be real, and if you fail to respond, your career will be over and you'll forfeit your pension. So if you want to keep your job and enjoy your beauty sleep, you'd best pray that animal is still able to wag its tail and play fetch.'

All the colour ran out of the indolent guard's face, and, having made his point, Seamus followed his partner back out onto the street.

7

'Joe Keenan's not the guy,' Seamus said as soon as they were outside.

'No,' Jessie said. 'He isn't.'

They crossed the road and got into the MG.

'So what next?' Seamus asked.

'I'm going to go and see if I can't get social services to arrange for Joe to see his kid.'

Seamus chewed his lower lip for a moment.

'I don't have a problem with him seeing his son,' he said. 'But it isn't *usual* when a man is in custody. Not over the short term anyway. Why are you so keen on them being reunited so soon?'

'The boy was there when the bodies were found, and it seems to me that no one has talked to him at all about what he saw. If these two have been living in the wild for quite a few years, the kid might have a perspective on things that could be useful. We've a killer at large in a small community – we need all the input we can get to eliminate the threat.'

'And we can't talk to him without an adult present,' Seamus said, following her line of logic.

'Exactly. We can kill two birds with one stone. Will you go out and have a look at the burial site?'

'Will do. I'll call the dog warden too. Make sure that animal doesn't get put down.'

Jessie was entering coordinates into the Google Maps app on her phone and paused, giving her partner an odd look. 'You seem very bothered about the dog, Seamus.'

He shrugged, looking uncomfortable at having attention drawn to it. 'I dunno. No reason for the poor animal to suffer, is there?'

'Did you have a pet dog you loved when you were a boy?' Jessie wanted to know. 'Or maybe your mam wouldn't let you have one.'

'Don't feckin' analyse me, Jessie Boyle!' Seamus said, giving her a hard look as he climbed out of the car. 'I'll see if Waters can loan me a squad car for the afternoon.'

'Good idea. I'll ring when I've spoken to social services,' Jessie called after him. 'Will you organise some accommodation for us too? It looks like we're going to be here for a few days at least.'

'Not quite the open-and-shut case we thought it'd be,' Seamus said.

'Which is why the commissioner sent us, I suppose,' Jessie said. 'I'll see you soon.'

And she did a U-turn in the main street and turned the orange sports car for Carrick-on-Shannon, where the offices of the social work department were situated.

8

Jessie called Terri Kehoe during her drive.

As well as being something of a genius when it came to computers and the Internet, Terri was a historian by qualification and a genealogist by trade, meaning she was an expert in following the trajectory of a person's life, tracing their family line through myriad records and databases. Terri had been able to use these skills to assist the police in a murder case involving a dispute over a land title, and in so doing was instrumental in bringing a killer to justice. This brought her to the attention of Dawn Wilson, believing her ability to track down obscure information, not to mention her command of technology and familiarity with the more far-flung corners of the Internet, would be of huge benefit to the new task force.

Terri was in her mid-twenties, a diminutive girl who tended to dress in a style Jessie referred to as 'goth light' – almost all her clothes were either black or purple, and her hair was dyed a violent shade of blue. Having grown up in the care system, Terri still grappled with anxiety and low self-esteem, but these never got in the way of her work, and both Jessie and Seamus (who always called Terri 'little sis') relied on her as a valuable asset and a trusted friend.

Terri answered Jessie's call on the first ring. 'Hey, Jessie. How's Leitrim?'

'Hiya, Terri. It's very... rural.'

'Yes. I... um... I would have expected that really.'

'How goes the office?'

'Good. I've rented us a suite in the Elysian Building, which is very central and has high-speed fibre broadband. It's *so* fast, Jessie. You're going to love it.'

'Terri, when has broadband speed ever excited me?'

'I know. Believe me though, it's cool. Did you know the Elysian is the tallest building in Cork, and the second tallest in Ireland?'

'I did not know that.'

'Well it is.'

'What's the tallest?'

'The Capital Dock in Dublin. It'll be brilliant to be able to work with the computer research department at the university here in Cork. They've assisted on all kinds of cases in the past, and I can't wait to see their skills first-hand.'

'I have a feeling they'll learn more from you than the other way around. Terri, can you chase something up for me?'

'Of course. Name it.'

'I'm trying to fill in the blanks on the main suspect in the case Seamus and I are working. Well he's the *only* suspect actually.'

'What do you need?'

'Will you check the records for a Davey Dunnigan – he's a detective I think, or at least he was? Our man here, Joe Keenan, claims he assisted him on a case involving a Mother Joan. This Dunnigan guy went to Northumberland looking for her, and Keenan and his family helped him out apparently.'

'You don't believe him?'

'Quite the opposite. I think he's completely believable actually. But we need to do our due diligence. Will you have a look and get back to me?'

'No problem. I'll call as soon as I learn anything.'

'I know you will. I'm also going to send you the details of a type of dental cap made of a particular type of porcelain. Could you see what dental surgeries in Ireland use it?'

'No problem.'

'I'll attach a physical description of what one of the victims here would have looked like before they met their end. When you have the dental surgeries, call around and find out if they gave caps to someone meeting that description within the past two months.'

'I'll get working on it. Tell Seamus little sis says hi.'

'He'll be delighted to hear that. Talk soon, Terri.'

'Bye.'

And they hung up.

9

Terri and Seamus didn't know it, but while Jessie was visiting the social workers, the pair were individually investigating Derrada Woods, though in very different ways.

In Cork, Terri was seated in front of her laptop, through which she was accessing the Garda PULSE system, which she had recently fine-tuned with a series of algorithms built specifically to help speed up the network's response time, which, while hardly sluggish, was too slow as far as Terri was concerned – there could be a lag of a second or more between entering your search parameters and getting results.

But it was those results that annoyed Terri.

PULSE, or Police Using Leading Systems Effectively, was the central database used by Irish law enforcement and contained information on all cases logged within the state. It worked along the lines of a linear filing system: the user entered a name, address or car registration number, and PULSE gave back whatever information it contained on that subject.

Or at least it did in theory. The network tended to focus on the first few paragraphs of a given report and was unable to adjust for misspellings or place names in the native Irish language, which many rural areas still used. This meant it could be unreliable when dealing with anything other than chasing up the criminal record of a suspect or trying to find out who owned a stolen car. Dawn Wilson, the police commissioner, had always believed the system unfit for purpose, and when she'd mentioned it to Terri a couple of weeks before she teamed her up with Jessie and Seamus, the young historian and tech expert had offered to take a look to see if she couldn't improve things.

Terri learned that cross-referencing was another serious issue for PULSE – small errors most search engines would recognise and attempt to rectify (Google picking up on a misspelling, for example – *did you mean* **Cavanaugh** *Street rather than* **Kavanagh** *Street*), PULSE had no such capacity to address, which meant much information that could have been useful was lost.

Fixing this problem wasn't a huge challenge for Terri, who had never been formally trained in writing code but had discovered from the moment she first sat in front of a computer that she and the machine shared a mutual understanding. And this extended to language. Terri read a few books on programming, but she worked mostly on instinct.

The tech expert saw PULSE as the computer version of Frankenstein's monster – a sad, beautiful soul that had been built with the best of intentions, but whose creator had never shown it much love. Terri was determined to fix that.

So it was that, when she learned Jessie and Seamus were heading for Leitrim, Terri entered *Ballinamore* and *Derrada* into the system. Within less than half a second, the screen before her filled with information.

It took her more than an hour to read through the summary pages on each of the files, and what she learned gave her immediate pause: there were thirteen cases specifically relating to Derrada Woods that remained open on the Garda books. Of these, nine were missing persons: individuals who had gone into the woods for a variety of reasons and had not been seen again.

Terri read about a schoolteacher who had gone looking for wild mushrooms and not returned; a birdwatcher who had come to Derrada to see a hoopoe, a rare visitor to Irish shores which had been reported in the vicinity of the woods, and had vanished without a trace; a metal-detectorist who was convinced Grace O'Malley had buried treasure deep in the trees, but had disappeared when he went into the forest in search of it. Of the nine, six were locals and three tourists or visitors to the area, all of whom had been swallowed up by the trees.

Though the disappearances spanned a period of more than twenty years, for them to have occurred in an area of such low population density made them worthy of note, and Terri found it remarkable that a major investigation hadn't been launched before now. The only reason she could find to explain it was that due to the limitations of PULSE (before her improvements, of course) the cluster of vanishings weren't flagged as connected. Due to misspellings of the relevant place names and some being logged as Derrada, others as Leitrim, still others as Ballinamore, each was filed under a different heading. Add to that the gaps of time between each one and no one had done any follow-up.

This would have been reason enough to alert Jessie that there was more afoot than they had at first thought, but the files offered yet more reasons to be wary.

The other four cases with links to Derrada that PULSE revealed related to bodies found in the woods, also over a twenty-year period. These remains were all of men who had died violently, all had been found close to the site where the Keenans had discovered their own collection of corpses, and – this was the part that really made Terri sit up and pay attention – not a single one of them had ever been identified.

None of their DNA was on file; nor were their fingerprints, and a trawl of dental records had similarly drawn a blank. Just like the bodies currently being examined in Galway, these four sets of remains seemed to belong to individuals who had dropped out of the sky, people without histories.

Whatever was going on in Derrada Woods, Terri surmised, had been going on for more than two decades.

———

While Terri was taking notes on the information she'd just collected, Seamus walked the perimeter of the Keenans' camp, keeping his eyes on the forest floor in front of him and his ears open. He was well aware the forensic team had already been over the site but wanted to get a sense of the feel of it, the atmosphere. And to see what the ground told him about the killer. The soft floor of the forest might tell many tales.

And if he was honest, he liked being in the woods too.

Growing up in Cahirsiveen, a small town in County Kerry, he'd spent a good deal of time outdoors. His mother, Katie, was a former schoolteacher and always had a great love for woodland and heath. From a young age, Seamus could tell the difference between the song of the *rí rua*, the chaffinch, and the *meantàn mòr*, the great tit. He pondered how, despite having left Kerry more than ten years ago, he still thought in Irish, the language he'd been raised speaking. There were many things – like the names of songbirds – that came to him in Irish first, and he had to translate them into English in his head before he spoke.

And he didn't mind the fact at all. If he was honest, he found the Irish names far more musical and beautiful. *Rí rua*, for example, meant *red king*, which summed up the place of the handsomely hued chaffinch in the woodland pecking order perfectly.

Seamus felt an affinity for wild things, and somehow, his native tongue facilitated that connection. As a boy, he'd known where to find the herds of red deer that ranged about the mountains, and on long summer days would make his way to crystal lakes amid Macgillycuddy's Reeks, the mountain range his hometown huddled beneath, and spend the daylight hours fishing for brown trout.

What this also did though was give Seamus a sense of how the land responded to the comings and goings of people. A place where many bodies had been buried should tell a story, lay out within its environs the tracks and trails used to transport such a grisly cargo.

Yet Seamus found no such trail in these woods. All he could discern was a silence, as if the woods themselves were holding their breath. The lack of trails made no sense to him. How were bodies being brought in and out without being physically carried?

He paused for a moment, kneeling so he could examine the ground closely. There were patches where the sun broke through the tree cover, and these had a thin covering of grass. The rest of the clearing was covered in a mix of dead leaves, pine needles and a kind of light brown humus, a combination of vegetation that had rotted down to form a rich, sweet-smelling substance that was like crumbling soil, but with larger particles. The top layer was compacted, but it wasn't hard for Seamus to get his fingers down into it and pull out a fistful.

Could the killer be covering his tracks? Seamus knew there were ways of doing this – he'd seen an episode of Ray Mears once where the soft-spoken survivalist had gone into the Alps with the Swiss Army and shown how they could disappear into the landscape so effectively no one would ever know they'd been there.

If they were dealing with someone with those skills, they were in trouble indeed.

As he walked through the tall trees, casting about in search of any sign of recently moved vegetation or something that might hint at a passageway through the undergrowth that could suggest regular usage, he emptied his mind, picking out the sounds of the woods about him. A *dreolín*, a wren, made its bubbling call from a thicket near his feet, and from a hawthorn tree a flock of *grànàin òir*, goldfinch, sang a tinkling song that sounded like water over ice.

Seamus was pausing to gaze at the spectacularly coloured little birds when he thought he caught a movement from the corner of his eye – something dark, too large to be an animal – off among the trees. Seamus Keneally wasn't easily scared, but he felt every hair on his body suddenly stand on end and a series of shivers run right down his back. He tried to shake the feeling, but it was no good.

He realised, in a flash of clarity, that he was terrified. And he had no idea why.

There was the movement again. It seemed to him to be impossibly fast, as if whatever it might be was travelling at an unnatural speed through the woodland. He turned sharply, his hand going to the handle of his Glock 17, but there was nothing there.

He looked back over his shoulder. In the distance he could see the location where the Traveller family had camped – a clear spot among a grove of oak, where the trees offered enough room between them to navigate a small van. There was a fallen log that could be used as a bench, and a ring of blackened stones showed where a fire had been lit.

Despite the fact they'd been gone for a few days, the campsite somehow still spoke of life, of a family who had eaten and laughed and chatted there.

Seamus turned slowly, due east. There, in his direct line of vision, about twenty yards off, he could discern the red-and-yellow line of crime-scene tape, which denoted where the bodies had been exhumed.

So near to where the family had lived was the place of death.

There! He caught a flicker of movement again and turned hard right, his gun in his hand now, sweat beginning to bead on his forehead. Once more, by the time he turned, whatever had been there was gone.

His gun held by his side, Seamus began to move slowly and deliberately in a clockwise direction. Whatever – *who*ever – he had seen couldn't have got far.

He came around a large cluster of rosebay willowherb that had gone to seed, the cotton-topped stalks so tall they came almost to his waist, when he heard something – it was so soft, it barely qualified as a sound at all – behind him and turned, his gun in front now, and called out, 'Stop! Police!'

He had a brief glimpse of a dark figure – little more than a silhouette – but then his legs were swept out from under him and he went down hard on his back. Seamus was trained in hand-to-hand combat, and he knew how to fall. Just before hitting the ground, he tensed his shoulders to protect himself from the impact and rolled as he hit, coming up into a kneeling position, the gun held two-handed in a shooter's stance.

And discovered he was facing nothing. All he could see was woodland.

How had they vanished so fast?

Too late, he realised his attacker was off to the side, just out of his line of vision and crouched low. Seamus, still kneeling, spun, but with the swift motion of a booted foot, the Glock was kicked from his hand.

Shit, Seamus thought. *Now I'm in trouble.*

The second kick came before this thought was finished and, connecting with his jaw, sent him reeling all over again. This time he was less prepared, and for a moment the universe spun and he went with it, and awareness left him for a time.

He came around with a start five minutes later, flat on his back on the forest floor, his jaw aching from where he'd been kicked, and his gun lying exactly where it had fallen.

He searched the area for an hour and found no boot prints.

It was as if his attacker had never been there.

Dawn Wilson, the recently appointed police commissioner of Ireland, sat at the burnished oak desk in her office in police headquarters in the Phoenix Park, in Dublin, and listened in silence while the Minister for Justice bellowed at her down the phone line.

'I do not understand why you've sent that team of yours to Leitrim on a case that is clearly already solved!' Minister Carroll said, irritation and no small amount of anxiety evident in his voice. 'I am looking at a computer screen at this very moment that contains so many files pertaining to organised crime, terrorism, far-right activity, foreign threats of all kinds... and you send your best people to the arse end of nowhere to investigate a case that doesn't need investigating?'

Dawn pushed her chair back slightly and placed first one foot then the other onto her desk. Six feet two in height, her red hair pulled back into a neat bun, Dawn was dressed in the distinctive red-trimmed blue uniform of her rank. Casting an eye on the Superman clock she'd placed just above the office door, she noted the call was now entering its fifth minute, and, so far, she had said only the words 'Hello, Minister'. Which she found puzzling. The discovery of more than ten bodies was, to her mind, a significant enough emergency to devote whatever resources she had at her disposal, and she was deeply concerned about the threat they presented – there was no way to ignore that someone was killing people in large numbers in County Leitrim, and she had to assume they were planning to continue their lethal activities.

It was the job of her and her people to stop this killer. Yet she was being told to pull back.

It didn't make a lot of sense.

'I have been reliably informed by the Gardaí on site that an arrest has been made and that they are confident they can make the charges stick. What else is there for your people to do?'

Dawn waited to see if this was a question she was actually required to answer, and, finding that it was, said, 'There is the matter of the identification of the bodies, which so far seems to be baffling everyone involved. And there are some clear problems with the man who has been arrested. I want his case re-examined.'

'So order a review and let the people on the ground address it!'

Dawn cleared her throat and took a deep breath. She was beginning to become irritated by the minister's manner. Technically, she was answerable to him, but in actuality he had never been a member of the police force and had only the most cursory knowledge of what the job involved. Which meant he was giving her a hard time because someone had told him to.

Dawn was inclined to ask him who, but decorum stayed her hand, and she ploughed on stoically, attempting to explain her reasons for sending Jessie and her team in.

'I've had a look at the file on the man currently in custody, and I'm dissatisfied that he's responsible. The fact he reported the remains is only the first of many problems. Then there's the woods where the bodies were found.'

'What about them?'

'They've triggered a few red flags here.'

There was an uncharacteristic silence at the minister's end of the line. Then: 'What the hell is that supposed to mean?'

'Well, you know the new investigative task force you were just talking about?'

'If I was just talking about them, I obviously do.'

Dawn, a native of County Antrim in Northern Ireland, had recruited the three members of Jessie's team shortly after she'd been given the position of commissioner. She and Jessie had attended Trinity College together in the early 1990s and had become fast friends. When Jessie's career took her to London, where she rapidly rose through the ranks of the Met, Dawn kept a watchful eye on her old classmate, and when faced with a seemingly impossible case involving serial abductions and a killer who seemed to have evaded capture for many decades, Jessie was the first person she thought of to head up the investigation. Seamus, a detective who had shown his grit and loyalty under fire and who had a deep respect for the routine aspects of policing, seemed a good counterpoint to Jessie's devotion to psychological profiling and behavioural science.

And then there was the third member of the group.

'One of them is named Terri Kehoe and she is a very talented young lady,' Dawn explained. 'She's something of a whizz when it comes to computers and networking and the like, and she's done some work on the interface I have with the PULSE system here at HQ.'

'You allowed a civilian to meddle with the police computer IT network?'

'Terri is a trusted member of my task force,' Dawn said firmly, 'and therefore has whatever security clearance I see fit to bestow upon her, civilian or not.'

'My understanding is that type of thing needs to be discussed at departmental level,' the minister growled.

'Then you *mis*understand,' Dawn said stiffly. 'Terri has developed a couple of rather nifty little algorithms that have made the system much more effective. For example, when word on the Leitrim burial site came across my desk, Terri was able to enter the location, and what do you know? There are over a dozen unsolved murders and disappearances connected to Derrada Woods that seem to have been left to gather dust. There was never any interest from Garda HQ because they've all been filed separately and under different addresses.'

The minister made a grumbling sound. 'Some form of clerical error, I expect. Nothing to be alarmed about.'

'I *am* alarmed though,' Dawn insisted. 'Derrada was spelled five different ways across the files I was able to retrieve, and in one instance barely mentioned at all. Ballinamore was sometimes given as the location, and in one instance, all that's mentioned is that a body was found in rural Leitrim.'

'This is surely not unusual,' the minister offered.

'Whether it is or not is moot,' Dawn said. 'It's just not good enough. The local guards in Ballinamore investigated some of the cases, as did the Sligo detective squad, but there hasn't been much consistency. If Terri hadn't worked her magic, those cases *still* wouldn't have been brought to my attention. But they have been now. And I want them looked into.'

'Commissioner, might I just say that the priority here is resolving the issue of the ten and some bodies currently lying in the medical laboratory in University College Galway?'

'I couldn't agree more, Minister. But prosecuting a man who may or may not have anything to do with those deaths will not help their families grieve. As of right now, those bodies cannot be given funerals as we don't know who they are or who might be waiting up at night for news of their whereabouts. My team may well be able to do something about that.'

The minister sighed heavily. 'One week, Commissioner. I am giving your exalted team one week to justify their presence in Leitrim. After which I want them rerouted into something more suited to their... their unique talents.'

'A week is all they'll need,' Dawn said, hoping she wasn't overselling her team. 'Probably won't even take that long.'

The minister muttered ominously about having enough rope to hang oneself before hanging up.

And Dawn Wilson wondered what it was about Derrada Woods that seemed to bother him so much.

11

Terri rang Jessie while she was on her way back from her visit to social services.

'Joe Keenan was involved in a case that was being investigated by David Dunnigan, a criminologist who worked as a consultant with the National Bureau of Criminal Investigation from 1997 until last April,' she reported.

'What happened last April?'

'He resigned his position and moved to Greenland.'

'Just like that?'

'It's a pretty complicated story, but from what I can see it's all mixed up with this trip to Northumberland you mentioned. In his report, Dunnigan makes reference to an Irish Traveller who acted as his guide when he was in Kielder. It makes sense it was the same person.'

'So his story checks out,' Jessie said. 'I think we can conclusively chalk Joe Keenan up as innocent.'

'Okay,' Terri agreed. 'Is there anything else I can do?'

'Just to get Glenn off my back, let's have some forensic evidence to close the deal. Will you check the footage from traffic cams between Rosslare Europort and Ballinamore,

Leitrim? Go back one week from today. I'm looking for a 1986 Ford Transit van, registration 2435 ZY. It should show up on the passenger list on a ferry coming from Fishguard too. That'll put the whole thing to bed once and for all.'

'I'll get working on it,' Terri said. 'Jessie, if this Keenan person didn't kill all those people, who did?'

Jessie laughed a dry, humourless laugh. 'I think that's what Dawn has sent Seamus and me out here to learn,' she said. 'Of course, if we find the real culprit, we'll also be clearing Joe. Which is my job.'

'The commissioner has had me looking at some cases relating to Derrada Woods. I can't say for certain they're directly linked to the bodies discovered, as those don't seem to relate to any known missing persons, but there are a number of extant disappearances in the area, and several unsolved homicides all linked to those woods going back more than twenty years.'

'Really? How many is several?'

'Thirteen.'

'All based around Derrada?'

'Yes. I'll send you on the files, but it seems that people have a habit of wandering into those woods and never wandering back out again. Among the baker's dozen are four dead bodies discovered at various points around the woods. And would you like to hear something interesting about them?'

'Of course.'

'They remain unidentified. The police were completely unable to find out who those people were.'

Jessie thought about that. 'So the unidentified bodies that have just been exhumed aren't the first in Derrada.'

'No, Jessie. They aren't. It looks as if whatever is going on in Leitrim has been happening for a while.'

'Why am I only hearing about this now?'

'I did some work on the algorithms PULSE utilises. Once

they were fine-tuned, the system was better able to cross-reference past cases. You don't need to know the intricate details. What matters is that you appear to be in a violent crime hotspot.'

'Okay. Please send them on. As soon as you're finished setting the office up, get yourself up here. You know we'd be delighted to see you.'

'I'll be in touch.'

'I know you will, Terri. Talk soon.'

12

Dawn Wilson sipped coffee from a large mug emblazoned with the Batman insignia (a gift from the team in Pearse Street, which had been her last command before taking up the job of commissioner) and leafed through the report of the forensic team that had retrieved the bodies from Derrada Woods.

The bodies were all found in the upper strata of soil, though it seems reasonable to assume they had originally been placed at a deeper level. Heavy rainfall within the past three months will have caused the soil particles and humus to expand, pushing the remains closer to the surface.

Fragments found in the ear cavity of Remains #1, #4 and #7 indicate they had been placed in subsoil, and the pollen and plant remains found attached to them suggest an original depth of approximately two metres. The area of the clearing where Remains #9 was recovered contained soil made up of a lot of decayed vegetable material, mostly rotted wood, and investigators were able, at a depth of fifty-six inches, to recover the indentation of a bladed digging tool. Analysis shows this was too small to be a standard spade or shovel, but several suggestions have been made as to its provenance: possibly a tool like a mattock or a wide-bladed farming hoe.

Dawn paused and considered this. It seemed odd to her that someone burying a body in the woods, a task they surely would want to complete as quickly as possible, wouldn't use the most effective tool for the job. The two implements suggested in the report would be good for breaking up the earth, but not for moving it out of the hole to make space for the body itself. Maybe that was what had happened and the shovel just hadn't left marks showing it had been used. Shaking her head, she went back to the report.

Derrada Woods, sometimes referred to locally as the Forest of Derrada, are all that remains of a tract of mixed woodland that at one time ran from the border of Donegal right the way to the edge of the Burren, in Co Clare. The woods still contain remnants of Neolithic and early Celtic settlements, and according to the Ordnance Survey, there is, in a clearing in the centre of the forest, a burial mound said to have been the resting place of a local chieftain. The woods are a designated wildlife reserve and are maintained by Coillte, from whom permission had to be sought before we carried out our forensic investigation.

It should be noted that Derrada is, due to its archaeological significance, an area of historical importance, enforced by a preservation order held by the Office of Public Works. It is the opinion of Forensic Science Ireland that further excavation would be justified, but to do so would require an overturning (or at the very least suspending) of that preservation order. It would be expedient to pursue that through legal channels without delay.

Dawn made a note to do just that in the morning.
Before going home, she texted Jessie.

The Minister says you have a week before he's pulling you to work on something else. So make your time there count. Something weird is going on, and I'm fucked if I know what it is.

Jessie responded almost immediately.

Agreed. Nothing about this is right. I don't know if a week will be enough, but we'll do what we can.

Dawn paused for a moment before messaging back.

I'll try to extend it for you. But I'm not making any promises.

Little did Dawn know that things would reach crisis point long before a week was up.

CASE NOTES ON LEITRIM BURIAL SITE – TRANSCRIBED FROM AUDIO JOURNAL KEPT BY JESSIE BOYLE

7 NOVEMBER

It's tempting to leap to the simplest conclusions in this case, and if I'm honest, a part of me wants to do just that. The physical evidence is that an isolated, rural site is being used as a burial ground for multiple human remains. There are various explanations that could be moulded to fit that fact, and it seems the police are already inclined towards one of these: that we are dealing with a Traveller feud.

I am not greatly experienced with the Travelling culture in Ireland – growing up in inner-city Dublin, I was of course aware of that ethnic minority, but the truth is, my life didn't cause me to cross paths with them in anything other than the most cursory of ways. However, I did take a course in sociology as part of my training, and I came across a few Traveller families during my work with the Met.

So the following conclusions are based on that. I will make a point of researching my ideas over the coming days, and I hope my relationship with the Keenans will enlighten them further.

But in the meantime, here goes:

The psychology of the Travelling people is, as I understand it, wrapped up in their nomadism. Everything they do: how they raise and educate their children, how they arrange their marriages, how they engage with their faith – all are rooted in the concept that no one will be in one place for long. This is hard-wired into the Traveller psyche. It is central to how they view themselves.

Even their feuds tend to be carried out with this in mind. Confrontations usually occur at a prearranged location, often at a horse fair or other social gathering. In other words, they bring the fight to a static setting, rather than facing off along the road or at their campsites. And this is another important point: the places where the Travellers camp are seen as sacred spots. Their families will have frequented them, sometimes for hundreds of years. The Irish Travellers see the earth as sacred. They all proclaim to be Roman Catholic, but in practice their creed is much closer to paganism in lots of ways.

The Celts worshipped the earth goddess, Danu, and the Travellers see Mary, the mother of Jesus, as being closely linked. I find it hard to believe they would sully the ground in a location near where they regularly camp – and Waters and Glenn both tell me Travellers do camp in and around Derrada and Ballinamore often.

Based on all of this, I feel we are not looking at a Traveller feud.

I'm going to summarise my thinking.

Firstly, I cannot see all the bodies being placed in one location – Travellers would distribute them at disparate places as they move about the countryside. Burying them on top of one another would be seen as disrespectful in terms of how the Travellers feel about the treatment of the dead. As I understand it, burying even a rival without the proper honours would invite bad luck, and a charnel pit would be viewed as abhorrent in the extreme to a Traveller.

Secondly, I feel these sites would be far away from traditional campgrounds and halting sites. Travellers would not wish to taint the places they live by placing bodies in the ground near them.

In short, this does not feel like a Traveller feud. It feels like something else.

We are dealing with a serial killer. Though one unlike all the others I've encountered.

Seamus had booked them a couple of rooms in the artfully named Commercial and Tourist Hotel on Ballinamore's high street. It was nearly six o'clock when Jessie parked the MG outside, and she was delighted to discover the place was far more comfortable than the name suggested. She had just closed the door when Dawn texted her, and she read the message with an emerging sense of just how challenging their situation was becoming. Deciding there was nothing she could do about it, she had a hurried shower before joining Seamus in the restaurant for dinner.

When she got to their table, she could see he'd been in an altercation – one side of his face was bruised and swollen.

'What happened to you?'

'I was jumped in the woods near the burial site.'

'Did you get a look at them?'

'Someone dressed in black. That's all I've got. And don't give me a hard time over it either. I'm mad enough at myself already.'

'Did you have physical contact with him?'

'A boot to my jaw. Nothing more, so there was no skin

under my fingernails to try to get DNA evidence from. Whoever they were, they knew how to fight. Put me down in two moves.'

'Were you knocked out? Do you need to see a doctor?'

'I was briefly stunned. I've had worse.'

Jessie nodded. 'They know you were police?'

'I identified myself, yes. I'm not a rookie, Jessie.'

'I withdraw the question.'

'Good.'

'It looks like someone doesn't want us poking around the area then, doesn't it?'

'It really does. How'd you get on with everything else?'

'I had to jump through a few hoops to get Joe a visit with his son,' Jessie said. 'Did you know that social workers clock off after five in the evening? I mean, what the hell is up with that?'

As she spoke, a waitress arrived with their food.

Seamus had ordered a starter that was described on the menu as 'a sharing platter for two'. It contained barbecue ribs, onion rings, cocktail sausages and what looked to be prawns wrapped in bacon, along with several different dipping sauces. Jessie had a bowl of vegetable soup.

'I'm assuming families mustn't go into crisis outside of office hours,' Seamus said.

'Seriously. Sometimes I despair,' Jessie agreed as her partner picked up a rib, taking a sizeable chunk of meat from the bone in one bite.

The rib was covered in a sticky sauce, which Jessie reckoned she would get all over her face, fingers and clothes if she attempted to consume it. Seamus, on the other hand, seemed to possess the ability to eat the most challenging of foods without ever getting a drip on his person. Jessie noted he held the cut of meat delicately between his thumb and index finger, using the short section of bone that protruded from the end as a kind of handle. As she watched, a deep ochre drip ran down the end of the rib and looked about ready to drop onto the front of Seamus's wrinkled, though otherwise quite clean, shirt.

Somehow (he didn't seem to be looking, so Jessie had to assume it was instinctive), the detective tilted the rib so the rivulet of sauce halted in its descent and oozed back the way it had come, saving his shirt from injury.

'You arranged for them to see each other though?' Seamus asked.

'I had to get Dawn to make a call – apparently my word wasn't good enough – but yeah. Two thirty tomorrow. One of the care staff is bringing the lad to the station. It's not ideal, and I tried to suggest an alternative, like maybe the local community centre, but Waters insists Joe is a flight risk. So he has to stay in his cell for the visit. The boy can talk to him through the bars. Which I think is pretty shite, but I suppose Joe's in a better position than he was before we got here. Did you have any luck with the dog?'

'Still alive, thank goodness. The dog warden seemed a nice chap, to be honest. Said Rufus, the dog, seems a bit depressed. Actually asked if there was any hope the residential unit might allow the wee lad to have him while he's there.'

'Might be worth checking,' Jessie said.

'Can you see them going for it?'

'Not really. But it can't hurt to ask.'

Seamus munched the last morsel of meat from the rib and placed the bone back on the plate. He had a tiny dab of sauce on his thumb and finger, which he removed delicately with his napkin, but other than that he'd escaped without so much as a blemish. Jessie told him about her conversations with Terri.

'So let me get this straight,' Seamus said. 'There are thirteen other cases connected with Derrada Woods?'

'There are.'

'Some of which are local people who were reported as going into the woods and never being seen again?'

'Yes.'

'But there are also four unidentified bodies, four remains of unknown people beyond our ten?'

'There are. Whatever's going on here, it's been happening for a while.'

'And the detective Joe worked with in England?'

'It seems Joe really did work with an Irish criminologist on a tough case in England earlier this year – Terri confirmed it. If we can show that he has, in fact, only been a friend to the police, not to mention his being out of the country when quite a few of those bones were put in the ground, there's no reason not to rule him out as a suspect. Which means we can focus on what's really going on here.'

'Any thoughts on that?'

'We can't rule out the Dunnes, the group who are after Joe. It seems they do pass through here from time to time, so I'm wondering if we should be looking into them some more.'

'It's a place to begin,' Seamus agreed. 'But if I'm honest, I don't see it.'

'This far north, I also wondered if it might be something to do with either republicanism or some kind of sectarian unrest in the Six Counties.'

'Possible,' Seamus said, dunking a bacon-coated prawn into a ramekin of sweet chilli sauce. 'I had another thought too.'

'Go on.'

'Might the bodies belong to some kind of community burial site?'

'Where all the dead have been shot or worse?'

'There are some strange religious groups out there at the moment. I know it seems far-fetched, but I think it's worth exploring. Find out if there are any weird cults operating in the area. Some of those real tinfoil-hat wearers are so paranoid, they might not have permitted any of their DNA information to be stored.'

'Well it can't hurt to look. Are you really going to eat a main course after that?' Jessie asked, no longer able to contain her amazement.

'This is the first thing I've eaten since lunch!' Seamus said, sounding offended. 'I get low blood sugar, you know.'

'Yes. You have told me that before.'

'I waited for you to get here so you wouldn't have to eat dinner on your own,' Seamus went on, looking very glum. 'Even though I was *starving*.'

'And I appreciate that,' Jessie said and decided to steer the conversation back to the case. 'Have you formed any other theories on the source of the remains? Any that don't involve death cults?'

'I'd be leaning towards some kind of gangland activity,' Seamus said, still sounding a bit miffed. 'You've got a mix of execution-style killings alongside a number of deaths where extreme prejudice was used. The bodies show evidence of torture, and that's not a Traveller feud. Travellers sometimes use lethal force, but they're more inclined to shoot you in the belly with a shotgun than paralyse you and bury you while you're still breathing. This is something else, Jessie. Joe and his people are just easy targets.'

'That's a possibility,' Jessie said. 'But I keep coming back to the fact the DNA in these cases is not on the system. And that detail *has* to tell us something about the killer. And I think we're dealing with one killer here, Seamus. I'm not discounting the idea of a crew, but my gut is telling me we're looking for one person.'

'It is curious,' Seamus said as he popped the last cocktail sausage into his mouth and chewed. 'I've heard there are hackers you can pay to wipe your details from the Internet. Could that be what we're dealing with here, but maybe in reverse?'

'A killer who has the details of their victims removed, to prevent them from being detected?'

'Terri might be able to look into it,' Seamus said.

'She's going to be a busy girl,' Jessie agreed.

Seamus was just attacking his main course, a Thai green curry, when Jessie's phone rang.

'Waters,' she said to Seamus as she picked it up. 'Hello, this is Jessie.'

'You'd better get out to Derrada right away,' the guard said without preamble.

'Care to tell me why?'

'Another body has shown up.'

'Someone dug another one up?'

'This one wasn't buried.'

'We're on our way,' Jessie said.

The body was lying flat on its back on the forest floor three hundred yards from where Joe and Finbar had camped. The area was illuminated by floodlights when Jessie and Seamus, wearing protective white jumpsuits to prevent contamination of the scene, went to stand with Julia Banks to gaze down at what had once been a person.

Jessie had a terrible sense of déjà vu. It took her a few seconds to realise she was reliving the awful moment she'd come upon the body of her former partner in the Met's Violent Crimes Task Force (and also her lover), William Briggs, his torn and bloodied form left in the tidal silt of the Thames near Southwark by a serial killer working under the name Uruz.

Jessie forced the feelings of horror and devastation deep down into herself, into the stillness that lay at her core, and focused her attention on the form lying on the woodland floor at their feet.

She would have her chance to make Uruz atone for what he'd done. For now, there were other matters pressing.

'You don't need me to tell you that I can't give you an official cause of death yet,' the pathologist said. 'But informally, there's what looks to be a puncture wound to the back of the neck that would have severed the spinal cord and paralysed the victim and then cut off their air supply, thereby causing death by suffocation.' Julia had a clipboard and was writing copious notes as they spoke.

'That and everything else!' Seamus said, looking a little green about the gills.

'Am I right in thinking...' Jessie said, pointing, and Julia interjected, 'Yes. They've been scalped. Like in the old Westerns.'

'Time of death?' Seamus asked.

'Again, I won't be able to say for certain till I get him on the table, but from the fact decay hasn't yet set in and the wounds remain quite moist, we're looking at within the past twelve hours.'

'Can you give us anything else?' Jessie asked. 'A ballpark figure on the age, for example?'

'I haven't had him on the table yet. Everything you're asking me requires guesswork. I don't like doing that.'

'I won't hold you to any of it until you've confirmed,' Jessie said. 'But it would be wonderful to have something to go on.'

'All right,' Julia sighed. 'Victim is, giving my best guess, approximately thirty-five years old. I *can* tell you that he is five feet nine inches in height, and, just like the others, appears to have been in excellent physical fitness before he met his end. I'm going to assume the scalping was done for a reason, as was the removal of various patches of skin from the arms and abdomen.'

'Tattoos?' Seamus asked.

'Yes, or scar tissue that may have been seen as an identifying feature. You do see people with head and face tattoos now, so it's not impossible, but I'm inclined to believe the scalp was removed because the victim carried the mark of some kind of recognisable injury. Statistically, I believe it's more likely.'

'Would such an injury show up in the bones when you examine them?'

'I've already had a cursory examination – our killer was kind enough to reveal the skull for me, saving me some trouble later. Yes, this chap took a blow to the head some time ago, and it left a mild dent in his skull in the front right-hand quadrant. I'm going to guess the hair grew back white in that spot – which is not unusual – and that's why the scalp was taken.'

'Wouldn't it just have been easier to shave his head?' Seamus asked.

'Actually, no,' Julia said, looking up at him. 'The scalp comes off very easily. If the killer knew what they were doing, they'd have peeled it away in a matter of seconds. Shaving the head would be much more labour intensive.'

Jessie was gazing at the bloodied remains.

'If it is scar tissue, the victim could have been very active,' Jessie said. 'Could we be looking at an extreme-sports fan? A free-runner perhaps, or a mountaineer?'

'Possibly,' Julia said. 'I know you need to use some imagination to see beyond the injuries, but he had an athletic build. Slim, but strong.'

'He was found here? Just lying on the ground in the open?' Jessie asked.

'Exactly as you see him.'

'This is maybe ten yards from an active police crime scene,' Jessie said.

'I'm aware of that,' Julia remarked. 'I'm still *working* that crime scene.'

'So the killer snuck in, right under the nose of the police, and left *another* body, this time in plain view, not even buried?' Seamus asked.

'That would seem to be the case, yes.'

Jessie shook her head. 'Seamus, we've got some work to do.'

'As do I,' Julia Banks said. 'So unless there's anything else I can do for you two?'

'Thank you, no,' Jessie said. 'You'll keep us posted?'

'As soon as I know anything, you will too,' the pathologist said.

15

'It looks like we're dealing with a complete psychopath, doesn't it?' Seamus asked as they drove back to town.

'A sociopath certainly,' Jessie said. 'But I think it might be more complicated than that too.'

'Complicated how?'

'There could be one of two things going on.'

'I'm listening.'

'We might have just seen a serial killer marking his territory – basically a warning to us to back off.'

'You're telling me this person is crazy enough to think they can scare the entire Irish police force off by dumping a mutilated body right in the middle of their forensic investigation?'

'Think about it,' Jessie said. 'Whoever we're dealing with has just shown us they can move about in the woods undetected and can continue to kill and deposit corpses without us catching so much as a glimpse of them. That's a very potent message: this is my territory, you're powerless to stop me, so you might as well just stop trying.'

'But they can't really think that will work,' Seamus said.

'Surely the woods will be combed top to bottom now until they turn up wherever this person is holed up.'

'I doubt anything will be found,' Jessie said. 'Our killer is very, very careful. Of that I'm certain.'

'You said there was another thing?'

'Yes. And this one might even be scarier.'

'Excellent. I love that we can always go scarier.'

'We might well be seeing them reaching crisis point. What if he's reaching the end of his journey? What if he's ready to make his final stand?'

'By revealing himself, you mean?'

'Yes. He could be getting to a place where he doesn't care about concealment or subterfuge anymore, and actually wants us to know he's there, is killing and will kill again.'

'Well either option leaves us with just one course of action.'

Jessie threw her partner a glance. 'What's that then?'

'We have to stop the bastard before he kills again.'

'Simple,' Jessie agreed. 'Simple and foolproof.'

'Which is just as well,' Seamus mused. 'So how do we begin to do that?'

'By speaking to someone who knows the woods,' Jessie said. 'And I think I know where to begin.'

16

But that couldn't happen until the following morning, so they went back to the hotel bar to have a drink before bed.

They had just sat down when an elderly man, who had been sitting at the bar over a large bottle of Guinness, made his way over to their table.

'Ye're the polis from Dublin, I take it,' he said.

'I wasn't aware our presence was widely known,' Jessie said. 'But yes. I'm Jessie and this is Seamus.'

'And you're here to find out what killed those poor souls in the wood.'

Seamus threw Jessie a look. 'You know about the remains that were found?'

'Everybody knows about the mass grave sure,' the oldster said. 'This is a small town, and there's been Marias and Garda cars and fellas wandering about the countryside in protective gear with surgical masks on and I don't know what else. I went out to have a look to see what all the fuss was about and a young girrull in a Garda uniform turned me around, very polite like, but she was firm enough. I seen the crime-scene tape though. And the shapes on the ground covered over in tarpaulin.'

'And I take it you weren't the only person who wanted to see what was going on,' Jessie said, thinking that their job had just become exponentially more difficult – nothing clouded the clarity of an investigation like local gossip.

'Ah sure, not much happens around here,' their new friend said. 'Takin' a wee look wasn't goin' to hurt anyone, was it?'

'Would you like to sit down?' Jessie pushed a chair out for him to join them.

'Don't mind if I do.'

The old man took the proffered seat, emitting a kind of satisfied groan as he relaxed into it.

'This is mighty neighbourly of ye both,' he said and then looked sadly at his almost empty glass. 'What would be even more friendly would be if you were to stand me a drink. My pension isn't due for another coupla days, and sure, amen't I here with an awful thirst on me?'

'A large bottle, is it?' Seamus asked.

'And a ball of malt,' the old man said, grinning. 'You're a grand lad, so y'are.'

'I didn't catch your name,' Jessie said, sipping her glass of Glenfiddich as Seamus made for the bar.

'Oliver McGee,' the old man said, extending his hand for her to shake. 'But everyone hereabouts calls me Ollie. Just like in those old movies: Laurel and Hardy. D'ye remember them? Stan and Ollie. He was the fat lad, so the name doesn't really fit a skinny chap like me, but I don't mind.'

Jessie laughed. 'They were a little before my time, but I know what you're talking about.'

The old man was about five feet four inches, with a tousle of thin white hair forming a cloud about his head. He was dressed in a purple cardigan that had more than a few holes in it over a brown-and-white checked shirt and grey slacks, the trousers dappled with myriad stains and smudges, some of which looked to be food, the genesis of the others a little harder to discern.

Ollie's eyes though were alive with wit and intelligence, and Jessie liked him immediately.

'So how much more do you know about the mysterious goings-on in Derrada Woods?' Jessie asked him.

'Well I know they've arrested that tinker fella.'

'You're alarmingly well informed.'

'I keep me ear to the ground,' the old man said, winking. 'I used to be a teacher. But that was long ago. Now that I'm gone beyond my eightieth year, I don't have much else to do but stick my nose in where it's not wanted.'

He laughed heartily at that and was still tittering when Seamus returned with his drinks.

'The whiskey is Jameson,' he said. 'I hope that's okay.'

'Well I see you either got me a double or Jimmy behind the bar has developed a more generous pour than usual, so I won't be the one to complain.'

'Did you meet Joe, the Traveller who's been arrested?' Jessie asked.

'I did. I called on him and his boy when they arrived here a week ago. My father always had great respect for the Travelling people, and he passed it to me. I had an old metal pail needed mending, and though a lot of the younger Travellers don't have the tin-smithing skills anymore, I wondered if he might do a job on it for me. And you know what? He did, and he wouldn't accept any money for it neither.'

'That was kind of him,' Jessie observed.

'I was shocked when I heard they'd taken him in for killing those people.'

'You didn't think he seemed the type?' Seamus asked.

'Well that's true, he doesn't strike me as a murderous sort, that young man,' Ollie said. 'But sure, 'tis more than that.'

'More how?' Jessie asked.

'There's something bad living in the Derrada Woods,' Ollie said. 'There has been for a very long time, and I think it's what took those people. It's been taking souls almost as long as Christians have lived in this part of Ireland, and it's going to keep doing it until someone is brave enough to stop it.'

'What are you talking about, Ollie?' Jessie asked.

'You probably won't believe me,' Ollie said, taking a long swallow of his whiskey and chasing it with a slug of Guinness.

'Why don't you try us?' Jessie said.

'I'm talking about the *néamh mairbh*,' the old man said, his voice falling into a hush.

Jessie looked to Seamus.

'*Néamh mairbh* means half-dead, or undead,' he said.

Jessie raised an eyebrow quizzically.

'The Abhartach lives in those woods,' Ollie continued. 'St Eoghan buried him standing upright in a grave deep in the forest, with a stake through his heart made of pure ash wood. But the rod withered over time, and when it crumbled to dust, he came back.'

'You're saying a ghost killed those people?' Jessie asked.

'Abhartach is much worse than a ghost,' Ollie said. 'Abhartach is a vampire. And he's been hunting the woods of this place for eight hundred years.'

PART TWO

WHISPERS ON THE WIND

7–8 November 2018

'And into the forest I go, to lose my mind and find my soul.'

John Muir

17

'Do you know how some places just seem to draw evil to themselves?' Ollie asked Jessie and Seamus.

'I've heard of places that seem to be like that,' Jessie agreed. 'But you know, if poverty or crime or even warfare is a feature of your world, then it can seem as if a particular location is attracting unhappiness. It isn't though.'

'That sounds like the answer of a philosopher,' Ollie said, tutting and shaking his head. 'There is nothing that can explain the awful events that have focused around those woods except that the place itself is evil. And it all began with the Abhartach.'

'A vampire?' Seamus asked. 'You really believe Dracula lives in the woods just outside town?'

'Dracula is a fictional creation,' the old man sniffed. 'The Abhartach is the historic figure who inspired him. People credit some Romanian warlord, but Bram Stoker was Irish. The tale I'm about to tell you was the real basis for his novel.'

'So who was the vampire Abhartach?' Jessie asked.

'He didn't start out a vampire,' Ollie said. 'They never do. In the beginning, Abhartach was just a man, though an evil one, for sure.'

'So what – he got bitten by a bat or something?' Seamus asked, laughing.

'This is no laughing matter,' Ollie said, giving the young detective a hard stare. 'These are serious things I'm telling you about.'

He paused for a moment, looking into the glass that had recently contained whiskey.

'And it would be an easier tale to recount if I had another ponger of fine spirits to bolster my nerves.'

Sighing deeply, Seamus went to the bar, returning with the old man's glass replenished.

'Good man. May a blessing be on you and your whole family.'

'You were about to tell us the story of Abhartach?' Jessie reminded him.

'I was, to be sure. My tale begins in the fifth century after the birth of our Lord. The land hereabouts was divided into many small baronies in those days, each ruled over by a different warlord or chieftain. Abhartach was one such, and terrible and cruel he was. It is said he would put his subjects to death on a whim in the most horrible of ways, and he terrorised everyone so badly that eventually it was decided he had to go. Well they employed a hero from Mayo named Cathain to come and do the job, and indeed it seemed he had earned his money, for didn't he come back to the fort dragging Abhartach's body behind his chariot, and the evil creature was buried in the woods.'

'That wasn't unusual in the early medieval period,' Jessie said. 'Lords and chieftains were constantly getting knocked off to make way for the next ruler.'

'You may be right, Jessie, but this story is *not* usual. I give you my word on that. There is *nothing* usual about the Abhartach.'

'Doesn't the word mean *dwarf* or little person?' Seamus

asked. 'It's old Irish and not really used anymore – probably not very politically correct.'

'They do say Abhartach was a man of very small stature,' Ollie agreed. 'I don't think his size had anything to do with things though, for in spite of it he was a fearsome warrior. But let me finish the story.

'The night Cathain returned triumphant, there was a feast, but on the stroke of midnight, a great cry arose from the guards on the walls, for they spied the Abhartach, all stained with mud and leaves, approaching the keep from the treeline. He had returned. Cathain was called from the feast to finish the job he claimed he'd started, and he did so, but the next night Abhartach was back, and the night after that again. Finally, a Christian saint, Eoghan, who lived in a cave nearby, was called upon, and he slew the dwarf with an ash stake through the heart and buried him, still so impaled, in a mound in the centre of the woods, with a mighty stone atop, carved with a cross.'

'Surely that would hold him,' Seamus said.

'It did, for a time,' Ollie said. ''Twas the ash rod that bound him, and ash is strong, but it will eventually rot and decompose. And when there was no longer a single shard of it left, the Abhartach was sure to rise again. And he did.'

'You think he drew evil things to the woods here,' Jessie said.

'I do. The facts speak for themselves.'

'And what are the facts?' Jessie wanted to know.

She was sceptical but had long since come to understand that no information learned during an investigation was completely useless, no matter how far-fetched or sensational. Even the most lurid nugget could hold a grain of truth.

'I'll need my glasses refilled before I tell you that,' Ollie said, looking expectantly at Seamus.

18

'I could tell you about a group of pirates Grace O'Malley sent to Derrada to negotiate a trade agreement with the local farmers, who were picked off a man at a time until there were none remaining to complete their deal,' Ollie said. 'Or I could regale you with the tale of some Free Staters who buried a cache of arms in the woods in 1922 but finally abandoned it because they said the ghost of a deformed child haunted the area, and they became afraid to go there.'

'Haven't you just told us those stories now?' Seamus asked.

'I could tell you about those awful events,' Ollie went on, ignoring him, 'but I have a much more recent tale to tell you.'

'Go on then,' Jessie said.

'In 1967, two young children went missing during a nature walk on a farm on the outskirts of the woods. A search party was launched, made up of Gardaí and local volunteers. They searched the woods for a week, and finally one of the children, a girl named Bridget, was located, close to death, near a mound in the centre of the forest. She was delirious and kept repeating the words: *he wanted us to lie with him; he wanted us to lie with him.* The police thought the kids must have been abducted by a local pervert, but after an examination, it was clear the girl hadn't been sexually molested. She had lost a lot of blood though, from deep gash marks on her neck and wrists. Her friend, a little boy, was never found.'

'I've never heard of this case,' Jessie said. 'I would have thought it would be quite well known – Ireland is a small country...'

'It was never reported in the papers,' Ollie said. 'The local county councillors hushed it up. People were embarrassed. But I'm here to tell you, it happened. I was part of the search party that found her.'

'Did she recover, the girl?' Jessie asked.

'I wish to heaven she did, the poor cratur,' Ollie said, making the sign of the cross. 'She died a week later.'

'I'm sorry,' Jessie said.

'It was an awful thing,' Ollie said. 'But terrible events happen in those woods all the time, and they're still happening. Two Gardaí were shot in Derrada when they went in to rescue an industrialist who'd been kidnapped by gangsters back in 1983. I heard murmurs that the polis weren't the target those bullets were intended for. The criminals were shooting at something in the trees that terrified them, and the Gardaí just got in the way.'

'Firefights get messy, Ollie,' Jessie said. 'People often die when guns are discharged. I've seen it first-hand.'

'I'm just tellin' you what I heard,' the old man said. 'Two years ago, the body of a young man was found in a clearing not far from where those bones have just been discovered. The cause of death was never reported in the papers. Which makes me think there was a cover-up, just like with the children in 1967.'

'Why would anyone cover up the actions of a vampire?' Seamus asked. 'Isn't it far more likely something else is at the root of what you're describing?'

'I know what I know,' Ollie said. 'The powers that be – the government, the church and the police – have let it hunt here, in the quietest part of this island, for eight centuries. I don't know why, but I think they want it here. Maybe it's best left, don't you think? Some things are better undisturbed.'

'I disagree,' Jessie said. 'If someone has been killing people, they need to be stopped.'

'There are some things shouldn't be tampered with,' the old man said. 'If I were you, I'd turn around and make for home. This is not going to end well. Mark my words on that.'

'Thanks for the vote of confidence,' Jessie said.

But the old man drained both his glasses, nodded at the two detectives and scuttled out of the bar. He had, it seemed, said what he'd come to say and had nothing more to add.

19

Terri sat in the team's newly appointed offices in Cork, using the computer laboratory she'd just finished building. Dawn Wilson had told her to design the system of her dreams, and that was what she'd done, expecting it would be way too expensive, but the commissioner had signed off on it without batting an eyelid. It was made up of three interlinked terminals, each with different specifications to make them ideal for a disparate set of tasks.

Terri had ordered the new hardware with a carefully chosen list of modifications that would make her work easier – the last case she, Jessie and Seamus had worked involved her hacking into Instagram to retrieve a set of deleted personal messages, and she wanted to make sure she had the right tools should she be called upon to do so again.

And now she did.

The Elysian Building was quiet this late in the evening, most of the other workers long gone home for the night. Terri, who didn't really have a life outside of her work, was making her way through the traffic-cam recordings relating to Joe Keenan's Transit van.

So far, she had tracked the vehicle's movements halfway across Ireland, beginning with footage of the van arriving into Ireland through Rosslare, where it cleared customs without difficulty. The van moved from Wexford to Wicklow, and then seemed to do a U-turn and travelled to Tipperary, which made no sense at all. Terri wondered if Joe was simply wandering aimlessly, but the fact he never remained in one place for more than five hours led her to believe he was not, in fact, just going for a drive.

'He's running evasive manoeuvres,' Terri said to herself. 'He's covering his tracks.'

Terri continued to track the van's movements, making a note of each point in its trajectory as she did. It was about eleven thirty when she came across a recording of the van parked in a layby on the M6 motorway. The Transit pulled in at ten thirty on the night of 23 October. Terri watched as Joe climbed out of the driver's-side door. A small dog followed him, and a boy came around the front of the van, obviously having come out of the passenger side. They disappeared into the darkness beyond the hard shoulder (she assumed they'd gone into the waste ground to relieve themselves), then returned and got back in, all three of them climbing in the sliding door at the side of the van, clearly intending to sleep.

Terri scrolled the footage forward. This stop lasted only three hours before a dishevelled-looking Joe emerged, got into the driver's side without delay and the van pulled away.

Terri let the video continue to play while she made a note of the location and times, and was looking back up at the screen to load the next piece of footage when she saw a car pulling in at the exact same location the van had so recently vacated.

It was a blue Ford Focus, and as she watched, a man climbed out. It was hard to put an age on him in the poor-quality video footage, but he was certainly thin and dark-haired, dressed in a loose denim shirt worn over jeans. Terri could see his face was wedge-shaped. Angular. And though he looked small, probably not much more than five feet five inches or so, his movements had an economy about them, an ease that spoke of lethality.

He paced up and down for a few moments, seemingly hunting about as if he was looking for something. Suddenly he kneeled and seemed to be examining the ground. For a moment, Terri wondered what exactly he was looking at, but then she understood: the tyre tracks. The man removed a phone from the breast pocket of his shirt and took photographs of the tracks, then stood, got back into his car and drove off in the same direction as the Keenans.

Terri rewound the tape and zoomed in on the registration plate of the car. She had a feeling it would come up on the system as having been stolen, or very possibly not existing at all, but that didn't matter. She could use the plate itself to track the car.

It was no surprise to Terri to learn that the Keenans had picked up the Ford Focus one day after they'd arrived in Ireland. Initially it had been five hours behind them, but slowly and surely it had caught up. On the first of November, the day Joe, Finbar and Rufus arrived in Ballinamore, the thin man in the Ford Focus got into town only thirty minutes after they did.

And there was no footage on any of the traffic cameras of him leaving.

20

Dawn Wilson was curled up on her sofa halfway through Zack Snyder's *Justice League*, a film she'd watched once before and was giving a second viewing to ascertain whether or not it was completely devoid of any redeeming features. So far all she'd come up with was that Jason Momoa made a way cooler Aquaman than any version she'd ever imagined and she was trying to work out if his characterisation was based on any of the elements she'd read in the comic books she'd collected since she was a kid when her phone rang.

The words *Number Withheld* flashed on the handset's screen. This wasn't an unusual occurrence in Dawn's world, however, as many government offices were ex-directory, so pausing her movie, she tapped the green icon on the display.

'Dawn Wilson here.'

'Commissioner, this is Regimental Sergeant Major Stewart O'Driscoll, at the Department of Defence. I apologise for the lateness of the hour, but I do need to speak to you about a matter of some urgency.'

'That's quite all right, Sergeant Major. Late phone calls are one of the perks of the job. What can I do for you?'

'I believe you have a team working on a case in Leitrim? Some human remains found in an area near the town of Ballinamore?'

Dawn sat up a little straighter. 'I'm wondering how exactly you came by that information.'

'That's not really important, Commissioner.'

'Begging your pardon, but it is.'

'You ran some searches on Derrada Woods through a government-controlled computer network.'

'Which I understood was encrypted.'

'It is. But not to me or my people.'

'Who exactly are your people, Sergeant Major? Within the Department of Defence obviously.'

There was a lull, and Dawn knew the man was considering answering the question. She suspected that while O'Driscoll most certainly had an office within the department, he worked for people whose reach went much further and higher than most civil servants.

After a moment he said, 'Sections of Derrada are owned by the Irish Defence Forces. We've used it as a training ground for some of our more... *special* operatives in the past, and while that practice has been discontinued, it remains an area of interest to us.'

'I wasn't aware of that. It doesn't appear in any of the information I've seen.'

'It's not a... commonly known fact. The kind of activities that are conducted in the area are not ones the public needs to know about. So I'm requesting, in the interests of professional courtesy, that you and your people behave with a modicum of discretion.'

Dawn couldn't stifle a guffaw. 'Sergeant Major, with the greatest of respect, who do you think you're talking to?'

'Commissioner—'

'It's my turn to talk now!' Dawn spat. 'I've had the Minister for Justice shouting down my ear this afternoon, asking me to instruct my team to, basically, do the bare minimum in their investigation, and to withdraw if they haven't found a smoking gun within seven days. Now I've got you on the phone in the middle of the night asking me to step carefully? What exactly am I supposed to be wary of? What might my representatives stumble over out there in the woods?'

'We launched our own investigation in Derrada a number of years ago.'

Dawn waited for him to continue. When he didn't, she said, 'And?'

'And it was unsuccessful.'

'What were you looking into?'

'I'm not at liberty to divulge that information. All I'm asking is that you keep me informed of anything you might find,' O'Driscoll said. 'I would appreciate it if the operation could be wrapped up as quickly as possible, and that you pass anything you learn on to me.'

'Sergeant Major, the investigation will be finished when it's finished. I will not be advising my team to rush *any* aspects of what they're doing. People have died and are still dying, and we have an obligation to try and find out why and to bring the perpetrators to justice. That's what my job is: to supervise, facilitate and support that exact task.'

'Will you at least keep me in the loop?'

'If I'm instructed to do so by my superiors.'

The soldier responded with a cynical laugh. 'And who do you consider to be your superiors, Commissioner Wilson?'

'I am answerable to the Minister for Justice, Equality and Law Reform.'

'Carroll? You know he's nothing more than a farmer who has a seat in the Dáil because his father had it before him?'

'It's not my business to think about matters like that,' Dawn said, rather primly. 'It's above my pay grade.'

'Why don't I believe that?'

'Goodnight, Sergeant Major. I appreciate the call.'

'I don't believe that either,' O'Driscoll said and hung up.

Dawn sat for a long time, gazing at the frozen image of Ben Affleck's Bruce Wayne on her television screen, wondering what exactly it was about Derrada Woods that seemed to have so many people ill at ease.

'So what did you make of all that?' Seamus asked Jessie as they rode the elevator to the third floor, where their rooms were situated. 'The old fella knows how to tell a story, doesn't he?'

'Folk tales and superstition,' Jessie said, her head buried in her phone. 'Although, we do know there's a history of disappearances and unnamed corpses, so perhaps we shouldn't rule out everything he told us. I mean, we're obviously not dealing with an 800-year-old vampire, but someone is up to no good in the woods. And I think the legend of the Abhartach has become part of their cover.'

Jessie slipped her phone into her pocket and, when the doors slid open, stepped into the corridor.

'Derrada Woods are a dense, mostly untended area of forest covering just under 2,000 acres, which, according to what I've just been looking at on my phone, translates to about three-and-a-half square miles. In a country as small as Ireland, it makes perfect sense that people who are up to no good, or who want to hide things – guns, money or bodies – would be attracted to a location like that.'

'And where bad people go, mischief follows,' Seamus said.

'Exactly. Deaths and disappearances aren't exactly unheard of when a criminal element gathers.'

They arrived at the door of Seamus's room and paused.

'There's also a distinct possibility the story of a vampire was perpetuated by the criminals themselves,' Jessie went on. 'What better way to keep curious locals at a distance than having them think a monster is hiding in the trees? I wouldn't be one bit surprised if it was Grace O'Malley herself who started the whole legend. She may well have been using the area to hide loot she'd plundered from the British or the Portuguese or whoever she encountered that week.'

'That does make sense,' Seamus agreed, taking his key card out of his pocket.

'Look, let's not ignore it,' Jessie said as he unlocked the door. 'I'll be sure to get Terri to have a close look at the legend and see if there's anything useful there. But to be honest, I'm inclined to think it's a rabbit hole we don't need to go down this time.'

Seamus laughed. 'I'm not going to pretend I'm not relieved to hear that,' he said. 'I think I've had enough Celtic demons to last me a lifetime.'

'Agreed,' Jessie said. 'Night, Seamus. Tomorrow we begin the hunt for this killer, and in so doing get Joe fully off the hook. I don't think vampires are going to feature very prominently in us doing that.'

Jessie Boyle would remember those words in the days to come and wonder how she could have been so wrong.

22

Jessie was lacing her boots the next morning when her phone buzzed. Convinced it was Seamus, she opened the message without thinking.

You have come to the forest to fight the dragon that lives there, the message read. *I hope you find him a worthy adversary. He has some particular talents you should appreciate. I've been following this particular pilgrim's progress for many years, and the thought of you and he pitting wits intrigues me. I shall be watching with interest.* ᚾ

Jessie sat where she was, gazing at the message. It had been sent from an unfamiliar UK mobile number. She knew there would be no point in following up the source either, as by the time the SIM card was tracked down, it would be long since dumped.

Yet Jessie knew exactly who had sent the message. The symbol ᚾ represented Uruz, the serial killer who'd evaded Jessie during the last case she'd worked as a behavioural specialist for the Met's Violent Crimes Task Force. Jessie had followed a trail of clues that clearly implicated another suspect, someone who had a history of violence against women. All too late, she'd learned the evidence had been planted, but by then Uruz, who had managed to remain below the radar during her investigation, had absconded.

The failure had driven her to leave the Met, and she'd been close to giving up her career in policing. She almost certainly would have if Dawn Wilson hadn't approached her and persuaded her to head up a new investigative team.

Jessie had initially been reluctant, but Dawn had brought considerable pressure to bear, calling in an old debt Jessie simply couldn't refuse to honour: while they were both students, she and Dawn had, during a physical altercation, accidentally killed Jessie's abusive stepfather, a fact they had subsequently covered up. The man was a known criminal, so the authorities simply assumed he'd been murdered by a rival, and his death hadn't been investigated with any enthusiasm anyway. Dawn had kept Jessie's secret for more than two decades but had finally used it to leverage the behaviourist into joining her new investigative team with Seamus and Terri.

Yet Jessie's return to Ireland had not brought an end to Uruz's vendetta. He'd manipulated the first case Jessie had worked for Dawn, goading a serial killer to draw her into a cat-and-mouse game that had almost resulted in the entire team being killed. Uruz, it seemed, was in contact with a network of predators and seemed determined to make Jessie's life as difficult as he could. She'd hoped his failing to end her life in Cahirsiveen might cause him to skulk away and bother her no more.

But now he was back.

Jessie forwarded the message to an officer in the tech squad who went through the motions of following up Uruz's contacts with her, then archived the message in a folder on her phone.

She wouldn't allow herself to be distracted by it, but she knew she needed to remain watchful. Uruz being even peripherally involved was never a good thing.

23

The local office of Coillte, the Irish forestry service, was situated in a couple of rooms above Ballinamore's one and only café, and just after nine, Jessie and Seamus mounted the stairs to find a woman unlocking the door.

'Good morning,' Jessie said as they came to the landing. 'We're looking for a Robin McTiernan?'

'Yes,' said the woman. 'That's me.'

The woman holding open the office door to allow them access was probably forty years old and about five feet tall. She had long blonde hair done in a thick plait that hung down her back, and she was wearing a yellow fleece and green canvas trousers. Jessie noted her hiking boots were sturdy but well worn.

'We're investigating the bodies found in Derrada Woods,' Jessie said. 'You spend some time there, I believe. Have you ever seen anything suspicious? Anyone coming or going who shouldn't be?'

The woman followed them into her workroom. Photographs of birds, animals and butterflies covered the walls, as did a selection of maps of various parts of the county, and the desk was buried under heaps of folders and binders.

The space had a cosy, contented feel – Jessie got the impression that the forestry worker loved her job, and while the office didn't seem to be blessed with many modern conveniences (she couldn't see a computer, for example), it gave off an aura of calm industry.

'I actually don't spend a huge amount of time in Derrada,' Robin said. 'I'm in charge of maintaining all the woodland in Leitrim, and Derrada is what you'd call mature woodland, meaning it very much looks after itself. Woods, when they get to a certain age, are self-sustaining: the wildlife does all the heavy lifting itself – deer keep grass and bracken down, badgers clean up deadfall branches to line their setts, jays and wood pigeon reseed areas where there's been tree loss due to woodworm or other larval infestation. Every now and again I need to arrange a cull of rabbits, as the population can get out of control, and I try to enforce the various game seasons, but to be frank, that's the job of the police, and they mostly turn a blind eye.'

'But you do visit Derrada?' Jessie said.

'Oh yes. A couple of times a month I do a walk-through of the parts used by hikers to make sure the paths are kept clear and maintained, and I organise a weekly clean-up of the areas we permit people to camp – that's mostly done by students and volunteers, but I coordinate it. Every year Coillte does a census of the population of birds and mammals living in all our wooded areas, and Derrada is no different. So I manage the whole thing and collate the data.'

'What does that involve?'

'It's literally a count.'

'How do you count the number of birds and animals?' Jessie wanted to know. 'It doesn't seem possible with a wild population.'

Robin struck her as slightly eccentric but capable. Jessie

doubted the woman had much time for people. Her life was one dominated by wild things, and human beings were a necessary inconvenience. Would she be so irritated by them she might feel driven to harm them though? Jessie didn't believe so.

'We don't *literally* count each one of them. If we can be sure there are a certain number of great tits in a single acre of the woods, which is easy enough to establish, we can then quantify what there'll be in the entire 500 acres, taking into account sectors of dense tree growth which wouldn't sustain certain species. We do the same with all the other birds and animals.'

'Do you ever go into those really deep parts of the woods?'

'I have been to the centre, to see the burial mound, when I first came to work here. It's quite a hike. The interior is very wild and overgrown, so it's not for the faint-hearted. Hikers don't usually go there, so I'm not called to much.'

'You haven't been back there since then?'

'I've had no reason to, so no.'

'The interior of the woods showed no sign of recent visitation?' Jessie asked.

The forestry agent paused. 'Well there was one thing, now you mention it, but it was very minor. Only someone who knows woodland would have noticed it.'

'What was that?' Seamus asked.

'There was a pattern of what are often known as wilderness corridors worn through a section of the undergrowth. Getting to the clearing along the route I took was difficult, but once I got there, I was able to make my way right to the mound along one of these basically clear pathways.'

'And why is that worthy of comment?' Jessie asked.

'Pathways like that are created by large mammals usually: deer or boar.'

'I'm still unsure what you're saying.'

'I wouldn't have expected to see evidence of that type of activity in an area like the burial mound. The ground vegetation is just too dense, and as it's technically a clearing, there isn't enough tree cover to make large animals feel secure. So those corridors are a bit of an anomaly.'

Jessie and Seamus exchanged a look.

'Is there anything else that might have made them, Ms McTiernan?' Jessie asked.

'Well,' the forestry agent said, her tone almost joking, 'I suppose a person might. But what would anyone be doing so deep in the woods?'

'You're aware of the bodies that were found in Derrada?'

'Of course. Nasty business.'

'Have there ever been any reports of people moving about in the woods who don't seem to belong? People who obviously aren't birdwatchers or hikers?'

'I sometimes hear of kids going into Derrada to drink beer and smoke marijuana. As long as they take their rubbish away with them, I don't see the harm in a bit of teenage rebellion. Other than that, there are occasional idiots starting fires, people cutting down trees for firewood or lumber – I usually get the calls first, although once again I pass most of it on to the police. But if you're asking me if anyone reported someone mysterious burying human remains, then the answer is a resounding no. I was as surprised as the next person when those bodies were unearthed. To be honest, I thought they had to be archaeological remains. I was shocked to learn they weren't.'

'So you have no sense of who might be responsible?'

'None.'

'Would you have any thoughts on who the victims might be?'

Robin McTiernan paused, and Jessie could almost see the cogs turning in the woman's head.

'I do not. Whoever did it, I only hope they've moved on. I'm due to do the wildlife census in one month's time, and I won't feel comfortable wandering about Derrada if there's something bad going on in there. Knowing a killer may be on the loose almost makes me glad of the bloody poacher!'

Jessie perked up at that. 'Do you know who this poacher is?'

'Of course! Everyone does.'

'Would you care to tell me his name?'

'Richard McCarthy,' Robin said ruefully. 'I've always found him quite harmless, though there are rumours he has links to certain factions in the North. Loyalist paramilitaries.'

Jessie and Seamus glanced at one another, but Robin didn't seem to notice.

'I'm sorry I can't be of more help,' she said. 'Maybe this is all the Abhartach's doing after all.'

'If it is, we'll be arresting him,' Seamus said without humour.

Richard McCarthy lived in a small, thatched cottage half a mile on the Sligo side of Ballinamore. When he opened the door to their knock, Jessie was surprised to see he was a handsome young man in his twenties, his face almost feminine in its beauty, his thick head of dark brown hair worn long, down to the shoulders. Jessie put him at about five feet ten, with a slim, athletic build.

'I heard about the bodies,' he said as he busied himself making coffee in the cottage's small kitchen, which, along with the cooker, sink and a tiny worktop – on which sat a thick wooden chopping board and what looked to be a professional butcher's knife – had just enough room for a table around which the three of them could sit. 'I'm not sure how I can help you though.'

'The body is, as yet, unidentified,' Jessie said. 'Do you have any thoughts on who it might be? Are there any local feuds, disagreements, instances of bad blood...'

McCarthy paused for a moment – it was just for a second, and if Jessie hadn't been watching him closely, she might have missed it.

'We're in rural Ireland,' the young man said. 'The Irish countryside has a long memory. Arguments over land. Family animosity that dates back to someone's prize ram being stolen thirty years ago. Arranged marriages that went wrong. You'll find it all here.'

'You think the body in the woods was killed over an old grudge then?' Seamus asked.

McCarthy shrugged. 'I didn't say it was. I said it could be. We're right next to the border too. Politics and religion run deep here. I'd be inclined to look there first.'

Jessie noted the young man had an educated accent, with just a shade of British to it.

'You've spent some time abroad?' she asked.

'My mother was from Surrey, so I grew up speaking like I'm from the Home Counties,' McCarthy said, laughing. 'A lot of it got knocked out of me when I started school – Leitrim is something of a Republican stronghold as I'm sure you know – but they couldn't beat it all out of me.'

'And what exactly couldn't they beat out of you?' Jessie asked.

'The accent, of course. Isn't that what we're talking about?'

'I heard a rumour you've got some connections to Loyalist groups across the border,' Seamus said. 'Interesting that you're pointing to a political or sectarian cause for the murder. Is there a particular group locally you'd like us to look into?'

McCarthy guffawed. 'You heard the story that I'm a Loyalist paramilitary, did you? As I said, it's a Republican area. I'm English. People put two and two together and get nineteen.'

'So you've never been involved in Loyalist activities?' Jessie asked.

'My uncle brought me to an Orange march once. I didn't like it. That's as far as it went.'

'And if I was to check the database of the Special Detective

Unit, I wouldn't find your name listed as being tied to any Loyalist faction?'

'I encourage you to do so,' McCarthy said, smiling. 'I am many things, but a terrorist isn't one of them.'

Jessie gazed at the young man searchingly and couldn't tell if he was bluffing or not. There seemed to be a mild amusement dancing behind his eyes, as if he knew something she and Seamus didn't. McCarthy was so self-assured, he exuded the sense that he couldn't possibly be anything other than innocent of any wrong-doing. Yet Jessie wasn't convinced. His confidence struck her as a cover, a mask.

Richard McCarthy was hiding something. She was sure of it.

'I like Surrey,' Jessie said. 'Do you visit much? You must have family thereabouts.'

'Would you believe me if I said I've never been there?' McCarthy smiled, pushing the plunger on the cafetière. 'I've never been much further than Limerick actually, and that was during a school tour. I'm a bit of a home bird.'

'Don't you feel you're missing out?' Seamus asked, accepting the mug of coffee McCarthy held out to him. 'You've never been on a foreign holiday or even been to the zoo in Dublin?'

The dark-haired young man laughed. 'Leitrim is one of the few places you'll find in modern Ireland that still has substantial space where civilisation hasn't encroached. I can and do spend days at a time walking the hills and woods here, camping out or simply sleeping under the stars. I've lived my entire life here and still haven't seen all of it. Why would I feel any desire to spend my precious time lying on a sun lounger beside a chemical-filled pool in a grotty apartment complex in Santa Ponsa when I have everything my soul needs right outside my front door?'

'I suppose I should feel jealous of that,' Jessie observed. 'Not many people are so happy with their situation.'

'I consider myself blessed.'

'How do you earn a living, Mr McCarthy?' Seamus asked.

'I'm currently between jobs.'

'What was your last place of employment?'

'Perhaps saying I'm long-term unemployed would be more accurate.'

'You've never had a job?' Jessie said.

'Not a salaried position. I draw the dole, but I don't really see myself as without work. My engagement with the country-side is all I really desire.'

'That's something of a luxury though, isn't it?' Jessie asked. 'How do you afford the rent on this cottage?'

McCarthy sat back in his chair and eyed the two detectives. 'Are you going to be informing social welfare of anything I say here today?'

'We certainly don't *have* to consult with them,' Jessie said. 'At least, not unless you give us a really good reason to.'

'Well then can we just say that I supplement my income by doing a little informal trapping and shooting throughout the year.'

'You sell the meat?' Jessie asked.

'Most of what I eat I have shot, caught or foraged,' McCarthy said. 'So that's the main motivation for what I do. But yes, I provide game meat to quite a few suppliers, and then there are a number of private citizens hereabouts who like a nice pheasant or a woodcock out of season. I can provide that.'

'How much hunting do you do in Derrada?' Seamus asked.

'Dependent on the season, I'm there a lot. During the autumn I camp in those woods for weeks at a time.'

'Where do you camp?'

'Do you want me to show you on a map? There's a few different sites I frequent.'

'Would you please?' Jessie asked.

The man got up and went into the adjoining room, returning with an iPad, which he fiddled with for a moment, before putting it down on the table. Jessie had to stifle a smile as she and Seamus leaned in so they could see – the iPad seemed a bit incongruous in the olde-worlde setting of the cottage, and at odds with McCarthy's 'living off the land' philosophy.

'I've put a pin in the three locations,' he said. 'Woodcock prefer slightly boggy terrain, and occasionally shelduck will nest in the woods too. There's a clearing here' – he indicated a place in the north-eastern corner – 'which is like an island in the middle of a bog. I pitch the tent there on the solid ground and use it to strike out in search of the birds.'

Jessie noticed the location he indicated was perhaps a quarter of a kilometre from the burial mound in the wood's centre.

McCarthy pointed out another place he camped when hunting deer, and one more he liked because it gave him access to pheasant, who liked the brighter, less-crowded parts of the forest.

'Sometimes I'll go in search of squirrel,' he said. 'Some of the more outré restaurants are stocking it now, so I can spend a day or two roaming about looking for those.'

'I presume you do a lot of hunting at night,' Jessie said.

'Some, yes.'

'So it would be fair to say you've been in Derrada Woods at all hours of the day and night?'

'I've lived there for periods of time, which means I've been there all day and all night.'

'Have you ever seen anything out of the ordinary while you were in there?' Seamus asked.

McCarthy laughed. 'Of course I have,' he said. 'Those woods are ancient. They've got their secrets and their mysteries.'

'Could you be more specific?' Jessie asked.

'I've seen figures moving about through the trees in places where no human could walk without sinking into the mire. I've seen a white deer, so bright you would swear it was lit up by some kind of electricity, emerge from the shadows only for it to vanish without a trace as soon as I trained my gun on it. And I've seen other things.'

'Other things?' Seamus asked.

'Things I know can't have been there. But at night, when the shadows are long and the moon is blocked out by the clouds, the eyes can discern things the mind struggles to process.'

'What exactly are you referring to?' Jessie asked.

The poacher looked at her gravely. 'I've seen a disfigured child,' McCarthy said, and there was neither humour nor irony in his voice now. 'In many different parts of the woods. I think he's been there for a very long time. The memory of Derrada stretches back to before Patrick first walked on these shores. I wouldn't be surprised if something old and angry has made the place its home.'

And that was all Richard McCarthy would say on the topic.

25

They sat in the MG on the laneway outside McCarthy's cottage.

'What do you think?' Seamus asked.

'I want to see if he's active with any Loyalist group,' Jessie said. 'He's a charmer, and his body language suggests a significant level of self-control. I think he knows far more than he's telling.'

'He says he doesn't leave the area often though.'

'That'll be impossible to confirm if he spends all his time wandering the countryside, but it's worth asking Waters all the same.'

'He volunteered that he spends weeks at a time in Derrada,' Seamus said. 'I don't think he'd do that if he was guilty of burying bodies there.'

'He is a hunter though,' Jessie said. 'So he's good at killing things.'

'There's that,' Seamus agreed.

Jessie's phone rang.

'Hi, Terri,' she said. 'I'm here with Seamus, so I'm going to put you on speaker, okay?'

'Hi, little sis!' Seamus called, grinning and (much to Jessie's amusement) waving at the phone.

'Hey, Seamus! I have the name of remains number ten,' Terri said. 'It wasn't difficult to track down the dentists who use that particular brand of porcelain in their crowns, and it was a... um... a process of elimination after that. I got a hit on the third dental practice I tried. The deceased gentleman got his caps fitted four weeks ago.'

'Went to his grave with great teeth,' Seamus said, shaking his head. 'What an awful waste.'

'I hadn't thought of it like that,' Terri said. 'But of course you're right.'

'So you've got the name. What can you tell us about him?'

'Well that's the point,' Terri said. 'The person that name belongs to is a ghost.'

'I don't follow.'

'His name is Eugene Garvey, according to the credit card he used to pay for the dental surgery. He also used health insurance, so I could chase that up. Mr Garvey has a date of birth, a social security number, even an employment record. But that's it. Nothing else. He apparently worked in insurance but doesn't seem to have ever come up for promotion – or been disciplined either, for that matter. He hasn't been married, and his health insurance shows only the dental appointment. He seems never to have visited a GP or even had his appendix out. What comes up when I run a check on him is not the contents of a human life. It's a vague facsimile of one.'

'I can't imagine that stopped you,' Jessie said. 'I've known you to work around harder problems.'

'Of course I didn't just stop there,' Terri said, her tone showing she thought the point so obvious it barely needed voicing. 'I dug a little deeper.'

'How deep did you go?' Seamus asked.

'When I got his credit-card details, it was easy enough to

find a driver's licence, so I had a photo of what Mr Garvey looked like before his death,' Terri said. 'I ran it through facial recognition software on every government database I could access.'

'Any joy?'

'Yes. I got just one bite.'

Seamus laughed. 'Are you going to make us wait to find out?'

'No, of course not. It was the Department of Defence.'

Jessie sighed and rubbed the back of her neck. 'Well that isn't going to make things easy.'

'I'm not finished yet.'

'You mean it gets worse?'

'Mr Garvey's file was redacted. I couldn't gain access. And I tried every trick I know, which is a lot. What does that mean, Jessie? I think I know, but I thought I should ask before I do anything else.'

'I think it's fair to say that Mr Garvey was employed by the Irish military at some level that requires a security clearance you and I do not possess,' Jessie said.

'Which is why his DNA didn't show up on any records,' Terri said.

'Feck,' Seamus said.

'Precisely,' Jessie agreed.

26

Dawn Wilson sat opposite Judge Peter McAllister in his chambers at the Four Courts.

White haired and massively obese, the eminent legal mind was wheezing as he read through her request to have the preservation order on Derrada Woods frozen, which would allow Forensic Ireland to move deeper into the forest to excavate, as their report recommended. Beside her, Wilhelmina Barden looked worried. At thirty years old, she was one of the youngest lawyers the Irish police employed, and Dawn wondered if she had enough experience to cope with the cut and thrust of supporting them at this level.

'This is a very straightforward matter, Judge,' Wilhelmina said. 'Another body was found in the woods just last evening, proving that Derrada is an active site for at least one killer, possibly more. We're seeking leave to search for further remains the forensic team believe may have been buried in the surrounding clearings. Sonic imaging has shown masses that may well be skeletal forms, but the prevalence of tree roots and other buried matter mean the only sure way to proceed is to break earth.'

'I understand that quite well, Ms Barden,' Judge McAllister said, looking up from leafing through the papers the lawyer had furnished him with. 'But I am also very clear that those woods are an important heritage site. You can't just go traipsing around digging up places of historical significance, you know.'

'The report you have in front of you explains that we're proposing targeted searches,' Dawn said. 'Our intention is not to wander willy-nilly about the place digging holes. We're looking for the remains of people whose lives have been taken through violence and buried without ceremony or sensitivity.'

The judge placed the sheaf of paper on his desk and sat back. 'And you know for certain further bodies have been interred in these woods?'

'No, but it makes sense—'

'How does it make sense? As I understand it, you don't know who the bodies you *have* found are. This sounds like a wild goose chase to me, and one that could damage important archaeological data.'

'Judge, I wish to state in the strongest terms that you are making a mistake,' Dawn said.

'From what I've been told, what we're dealing with here is the result of a Traveller feud. I'm a big believer in letting those people sort out their own issues in their own way.'

'Even if that is the case, they are breaking the law,' Dawn said. 'Laws both of us have sworn to uphold!'

'You do it your way and I'll do it in mine!' Judge McAllister said. 'Your request is denied. Now if you don't mind, I have to prepare for court.'

And that, it seemed, was that.

27

Jessie scheduled a meeting in the station in Ballinamore for midday. Sergeant Waters, the officer they had met when they first arrived in the village to interview Joe Keenan, insisted that Glenn, the chief investigator from Sligo, be present, so Seamus, Jessie and the two local guards sat, while Terri joined them via Skype on Jessie's laptop.

'Before we go any further,' Jessie said, 'I know you're all aware another body was discovered in Derrada last night, and none of us needs to be Sherlock Holmes to deduce Joe Keenan did not commit that crime. Can we just accept he's innocent and release him pending further investigation?'

'I'm going to need a bit more persuasion than that,' Glenn said mulishly.

Jessie sighed and nodded. 'All right then. Terri, you're up. Tell the group what you've learned.'

'Joe Keenan and his son travelled to Fishguard via Irish Ferries from Rosslare on the nineteenth of February 2015,' Terri said. 'The registration number of his van was recorded by both Irish and UK customs. In fact, the vehicle was searched at the Welsh end, although obviously not very thoroughly, as no weapons were found. However, it's clear they were in the UK from then until they returned on the twenty-first of October of this year, once again on a ferry into the port of Rosslare.'

'Doesn't mean Keenan didn't return in between those times,' Glenn said.

'I've run a search of all other ferries and planes in and out of the UK in the intervening period,' Terri replied. 'He wasn't on any of them. I used facial-recognition software to check passport scans, but I got no hits. Unless he was smuggled in on a container or in the boot of someone's car, Joe Keenan was out of the country for two years and eight months.'

'Which proves nothing,' Glenn said. 'We've been over this ground, Jessie. He still could have been involved.'

'Traffic cameras caught the Transit van at various points between Rosslare and Leitrim, and we can now confirm that the story Mr Keenan has given us regarding his arrival into Balli-namore is completely accurate,' Terri went on. 'He took a circuitous route to get to you, but there can be no doubt he's been truthful. He could not have buried the majority of the bodies discovered at the site.'

'Okay, so he might be being honest about that,' Waters said. 'What was he doing at these other locations he visited on his way here?'

'Sleeping would be my guess,' Terri said. 'The van wasn't stationary for more than a few hours. He remained on the move and was clearly following a route he hoped would help him avoid detection. Unfortunately, he failed.'

'What do you mean by that?' Glenn demanded.

'This man followed the Keenans to Ballinamore,' Jessie said, producing a blown-up print of the man's image from the CCTV footage. 'Picked him up very shortly after he arrived back in Ireland.'

It wasn't a great likeness, but it gave a sense of the lean cruelty of the man.

'Do we know who he is?' Waters asked.

'He doesn't show up on any police files,' Jessie said. 'But we have to assume he's been sent by the Dunnes.'

'Joe has been upfront with us about the fact the Dunne clan are out get him,' Seamus said. 'And we suspect they are, in fact, a much more viable suspect for the human remains that have been unearthed.'

Glenn sniffed, and said, 'I told Jessie the Dunnes haven't been seen in the Leitrim area for more than twelve months.'

'They haven't been *seen*,' Jessie said. 'But that doesn't mean they haven't been here.'

'The Dunnes are connected with twenty-three unsolved murders,' Terri said. 'They're suspected of being actively engaged in gun trafficking, the smuggling of everything from heroin to Chinese medicinal herbs into and out of the country, and of controlling a robbery ring that has targeted the homes of wealthy business owners. The Dunnes were one of the first groups to use the tiger kidnapping technique – kidnapping an official who's a key-holder to a safe, and holding his family to force him to access the funds.'

'These are very, very bad people,' Jessie said. 'Thieves, smugglers and murderers whom you have admitted spend time in this part of the world, yet you've arrested someone who, from what we can tell, is visiting for the first time?'

'Someone who, it appears, is being hunted by these very same bad people,' Seamus chimed in.

'Have you asked him if *he* knows who his shadow is?'

'Not yet,' Jessie said. 'While he's locked up, it's a moot point, wouldn't you say?'

'I for one would like to know what kind of evil bastard Keenan has drawn to my part of the countryside,' Glenn seethed.

'I think you're missing the point,' Jessie said. 'This man Terri has found on the traffic cams is someone we should look at as a suspect. If the Dunnes are using Derrada as a burial site, and this is their operative, I would think it's a good chance we've got our culprit.'

'And we'll be pursuing that in due course,' Seamus said. 'For now, though, can we just agree Joe is innocent so we can get on with finding the actual murderer before he decides to leave us another message?'

Glenn glowered at the younger man. 'I don't think we have the authority to release him,' he said through gritted teeth.

'Isn't it lucky then that I do,' Jessie said. 'Here's a letter from Dawn Wilson, the police commissioner. It authorises Joe's release, on condition he remains local until the case is solved. I'll take full responsibility if he absconds.'

Glenn read the letter, his face like stone.

'You're making a mistake,' he said through gritted teeth then tossed the page back across the table, stood and stalked out of the police station, banging the door behind him.

Waters sat where he was, a sheen of sweat on his forehead, looking extremely uncomfortable.

'I have the paperwork filled out already,' Jessie said, taking it out her bag. 'Sign, and we can get Joe out of that cell and on the way to seeing his son. I had arranged for the boy to be brought to the local community centre for an access visit, but I think it would be much better if his father went to pick him up to take him home, don't you?'

The fat cop did as he was asked.

Much to Jessie's surprise, Joe didn't seem overly excited when Waters unlocked the door to his cell to inform him he was free to go.

'Not before time,' the Traveller said, 'but better late than never.'

'I hope you're not going to be any trouble now, Joe,' Waters said as his former prisoner pulled on his shoes and, standing up, stretched expansively.

'I wasn't any trouble before you took me in, so I can't see as I will be now.'

Waters stood back to permit Joe to leave. As he drew level with the guard, the Traveller paused, and for a moment Jessie thought he would strike the rotund cop. Instead though, he extended his hand.

'You treated me with as much kindness as you could,' Joe said, grinning. 'I'm grateful for it.'

Waters seemed a little uncertain how to respond to the gesture, but he accepted the other man's hand and shook it gingerly.

'Right,' Joe said, turning to Jessie, 'I'm going to need my boy, my dog and my van.'

'It's all organised,' Jessie said. 'Seamus is bringing your van around as we speak. It's been stored in a parking bay behind the station. You and I can go and get your son, and Seamus will pick up your dog. How does that sound?'

'Works for me.'

The Transit van was out front when Jessie and Joe emerged, and the Traveller swore with annoyance when he pulled open the side door and saw that the flooring had been taken up and the living area was in complete disarray.

'I hope to feck they haven't damaged anything!' he said. 'I've put a hell of a lot of time and love into this vehicle. It's the only home Finbar and me have, and there was no call to wreck it like this.'

'Police searches are a nightmare for the house proud,' Jessie said. 'I'm sorry, Joe. Would you like me to help you reorganise it before we go to pick up your son?'

'Sure you don't know where anything goes,' Joe said, and Jessie could tell he was trying to get his temper back under control. 'Give me half an hour. I think I can get it back in order, or as close as doesn't matter for the moment anyway.'

Joe proved true to his word, and thirty minutes later the floor was set back in place and the van looked reasonably tidy again.

'They've taken every scrap of food I had,' he told Jessie. 'Can we stop at the supermarket on the way back? I don't have time to go huntin' for tonight's meal. There might be somethin' in the snares I set, but I left them days ago, so if anything did get caught, the foxes will have it by now.'

'You're a free man, Joe,' Jessie told him. 'You can't leave

Ballinamore, but you can go wherever you want and do whatever you like within the town boundaries.'

'Am I supposed to be happy about that?' Joe asked, though there was no animosity evident in his voice.

'You're on your way to see Finbar,' Jessie said, patting him on the back. 'Be happy about *that*.'

The residential unit that had been Finbar's home while Joe had been incarcerated was a mile outside Ballinamore on the Donegal side, and it took them fifteen minutes to get there on the country roads. The unit was based in a large bungalow that had at one time been the home of Ballinamore's GP – the Child and Family Agency had bought it from him when the doctor had retired and moved with his wife to a villa in Spain. It had a large garden which the staff had filled with outdoor play equipment. Finbar was sitting on one of the swings when Jessie and Joe pulled up outside the gate in the Transit, and he immediately jumped off and ran to the wall to greet them.

'I've got the letters and odds and ends of paperwork the staff need,' Jessie said. 'If you two hold on here, I can get all that sorted.'

'I promise we won't abscond,' Joe said, winking at her. 'Will we, Finbar?'

The lad shook his head, and Jessie, deciding she was going to have to trust them, walked down to the house to deliver what she was by now thinking of as Finbar's release papers. What neither she, nor Joe and Finbar – who were locked in a tight hug – saw was the blue Ford Focus that pulled into a gateway about fifty yards up the road from the unit.

Invited inside by the member of staff who opened the door, Jessie didn't see the short, angular man getting out of the car. Joe and Finbar finished their hug (Joe cried a little, but Finbar pretended not to notice) and began to chat about everything that had happened in the few days since they'd seen one another, so they didn't see the man until he was almost upon them.

And it was only then that Finbar saw he had a gun.

'And the food is awful here, Da,' Finbar was saying to his father when he saw the dark-haired, hatchet-faced man striding towards them down the country lane. Finbar knew him immediately – he and his father had faced this killer before, and that he was here meant only one thing. Without slowing his pace, the man raised his hand and it had a gun in it – one of those square-shaped pistols everyone seemed to have on the TV shows the kids in the unit liked to watch.

'Da – gun!' Finbar said, and without looking, Joe wrapped his arms around the boy and threw himself over the wall, taking his son with him as the gunshot sounded.

Joe felt the bullet whizz above them through the air, but he didn't have time to think about how close it had been because he knew they had only a matter of seconds before the shooter was on them.

'Stay in by the wall and don't move,' he hissed at Finbar and then rolled away from his son and got his feet underneath him.

Casting about quickly, he spotted a child's folding table and wooden chair which had been laid out for a toys' tea party: pink-and-white plastic cups and plates with tiny spoons. Joe grabbed the chair and stood up just as the sharp-featured man reached the wall. In the super-focus that comes in moments of extreme crisis, Joe saw the muscles in the man's arm clench as he prepared to squeeze the trigger a second time, but before the movement could be completed, he swung the chair in a sweeping arc, connecting with the shooter's hand at the wrist and knocking the gun sideways.

Joe heard the detonation of the shot, but it went wide. The sound of wood splintering filled the country air as the chair shattered from the force of the blow, and their attacker staggered back, but the respite this offered was brief. The man brought the gun back up again and would surely have fired if a stone the size of a chicken's egg hadn't come sailing through the air and struck him squarely on the side of the head. The impact of it stunned the shooter momentarily, and he dropped to his knees. As he did, Joe turned to see Jessie standing on the lawn right behind them.

'Run!' she said.

The two Travellers didn't need to be told twice, and Joe, grabbing his son by the hand, took off across the lawn, heading for the fields that lay behind the house. Jessie waited until they had raced past her before jumping the low wall and driving her boot into the prone man's midsection, knocking him onto the flat of his back. The gun skittered from his hand across the tarmacadam of the road, and Jessie bent to roll him onto his stomach so she could cuff him, but before she could, the fallen gunman lashed out with his legs, knocking hers from under her and causing her to tumble backwards. The force of the fall stunned Jessie for a moment, and all the air was driven from her lungs.

Worried the shooter might have a second gun, Jessie forced herself to roll over and staggered upright just in time to see her antagonist scampering up the road towards his car.

'Jessie, are you okay?' Joe's voice cut through the irritation she was feeling at having permitted the man to escape.

'I told you two to make yourselves scarce,' Jessie said, giving Joe a reproachful look.

'I thought you might need a little help,' Joe said. 'That fella is no slouch when it comes to fisticuffs, if you know what I mean.'

'I'm all right,' Jessie said, rubbing her back, which she knew would be stiff and sore in the morning. 'But if I'm not mistaken, I think we have a serious problem.'

30

Julia Banks emailed her report on the newest body to Dawn Wilson, who in turn emailed it to Terri.

There was one item in it that fascinated Terri, and after she'd spent a few hours researching it, she cross-referenced the details and called Dawn.

'I've got some information I think might be useful,' she said.

'I'm listening.'

'The man who was left in the woods yesterday had been moved there from somewhere in County Clare.'

'And how do you know that? It wasn't in the report.'

'I used some forensic pathology.'

'I've heard the term, but I don't know what it means off the top of my head. I was a beat cop and then a detective, Terri, so I didn't worry too much about the science.'

'Forensic pathology is... well, it's fascinating,' Terri said, her tone betraying her excitement. 'One of the most useful methods of dating remains is through an analysis of entomological organisms found in the cadaver. Forensic Science Ireland sends their samples away to a lab in Germany to have them analysed, and results can take weeks or even months to come back. So I decided to follow up on it myself.'

'And by entomological organisms you mean...'

'Bugs,' Terri said. 'If you bury a body in the earth, things that live there treat it like a buffet at first, and when there's nothing left to eat, the bones and whatever skin remains are used as accommodation.'

'And there were bugs found inside our boy? I thought he was relatively fresh.'

'Professor Banks found the husks of several cardinal beetles in the mouth cavity,' Terri continued. 'She included quite a bit of detail on them in her report. Cardinal beetles are carnivores but are lazy hunters, so an entire body must have seemed very attractive to them. The mandibles of the dead beetles contained human blood cells, which means the cadaver was still relatively fresh when the cardinals encountered it.'

'How does this have anything to do with the location?' Dawn asked.

'Cardinal beetles are quite distinctive in appearance,' Terri said. 'They have a bright red shell. Their life cycle only lasts for one year, but during that time they shed their outer carapace just once. And always at a particular time of year.'

'Which is...' Dawn prompted her.

'June. The husks the state pathologist, Professor Banks, found in those remains had to have been left there in the month of June. It looks as if the body was killed, and probably buried, several months ago, and was then dug up and placed in some kind of cold storage, before being deposited in the woods in Leitrim.'

'And they were buried in County Clare, you're telling me?'

'Yes. You see, this is where I got curious. I thought I'd read somewhere that cardinal beetles of the type found in the body's mouth are primarily found in one part of the country. And then

I remembered. It's in County Clare. And in one specific part of County Clare.'

Dawn was quiet for a moment. 'Where exactly?'

'The Burren. There are quite a few species of plant, animal and insect that are only found there. The cardinal beetle just happens to be one of them.'

The commissioner thought about that. 'Does that help us at all?'

'I've got an idea,' Terri said, 'but for now, it's just an idea.'

'Tell me about it.'

'The other body we were able to identify, Garvey, was employed by the military, probably military intelligence.'

'He was.'

'There's a military compound in Clare called RDF Premises that is, according to some private chat forums I hacked into, a base of operations for G2, the Irish Intelligence Directorate. And they're just outside Ennis – not more than twenty kilometres from the Burren.'

Dawn whistled through her teeth. 'That's purely conjecture,' she said. 'But I'm not going to pretend not to be interested in seeing where it leads.'

'Will I dig some more?'

'Do, please.'

'I'll get working on it.'

'Good girl.'

And Dawn hung up.

Jessie had asked Terri to see what she could find out about the Abhartach, so while she set some search software through the Irish military database to see if there was any reference to personnel from Clare who might have been recorded as missing in action or absent without leave, she spent some time researching Irish cryptozoologists and monster-hunters, hacking into a number of obscure sites on the deep web. To her surprise, there was a very active community of people dedicated to pursuing legends, folktales and urban myths with complete conviction that they were based on fact, and it was on one of these forums that she came across a number of entries from a person with offices on O'Hagan Quay, right there in Cork City.

A person who claimed they'd had an encounter with the Abhartach.

What particularly attracted Terri to this individual was that they didn't fit the profile of the other monster-chasers she'd encountered on the various web pages and wikis. They were cut from a very different cloth indeed.

She made a note to visit them the following day.

It was seven o'clock by the time she finished her research and headed out to get something to eat. Terri had rented an apartment in Douglas, a suburb a short bus ride from the city centre, but she still didn't feel at home there yet. As had been her practice when she and the team had been based in Cahirsiveen, Terri brought a sleeping bag into the office and when she got tired simply went to sleep beneath her desk.

It occurred to her it might be an idea to buy some camp beds – Jessie sometimes worked all night too, so she expected the suggestion would meet with her team leader's approval.

Terri picked up a pizza (olives, anchovies and pineapple, a choice of toppings Seamus informed her was the weirdest combination he'd ever come across) at an artisan bakery and returned to the office, where she ate sitting at her desk, scrolling through images of pages she'd photographed during the day's research.

As she worked, Bettina, one of the cleaning staff (Terri knew them all by name) stuck her head in. Bettina was in her fifties and spoke English fluently, albeit with a trace of an Eastern European accent.

'You here for the night, Terri?'

'Yes, I'll probably sleep here, but if I decide not to, I'll lock up.'

'I'll set the alarm before I go, so don't forget you'll need to deactivate it if you're planning on leaving or you'll have the security guards and the police down on you.'

'I know. I expect I'll be staying anyway.'

'Okay, have a good night.'

'You too.'

When Bettina was gone, Terri turned back to her research. She still had no real sense of what they were dealing with in Leitrim. Someone was killing people – people who, it seemed, had a connection to the military – and was either burying or dumping the bodies in the woods, but surely this had nothing to do with a prehistoric vampire legend.

Common sense dictated that over the centuries, a piece of ancient mythology had evolved into a story local people told one another to scare and entertain – the rural equivalent of an urban myth. She googled the term.

An urban myth is a humorous or horrific story or piece of information circulated as though true, especially one purporting to involve someone vaguely related or known to the individual

That certainly fitted the situation in Leitrim. Many claimed to know someone who had seen the Abhartach, but from what Jessie had told her, and from her own research, there was no one living who had seen the creature and could tell of it first-hand.

Unless the individual she was hoping to meet in the morning offered her some compelling evidence. But she wasn't going to hold her breath on that one.

As the shadows grew longer in the room, Terri turned to some scholarly writings on the Abhartach legend. James

Charles Roy, an Irish American author and historian, wrote that the story of the Abhartach 'marks a clear demarcation point in the historical development of the Celtic people'. Paganism, Roy suggested, was giving way to Christianity, and the story offered an interesting perspective on that struggle. Terri sat back and thought about it.

In the story, the druids offered a number of suggestions as to how the creature might be forced to remain dead, but everything they tried failed, and the vampire returned, looking for blood. It wasn't until a Christian saint stepped into the breach that the creature's reign of terror had been stopped. But even that wasn't permanent.

Terri realised that what the story was really about was the wildness at the heart of the Celtic soul. You could tame it for a while, but the true essence of the berserker Celt wasn't going to be controlled. It would always find a way to creep out and make mischief.

She wrote up some notes on what she'd learned and sent a brief email to Jessie, which she copied to Dawn Wilson, giving an account of her work and outlining her plans for the following day. She then watched a couple of episodes of *Garth Marenghi's Darkplace* on her laptop (she was a huge fan of the tragically short-lived horror/comedy/hospital soap/spoof) and then unrolled her sleeping bag.

Terri was one of those people who found sleep with ease: once she closed her eyes, she would be unconscious within moments. That evening was no different. Three minutes after she lay down on the floor beneath her workstation, the historian's breathing had become regular, and as the clock on her computer screen showed 10 p.m., Terri Kehoe was already in a deep and restful sleep.

31

As Terri was finishing off her research, Jessie, Seamus and the Keenans were back in Derrada. Joe and Finbar busied themselves setting up camp while Seamus played with Rufus.

Jessie had just lit the fire with a box of matches Joe provided when Dawn Wilson rang.

'I ran a check on your boy Richard McCarthy.'

'And?'

'He's affiliated with two Loyalist groups, although neither are exactly hardcore, and one hasn't been active in about a decade.'

'When you say affiliated,' Jessie said, 'what are we talking about?'

'He was picked up during a riot in Derry in 2017, but he wasn't charged. Then, earlier this year, his name was given as part of a plea deal by a very nasty man called James Kilduggan as being a member of a faction of the Ballymena Brigade, a now defunct Loyalist strike force. They were linked to a number of attacks on Catholic housing estates in rural areas in spring 2018, though none of them were ever caught.'

'How serious were the attacks?'

'They were bad, but no one died. Cars burned out, windows of houses broken, anti-Catholic graffiti sprayed on walls where kids would see it going to school. Nasty, but low-grade stuff compared to some of what happens daily in the North.'

'He flatly denied being involved in Loyalist activity,' Jessie said.

'He lied.'

'It doesn't make him our guy, but it certainly puts him high on the list of suspects.'

'Keep an eye on him. And keep me posted.'

32

By eleven that night, Joe Keenan, Finbar and Rufus were comfortably under the trees on the edge of Derrada Woods. Jessie and Seamus sat on a fallen tree and sipped tea Joe made from water heated over the open fire. He and his son were perched on battered-looking folding chairs.

Seamus took a folded copy of the picture of the man who'd trailed Joe to Leitrim and passed it over.

'This is the man you butted heads with today,' Seamus said. 'Do you know him?'

Joe unfolded the page deliberately and examined the image. 'Oh, I do indeed. His name is Beezer Muldoon. He's a hunter the Dunnes use.'

To Jessie's surprise, he passed the page to Finbar, who looked it over briefly before handing it back to Seamus.

'He arrived in town shortly after you did,' Jessie said. 'He'd been tracking you for days. He wasn't successful today, but we have to assume he'll try again. Which means you're in serious danger.'

Joe nodded thoughtfully. 'I don't suppose old Waters would feel inclined to give me my guns back.'

'Those unlicenced weapons they found hidden under the floor of your van?' Jessie laughed. 'No. I don't suppose he would. Have you encountered Mr Muldoon before?'

'Oh yes. I've tangled with him once or twice, and on each occasion, I barely got away with my hide intact. He's as bad a man as you'll find above ground. But sure, you got a taste of that yourself, didn't you?'

'Whatever you did to the Dunnes, it really upset them, didn't it?' Seamus said.

Joe shrugged. 'If you're going to do a job, you might as well do it right.'

Seamus eyed the older man for a moment as if he was considering forcing the issue and asking him outright what had occurred, then seemed to think better of it. Joe clearly didn't want to divulge the information, and in the end, it didn't really matter.

'Thank you for everything you've done for me,' Joe said suddenly. 'Ye owed me nothing but you helped anyway. There's not many would do that.'

'You're innocent of any wrongdoing,' Seamus replied. Rufus was lying at his feet, and he reached down and scratched the dog's ears fondly. 'So that makes it our job to help you. We appreciate your thanks, but they're unnecessary.'

They drank their tea in silence for a while.

Jessie, who had spent most of her life in cities, thought the sound of the wind through the night-time trees was quite beautiful – she realised she had never taken the time to appreciate nature before and wondered if all this crime-fighting in rural Ireland might be altering her perspective somewhat. She had to admit she felt a very long way from home, but to her surprise, that didn't make her uneasy. She was out of doors on a pleasant night with Seamus, whom she thought of as a close friend, and in a very short space of time she had come to like Joe Keenan very much too.

'What are you going to do about them bodies?' Joe asked after a few moments had passed. 'Someone put them there. It'd be good to know who it was, so the Gardaí can stop bothering me about it.'

'That is precisely what Seamus and I are here to find out,' Jessie said.

'How?' Joe asked.

'By doing what we do.'

Joe gave her a look that told her he would very much like to know what that was.

'We've already begun interviewing people,' Jessie explained. 'We'll ask questions and examine the answers we get, and those answers will suggest other questions, and those answers will pose more questions, and as we go around asking people, we'll build up a picture that will hopefully give us a sense of what's going on.'

'That's the theory anyway,' Seamus said with a grin. 'Although I have to say, right now, I like Beezer Muldoon for this. My guess is he's a regular visitor to the area, and the bodies are here because of him. If only we could find some eyewitnesses to put him here.'

'Maybe you should ask the boy if he saw anything,' Finbar suddenly said.

He'd barely spoken since the attack at the residential unit that afternoon, so it was a surprise to Jessie and Seamus to hear his voice.

'Do you mean one of the kids in the house where you've been staying?' Jessie asked.

The lad shook his head.

'Someone you've seen in town?' Seamus ventured.

'Come on – speak up, Finbar,' Joe said, though not unkindly. 'Tell us who you mean.'

'The boy in the trees,' Finbar said, looking at his father as if this was the most obvious answer in the world.

Jessie sat forward, gazing intently at Joe's son. 'You've seen a little boy playing in the woods?'

'I saw him on the first night we was here,' Finbar replied.

'Where, Finbar?' Seamus asked.

'Over there.' The boy pointed to his left, indicating a direction that led deeper into the forest rather than back towards town.

'What time did you see him?' Jessie prompted.

'Late.'

'Late like now?' Seamus suggested.

'No. It was *really* late. I'd got up 'cause I needed to have a pee. Da was asleep, and me 'n' Rufus went out into the woods so I could go.'

'We have a chemical lav in the van, but we don't use it unless for solids, if you get my meaning,' Joe said primly.

'Do you recall Finbar leaving the van, Joe?'

The boy's father shook his head. 'I didn't turn in until after midnight that day,' he said, 'so it must have been after that, but I'm a heavy sleeper. If Finbar says he went, you can be sure he did. His word is good.'

'How far did you go from the van?' Jessie asked.

'I can show you,' the boy said.

Jessie nodded, and they all got up and trooped through the trees for about twenty yards, using the torches on Jessie and Seamus's phones to light the way.

'This seems quite a long way to trudge in the middle of the night,' Jessie said.

'Da always says you don't pish where you live,' Finbar explained. 'And you don't use the same place every time neither. It starts to stink and attract rats and such.'

'Very wise,' Seamus said, for want of anything better to say.

'It was here,' the boy said after a minute or so.

'You're sure?'

'I remember the holly bush,' Finbar said, and Jessie swung

the beam of her torch onto the plant the boy was pointing at, its spiky leaves such a dark green they were almost black in the night air.

'Tell me what you saw,' Jessie said. 'Try to remember as much detail as you can.'

'I was standing right here,' Finbar said. 'Right at this tree.'

'If it was so late, you must have been tired,' Jessie offered.

'I was sleepy,' Finbar admitted, 'and I just wanted to get back to bed.'

'Are you sure you didn't dream the boy?'

'Rufus started to growl, and that woke me up. He only growls if there's strangers about, so I thought we might be in trouble.'

'You reckoned it might be the Dunnes?' Jessie asked.

The boy nodded. 'It wasn't though,' he said. 'It was just a kid.'

'On his own?' Seamus asked.

Finbar nodded again. Jessie was starting to understand that he only spoke when he had to. Which meant his story was, most likely, true, or he thought it was, at the very least. This was not a child who sought attention or was prone to flights of fancy.

'Didn't you think that was strange?' Jessie asked. 'For a child to be on their own in the woods so late?'

'I was on *my* own,' Finbar said, and there didn't seem to be an argument to that.

'How far away was he from you?' Jessie wanted to know.

'See that oak tree over there?'

'Which one is that?'

'It's the one with the split trunk. Looks like a capital Y,' Finbar said.

Jessie cast about until she found the tree. 'How far away would you say that is?' she asked Seamus.

'About twenty-five yards.'

Jessie thought that seemed an accurate guess. It was close

enough to see, if there was light. The dark would make things much more difficult though.

'How could you be sure it was a boy?' she asked Finbar. 'You said it was the middle of the night...'

'I knowed he was a boy because he was small,' Finbar said. 'Maybe even smaller than me. I could see because of the moon. It wasn't full, but it was very bright – not like the day, but I could see him real clear like.'

Jessie cast Seamus a look, and he googled it.

'If the lad says the moon was bright, then you can be sure it was,' Joe said testily.

'I'm gonna be honest and say I haven't a clue,' Seamus said. 'According to moongiant.com the moon was in a "waning gibbous phase" but what that means I can't tell you.'

'I'm sorry, Joe, but we have to check,' Jessie said before turning back to Finbar. 'What did he look like, this boy? Was he playing?'

'He was walking,' Finbar said. 'He had a bag on his back and a hat on his head, and a long coat.'

'What colour were they?' Seamus asked. 'Could you tell?'

'They were green and brown.'

'Do you mean camouflage colours?' Jessie asked. 'Like a soldier would wear maybe?'

'Not like a soldier,' Finbar said, shaking his head. 'More like what me and Da wears.'

The Keenans seemed, despite their lifestyle, not to wear clothes specifically designed as outdoor wear, yet for all that, their garments were certainly chosen to blend into their surroundings and were made of hard-wearing fabrics: denim, linen and wool. Jessie wasn't sure what this meant in relation to the child Finbar had seen: could he be another Traveller perhaps? She filed the information away in her head for future consideration.

'Did you see his face?' Seamus said.

'Only for a moment,' the boy said. 'Rufus barked, and he looked over.'

'So you got a good look at him?'

The youngster nodded.

'There was something wrong with it,' he said, his voice a hushed whisper.

Jessie suddenly became aware that, above them, bats – tiny pipistrelles, which looked for all the world like black sparrows in the shadows thrown by their torches – were flitting among the branches of the trees overhead. It made her think of the stories Ollie had told them, tales she wanted to ignore but which seemed determined not to go down without a fight. She shivered, despite herself.

'How do you mean there was something wrong with him?' she asked, feeling a knot in the centre of her stomach.

'It was like the skin on his face was moving – like water maybe,' the boy said. 'It seemed as if there was ripples in it.'

People spoke of seeing a deformed child, Ollie had said. This had to be a coincidence.

What was going on here? Jessie wondered. What had she and her team stepped into this time?

'Do you think he saw you?' she asked, forcing fear from her mind.

The boy nodded.

'How do you know that?'

'He stopped walking and he looked right at me,' Finbar said. 'He looked at me and I looked at him. And then...'

The three adults were all gazing at the lad expectantly. The only sound in the night-time woods was the wind through the branches.

'What, Finbar?' Seamus asked. 'You don't have to be afraid, lad. You've done nothing wrong.'

'He put his finger to his lips, like he was telling me to

"shush",' Finbar said. 'Like this was our secret, his and mine. And then he turned and kept on walking.'

'Deeper into the trees?' Jessie asked.

'Yes.'

'Brilliant,' Jessie said to no one in particular. 'Just brilliant.'

33

Terri awoke with a start. She lay gazing at the ceiling for a moment then reached over and picked up her phone, which was sitting on an office chair charging. The display told her it was 3.35 a.m.

Terri couldn't remember the last time she'd experienced disturbed sleep but wrote it off as being down to overeating (she'd consumed the entire pizza, which was something she rarely did – if anything, Terri was prone to *under*eating) and too much caffeine right before bed (she'd had a cappuccino while watching *Garth Marenghi*, and while this would usually not have any impact on her, Jessie constantly chastised Terri for drinking coffee so late, and she assumed her boss's warnings were finally proving accurate).

As she gazed at her phone's screen, the historian also realised she had to pee. Yet again, this was an unusual occurrence for her, as she usually slept the entire night without having to visit the bathroom, but Terri reckoned there was a first time for everything, and, unzipping her sleeping bag, stood up and padded across the office towards the bathroom in stockinged feet.

She had just reached the ladies' room when, from the corner of her eye, she spotted that the main door to the office was wide open. And Terri distinctly remembered Bettina closing it as she'd left earlier that evening. The cleaner had a habit of closing the door and then turning the handle up, which caused a mechanism in the door frame to seal, keeping the heat in. Terri remembered hearing the 'click' as she did this.

So why, then, was the door open now? And most importantly, who had opened it?

She froze where she was, grasping the handle of the door to the bathroom, her full bladder aching dully as her heart began to beat faster. It suddenly occurred to her that she was the only person in the entire building. The office suite she'd rented for the team was on the fourth floor, which meant she had a long way to go to make it to the safety of ground level, and Bettina had commented to her at one stage that no one else ever spent the night in the offices. The alarm system, the cleaner had informed her, should keep her safe, as it was directly connected to both the offices of a security company and Cork City Police Station, which was less than thirty yards from the building.

It seemed that assurance had been somewhat premature, however. No alarm had gone off. No one was rushing to her aid. Terri realised, in a moment of terrifying clarity, that she was completely on her own – and very far away from assistance.

And she'd left her phone on its chair, right across the other side of the room.

She gazed about her, and her eyes fell on the wall of glass windows that fronted the office, overlooking the River Lee and the bustling dockside. She could see herself reflected in the glass. And in the darkness, over her shoulder, standing by the wall behind what was to be Jessie's desk, was a dark figure.

Terri couldn't make out any features, but she was sure it was a man dressed in black with some kind of face covering – possibly a balaclava or ski mask. Neither of them moved for several heartbeats. Then, in a rapid, lunging motion, Terri dragged open the bathroom door, threw herself inside and, running to a cubicle, flung herself in before bolting it shut, after which she squatted up on the toilet bowl and wrapped her arms around her knees.

Terri crouched there, trying not to breathe. In the absence of her phone, she began to count in her head, partly to ground herself and partly to keep track of time.

Don't panic, she thought furiously. *Focus on the numbers and you'll be fine.* As the thought crossed her mind, she realised how stupid it was, but she had nothing else, so clung to the idea in all its silliness.

She'd counted off a beat of 180, meaning three minutes had passed, give or take, when she heard the door to the bathroom slowly opening. A jolt of white-hot terror seized her so powerfully, she thought she might faint dead away, but somehow she retained her consciousness and remained where she was, teetering on the toilet seat, rigid with fear. The door stood wide for several long moments, as if whoever was there was deciding whether or not to come in. Terri held her breath. Then there was the sound of the door swinging closed, and slow and deliberate footsteps across the tiled floor of the bathroom. Terri expected that the cubicle doors would be tested, but to her surprise, the person walked as far as the end of the room, paused for a moment and then walked back.

She heard the door open and close, and then silence.

Only then did she realise that, at some point during the ordeal, she had wet herself.

She remained perched on the toilet until she reached a count of two thousand. Only then did she stiffly get down and, trembling, creep to the bathroom door. There she remained, listening closely to see if anyone was still in the office outside. Hearing nothing, she gingerly peeped out.

The office door was now closed, and a panicked investigation of the darker recesses of the space proved her to be completely alone.

Ten minutes passed before her hands stopped shaking enough for her to ring Jessie.

34

Ninety minutes later, Terri sat in the lobby of the Elysian Building while a team of crime-scene investigators went over the fourth-floor offices. She'd changed from her urine-sodden clothes into an old tracksuit she kept there in case of emergencies. She could still smell herself but knew a shower wasn't going to be an option for some time yet.

She spoke to Jessie over the phone. 'I've been into the alarm software, and I can't find anything out of the ordinary.'

'What does that mean?'

'That the alarm triggers throughout the building just weren't tripped.'

'How is that possible?'

'As I understand it, every building has a blueprint of where the alarm sensors are, but only the security company would hold that.'

Jessie was silent for a moment. Then: 'Theoretically, could you hack into the security company and get those blueprints if you wanted to?'

'Yes, I could.'

'Then someone else could too.'

'Sadly, yes.'

'I know I'm wasting my time, but the CCTV cameras in the building?'

'Shorted out at the circuit breaker.'

'Is this a naïve question, but shouldn't that have also tripped an alarm of some kind?'

Terri laughed drily. 'Whoever did it inserted a piece of silver foil – in this instance, a gum wrapper – between the cable and the board. Which prevented the alarm signal being sent. It's old school, but very effective.'

'And they didn't take anything?'

'Not that I could see, no.'

'Did they try to access any of the files on the computers?'

'I've set up a system which records every time the filing system is logged into,' Terri said. 'The last login that was recorded was my own.'

'You're not going to like my asking this but...'

'No, Jessie, there's no way this person could have hacked around that. And if they *were* good enough to do so, they wouldn't have needed to come into the office. They could have done it remotely.'

'Fair enough,' Jessie said. 'I had to ask.'

'I know. And that's my honest answer.'

'You got a look at them? The intruder?'

'Briefly. It was... it was just their reflection in the window, but I saw them, yes.'

'Tell me what you saw.'

Terri closed her eyes for a moment, trying to draw to mind the exact image she'd witnessed.

'I saw a person, dressed entirely in black, and their face was covered by something – maybe a balaclava, or perhaps a ski mask. I suppose it could have been a bandana pulled up over their mouth and they could have had a hood up maybe. I can't be entirely sure.'

'Did you get a sense of their height?'

'Ummm...' Terri thought about that. 'I'd say they were aver-age. They certainly didn't seem particularly tall or very small either. There was nothing remarkable about them.'

'What about their build? Did they seem heavy-set, or muscular, or skinny?'

'I'd say they seemed slender,' Terri said, right away. 'That was the impression I had. Slim, but strong-looking.'

'That's great, Terri,' Jessie said. 'That really helps. Did you smell anything out of the ordinary? Aftershave, or deodorant, or even BO?'

Terri paused before saying, 'No, I can't say I did. I was a good distance away from them, and in the bathroom there's all the detergents and everything, so that was all I got. I'm sorry, Jessie.'

'Don't be – it was a long shot anyway.'

'There is one thing I can add to the picture,' Terri said. 'I don't know if it'll help, but it might.'

'Go on.'

'I noticed the way they moved. When I was hiding in the stall and they were in the bathroom – I could hear their steps, but they weren't heavy. It seemed as if they put each foot down with, well, with purpose. Almost like a dancer might. With... um... well, with precision.'

'That's interesting,' Jessie said.

'Does it help?'

'It sounds like someone who's used to moving about in woodland, where putting a foot out of place might give away your location.'

'Does that ring a bell?'

'I'm trying to draw up a picture, so I might compare it to people we encounter as part of the investigation. There's someone Seamus and I interviewed recently, a poacher called

Richard McCarthy, who's slim and lives for weeks at a time in the woods.'

'Do you think it's him? Could he break in to the building through all the security measures?'

'I have no idea. But that leads me to another question: what were they doing there in the first place?'

'I've been thinking about that,' Terri said. 'And I can only come up with two possibilities.'

'I'm listening.'

'The first one is, I hope, being addressed upstairs right now by the crime-scene boys.'

'Which is?'

'The planting of a bug of some kind.'

'That was my first thought. The other possibility?'

'It was a warning,' Terri said. 'He was letting us know he could get to us if he wanted to. Jessie, I was digging about in the Department of Defence online registry again today. I'm wondering if that might have triggered a response.'

'I don't know if that's actually scarier or not,' Jessie said.

'All I know is that I *am* scared,' Terri sighed.

They were quiet for a while, then Jessie said, 'Uruz has been in contact with me again.'

'Do you think this might have something to do with him?' Terri asked.

'It doesn't seem his style.'

'In what way?'

'You're still alive.'

'Oh. I don't know whether I should be relieved or horrified to hear that. I think I'm both at the same time.'

'We can't rule him out though. I don't think you should sleep in the office anymore for the moment. It makes you too easy a target.'

'I... well, I'd already reached that conclusion on my own.'

'Good. I'd hoped Uruz would have skulked away with his

tail between his legs when Cahirsiveen didn't go as he planned, but it looks as if he's still watching us at least.'

'He knows you're in Leitrim?'

'He implied he knows the killer. And he knows I'm working in a forested area.'

Terri sighed and rubbed her eyes, which were itchy from lack of sleep.

'He *does* know you're in Leitrim then.'

'I think so, yes.'

'Are we looking at a leak within the NBCI? I mean, how is he getting this information?'

'I've thought of that.'

'It's worrying, Jessie.'

'So far, all he's done is taunt us from afar.'

'And bring you to the attention of a very dangerous serial murderer. And almost get both Seamus and myself killed.'

During their investigations in Kerry, Seamus had been abducted and seriously injured by an associate of the killer – a man Uruz had manipulated into drawing Jessie and her team into the case with a view to killing the behaviourist and those she cared about. That same killer had targeted Terri and ultimately tried to murder her. She'd managed to defend herself but had barely escaped with her life.

'Okay. Fair point. I was probably trying to persuade myself more than you that he's just a twisted personality who's playing games with us.'

'He's an unknown quantity,' Terri agreed. 'All we can do is be extra careful.'

'That goes for you too.'

'I promise, Jessie.'

'Good. Keep in touch, and let's hope we can all be together soon.'

'I hope so.'

And they hung up.

PART THREE
HEARING THE SONG

9 November 2018

'No one who loves the woods stays on the path.'

Millie Florence

35

Terri Kehoe stood outside the office block on Horgan's Quay in Cork City and checked her notebook for the fifteenth time that morning. She was there to speak to someone who claimed to have come face to face with a Celtic legend in real life, and the encounter had cost them dearly.

The research Terri had carried out told her this person was a monster-hunter, but in truth, she knew they were much more than that.

The standard cryptid hunter was a misfit, often unemployed, usually still living with their parents, generally seeking validation from their equally socially awkward peers and not seeming to care much what anyone else thought.

Not the subject of Terri's visit though. The individual she planned to interview was a former military operative, someone with a track record of excellence in their field and numerous commendations to their name. Their career path had looked to be secure until something had gone badly wrong for them.

Something that happened during training manoeuvres in Derrada Woods and changed the trajectory of their life forever.

The office block was a new build on the city's waterfront –

a large, mostly glass structure had been added to the home of an old shipping company, its black and crystal bulk rising above the River Lee in opulent splendour. There was a café on the ground floor, but the new block behind it contained work-spaces for everything from accountants to publishers to soft-ware engineers, and among these the person Terri had come to see.

Satisfied she knew where she was going, Terri found her way to the elevator, and rode it to the fourth floor, following the corridor right to the end, where she was met with a plain wooden door with a sign affixed at eye level: *O'Hagan – Research and Investigations.*

Terri knocked.

'Come in!' a voice hollered from inside.

The door opened to reveal a small, stuffy room, the only redeeming feature of which was a large screen window that offered a gorgeous view of the river and some old grain stores on the opposite side. The space contained little more than a large desk, behind which sat a middle-aged woman wearing a ragged-looking cardigan over a faded, loose denim shirt. Her complexion was sallow and her face lined, suggesting she spent a good deal of time outdoors. The woman's hair, which was dark brown shot through with grey, was worn long about her shoul-ders, and her pale blue eyes were lively and electric with intelli-gence. Terri thought her mouth, which was thin and pursed, betrayed a slight cruelty, but then, Terri was wary of most people.

'Can I help you?' the office's occupant asked.

'You're Emer O'Hagan?'

'That's what it says on the door.'

'Um... it doesn't actually...'

The woman sighed impatiently. 'Wouldn't you agree it *implies* it then?'

'You were a sergeant in the infantry corps of the Irish

Defence Forces up until March 2014? You were injured during a training exercise in Leitrim. Quite seriously injured, I believe.'

The woman looked at Terri with thinly veiled annoyance.

'I know by looking at you that you're *not* a soldier, which means you're a cryptozoologist. I've told you people before, do not come annoying me at my place of work!'

'I'm not a cryptozoologist. But I do want to ask you some questions. It's... it's quite important.'

Emer O'Hagan narrowed her eyes. 'Who are you, and what do you want?'

'According to the Defence Forces personnel files, you retired with full pension and set up your practice here as a private investigator. But from what I can see from your online activity, you spend as much time pursuing a case linked to your leaving military service as you do following unfaithful husbands or looking into insurance fraud.'

'If you don't tell me who you are right now, I will throw you out the door you just came in, and I won't be gentle,' Emer said, and although her tone remained moderate, the cut of that cruel mouth told Terri she would make good on the threat.

'Give me a second to explain please,' Terri said. 'May I sit down?'

There was only one other chair in the room, and Emer nodded at it, so Terri sat.

'My name is Terri Kehoe, and I work with the National Bureau of Criminal Investigation.'

Emer shook her head. 'You don't look or smell like a cop.'

'I'm not. I'm a historian.'

'And now I'm confused.'

'I'm working a case in Leitrim, and as part of it, my team has encountered a story you seem very interested in.'

The woman surveyed Terri through lidded eyes. 'You've been to Derrada then?'

'Not yet. My friends are there now though. I'll be going to join them later today.'

'I'd stay right here if I were you, and I'd tell your friends to come home.'

Terri paused for a moment, considering, before saying, 'Someone tried to break into my team's offices last night.'

'So?'

'I think it's connected to the case.'

'Why do you think that? You're police. They could have been looking for anything.'

'We're not working any other cases. I think a site or a search subject I utilised yesterday set some alarm bells ringing somewhere.'

Emer frowned. 'Were you followed here?'

'I... I don't think so.'

'Did you check? Were you careful?'

'Ms O'Hagan, I'm a historian. I wouldn't know *how* to check. I walked from the Elysian Building, and no one *seemed* to be following me. If that makes you feel any better.'

Emer shook her head. 'You're out of your depth,' she said. 'Abandon the case now and bring your people home. This is not going to end in anything other than pain for all of you.'

'Why do you say that?'

'Because those woods belong to him,' Emer said. 'I know, because I strayed into his territory, and I barely got out alive.'

'You're talking about the Abhartach,' Terri said, fascinated.

'That's what the locals call him,' Emer said. 'I'd been sent on a command training exercise. I'd almost made it through Derrada and could see the treeline about fifteen yards ahead. I was making a run for it when he hit me. Hard.'

'You're sure it was this Abhartach person?'

'Originally, I thought it was... well, I thought it was someone I'd met long ago, but when I *really* saw him, I knew he was something else.'

'What?'

Emer O'Hagan shook her head.

'It doesn't matter. It was then I realised he'd cut me. Deep. He had this huge blade – I'd never seen one quite like it before – and he opened me from the bottom of my ribcage to my pelvic bone. I remember... I was sure I was going to die. I've been in combat many times, but I had never felt fear like that. I'm not ashamed to admit that I was terrified.'

Terri watched Emer as she spoke. It occurred to her that this must have been an awful experience, that the woman had effectively been eviscerated, yet she spoke of it with a cool objectivity, as if she was talking about someone else. She was saying the words, telling Terri she'd been afraid, but they rang hollow, as if their emotional impact had long been suppressed.

'How did you get away?' Terri asked.

'He let me. One moment he was there, gazing out of those cold, dead black eyes, and the next he was gone. I managed to ring for help before I passed out. They patched me up, but I still have to shit into a bag.'

Terri detected just a hint of emotion as Emer said that – someone else might have missed it, but Terri, who had grown up in the care system, was used to dealing with people who worked hard at repressing their feelings.

Some pain simply couldn't be fully buried though. Shards of it leaked out, no matter how hard you tried.

'Why do you think he let you go?' Terri asked gently.

'So my team would know to keep away. The army sent in a crew to sweep the place, but they found nothing. He was long gone back into whatever hole he lives in by then. They never used those woods for training exercises again though. So he got what he wanted.'

'Why would he want that, Ms O'Hagan? Is the military a regular presence in Derrada?'

Emer shrugged. 'Now, not at all. Back then, it used the woods occasionally.'

'Don't his actions seem a bit like overkill then?'

'He was protecting his territory. He'd set a perimeter and I breached it.'

Terri took her notebook from her pocket and leafed through it. 'You're referring to military tactical defence manoeuvres.'

Emer shrugged again.

'Are you telling me this person has a military background? Like you do yourself?'

'I'm not telling you anything other than to get out of Leitrim.'

Terri wasn't a trained interrogator like Jessie or Seamus, but she was an expert researcher, and she knew when she'd stumbled onto an important piece of information. She decided to push the point. 'You'd recognise a fellow soldier, wouldn't you?'

Emer snorted at that. 'There are many different kinds of soldiers. Some are barely worthy of the title. You don't know what you're talking about.'

Terri blinked at that but scribbled in her notebook before putting it back into her pocket. The private investigator's reactions had told her everything she needed to know.

'Do you believe in vampires, Ms O'Hagan? On several entries on cryptozoologica.com you refer to the Abhartach as a monster. You're a trained soldier, someone who's seen action on three different continents. Surely you don't really think there's a mythical creature living in a forest in Ireland's smallest county?'

'What does it matter what I think?'

'You're hunting him,' Terri said. 'I've been following your activity online, and it's obvious you're trying to find out what's been going on in those woods. That's what my team are trying to do as well. Maybe we can help one another.'

Emer sighed deeply and ran her fingers through her hair. 'From the first time I ever went to a war zone, I came across monsters,' she said. 'They come in all shapes and sizes. I've seen people do things to one another that would make you wonder if they've forfeited their right to be called human.'

'And you think that's what the Abhartach is? Someone like that?'

'Whatever you want to call him, he's death,' the former soldier said, sounding tired now. 'The only advice I can give you is to get away from there and never look back.'

Emer O'Hagan stood and motioned at the door.

'I'm going to have to ask you to leave now. I have another appointment.'

And Terri did just that. The conversation, it seemed, was over.

36

Terri found a bench on the waterfront and rang Jessie.

'I just met someone who had an encounter in Derrada Woods,' she said after they'd said their hellos.

'That's interesting,' Jessie retorted. 'Because I had a similar conversation last night before you rang. With everything else that was going on, it didn't seem pertinent to tell you about it.'

Terri watched a herring gull weaving and bobbing on an air thermal above the River Lee.

'Someone is active in those woods, Jessie,' she said. 'And I believe Emer O'Hagan thinks they've at least got some military experience.'

'I'm beginning to think that's the case all right,' Jessie agreed. 'And let's face it, the military keep popping up in all of this.'

'It might not be so simple though,' Terri said. 'Emer said there are all kinds of soldiers.'

'So we could be talking about the Irish Armed Forces, or Northern paramilitaries,' Jessie said. 'We had considered them at the beginning of all this.'

'Well here's what Emer told me,' Terri said.

They exchanged their respective stories.

'I'm not sure what to make of it all,' Jessie said when they were done. 'It doesn't add up. Whoever this is could have let your soldier woman go and she never would have been any the wiser. Yet the Keenans are actually camping in the woods and Finbar sees him, but he just gives a wave and continues on his way. It's a huge contradiction.'

'He obviously didn't see the boy as a threat,' Terri suggested.

Jessie sighed and they were quiet for a moment.

'You say this Emer O'Hagan was on some sort of black-ops training manoeuvres?'

'That's what she told me. All I know is that Ms O'Hagan used to be a soldier. She writes about it on her blog, and she's listed on the Defence Forces website, although only as a regular officer – a lieutenant. I suspect she rose higher through the ranks than that. Intelligence operatives and the Ranger division wouldn't be listed.'

'Can you dig a little deeper?'

'Into Emer O'Hagan?'

'Yes. The victims of a killer tell you a lot about the killer themselves. She's the only surviving one we've got, so let's see what we can learn about her.'

'I... I think this was just a random attack though,' Terri said. 'Emer was in the wrong place at the wrong time.'

'That could be said for any victims,' Jessie said. 'We have to assume he'd been watching her and decided to strike. That says a lot in itself.'

'I suppose it does,' Terri pondered.

'I'm thinking the Department of Defence will have a record of the attack,' Jessie went on. 'It would be good to know what they gleaned from their investigation.'

Terri had her notebook out and was furiously scribbling in it, her phone clamped between her chin and shoulder. 'Will they be prepared to share that kind of information, do you think?'

'Give Dawn a shout and see if she can't grease the wheels a bit.'

'I could always try and hack into their system...' Terri said thoughtfully.

'You could, but instead, why don't you try to arrange a sit-down with someone who can help?' Jessie proposed. 'You'll learn more from a face-to-face chat than you will digging about online.'

'I can learn a lot online though,' Terri said, a bit put out at her research skills being called into question.

'I'm not suggesting otherwise,' Jessie said. 'But let's knock on the front door first and see if anyone answers. If they don't, we can always sneak in through the window.'

'So you want me to go to Dublin?' Terri asked.

'I think that's the most sensible course of action,' Jessie said. 'You can link up with us here when you're finished there. It'll be good to have the team back together.'

'Okay, Jessie. I'll do that.'

'Thanks, Terri. We'll be in touch soon.'

'You and Seamus be careful, won't you? I... I don't like what this case is turning into. This person, they're not just a killer. They're something worse, I think.'

'We're always careful, me and Seamus,' Jessie said.

'We both know that isn't true,' Terri said and hung up.

Okay, so I don't know why I'm even saying this here, but vampires do not exist.

There are psychiatrically disturbed people who believe they're vampires, and there's even a culture of sorts that has sprung up around them. It seems to be tied in with body dysmorphia where people have extra-long incisors surgically implanted and refuse to expose themselves to sunlight and engage in various other self-harming behaviours of that nature. But there is nothing to suggest that's what's happening in Ballinamore. What we have here is significantly different.

First of all, the physical traits these 'vampires' celebrate are all linked to the concept of being eternally young and beautiful. If you read Bram Stoker's Dracula *or any of Anne Rice's novels or even Stephanie Meyer's* Twilight *series you will find an army of youthful and ethereally gorgeous undead, all slim, tall and clear-skinned. They are swooned over by women and feared and admired by men in equal measure.*

The vampire said to haunt Derrada is a grotesque. He is stunted, scarred, terrifying. There is nothing seductive about the Abhartach.

That immediately sets him apart from the norm.

I have learned, of course, that in this part of Leitrim there is no such thing as 'the norm'.

The Abhartach is also a loner.

While the vampires you'll find in goth clubs in London or on college campuses in Dublin are a community, the Abhartach is very much alone. He is isolated, solitary, as much a hermit as was the old saint who's said to have imprisoned him in his tomb.

In short, none of it fits.

In the story of the Abhartach, we're not seeing the traditional vampire myth, nor an example of modern vampire lore either.

So where does that leave us?

The Abhartach is one of the proto-vampire stories. It was written before the accepted forms and tropes of vampiric legend had solidified. There is no garlic. No lack of a reflection.

The dark fable of the Abhartach is really about fear of 'the other'.

The little Celtic chieftain is described as being evil and cruel, but we aren't given examples of how this cruelty manifested itself. Isn't it highly likely he was just seen as an unacceptable ruler because he was physically different? And the idea that death could not even rid the land of his 'otherness' may well hint at a fear of the genetic heritage Abhartach left behind.

The creature wanting to consume the blood of the women of the clan, to absorb their life force, illustrates that fear, I think. The Celtic mind had no idea of genetics, but they did have a concept of bloodlines, and by drinking their blood, Abhartach attempted to take the reproductive power of these women and make it his own. Their energy would rejuvenate him in his living death.

Only the Christian saint, the embodiment of oncoming modernity, could stop him and save the clan from his evil.

That is the story that's been handed down from generation to generation in Derrada.

Has there been a demonic force haunting the forest here since the time of Grace O'Malley? Of course there hasn't. That's simply not possible.

Is there a person who fits the description of the old Celtic monster using the woods as a cover for serial murders? I have to accept that there is.

And while this may seem like an outlandish coincidence, then consider this: doesn't it make sense for a criminal with a very distinctive physical appearance to seek out a place where their physicality becomes a deterrent? If you can turn a weakness into a strength, you've achieved something significant.

I now believe that a serial killer came across a story that offered him an identity and a refuge, and because of this he came to the place where that story still lives and breathes. The woods gave him a place to hide not just himself but the fruits of his labours too.

The fear the story engenders kept everyone away. And when someone did get too close, he either killed them or made sure they were so frightened they would never come back.

We have victims whose business is secrets, who – in all the ways that count – do not exist. Gangsters. Government operatives. Spies. We have a killer who seems to have links to the military, and who has also made themselves into a ghost, dwelling on the fringes of society.

I've also been thinking about the disparate ways in which the victims were killed. My initial assessment was there could be more than one killer, and I shouldn't discount that. Emer O'Hagan, for example, is someone who has reason to be angry, and who has the skills and training to have dumped a body right under the nose of the police and then disappear into the trees. And Richard McCarthy, with his violent political affiliations, is worthy of consideration too.

And I must leave room that there could be someone else in the woods, someone I haven't even considered yet.

I need to know – and soon. People are dying.
It's time to draw that killer out.
It's time for an atonement.

37

While Terri was speaking to Emer O'Hagan, Dawn Wilson was painstakingly working her way through a report on staffing numbers in rural police stations when the phone on her desk rang.

'A member of the counter-terrorism unit is here to see you, Commissioner,' the receptionist said. 'Says he has information you might find useful.'

'Send him up, Barry, please, and thank you.'

'Right away, ma'am.'

A minute or so later there was a gentle knock on her door, and a low-set man, clad in a leather jacket and black jeans, whose hair was shaved down to little more than stubble, came in.

'I'm Dawn Wilson,' Dawn said, standing and offering her hand.

'Charlie Hamner,' her visitor said in a broad Dublin accent, shaking it and sitting in the proffered chair.

'I'm told you come bearing information for me,' Dawn said, sitting back.

'Yes, Commissioner. I heard you were looking to know

about a Loyalist operative named Richard McCarthy. An English youngster.'

'I was, yes. The word I got back was that he's pretty harmless.'

'With the greatest of respect to your source, they're sorely misinformed.'

'With the greatest of respect back to you, I spoke to someone I've worked with for years, and they've never let me down yet.'

'It's not as simple as that.'

'Explain it to me then, Charlie.'

'Loyalists were always pretty basic creatures, using simple guerrilla tactics to get the job done. Lately though, mostly by recruiting out of college and universities, they've got themselves some fresh blood who know how to use the online world to spread information and, most importantly, misinformation. A sort of digital whitewashing has been done on a few of their most dangerous operatives, and Richard McCarthy is one of those.'

'So he's got a few more claws than I've been led to believe?'

'Richard McCarthy spent some time in the Parachute Regiment in the UK before being thrown out for insubordination. He spent six months at Her Majesty's pleasure as a result of the court martial that followed, after which he got out of England and landed here. It seems he arrived with firmly held views on the religious and political landscape of the North, because he immediately started offering his services to Loyalist groups.'

'What kind of services?'

'He's highly trained in everything from hand-to-hand combat, firearms, explosives, wilderness survival, use of bladed weapons... this is a very dangerous man, Commissioner.'

Dawn nodded. 'Is he a killer though, Charlie? I've met guys and girls who want to blow up cars and damage property, but they'd stop short of murdering innocent people. Or even not-so-innocent people, if you want to split hairs about it.'

'I've been working the Loyalist groups for two years now, and I can tell you that I believe Richard McCarthy is responsible for at least three deaths. And I suspect him of being involved in another two.'

'So the answer to that is a definitive yes then.'

'He's a killer. As cold as they get. Don't believe his boyish good looks. Richard McCarthy is a bad man.'

38

Jessie was sitting in Murtaugh's Café on Ballinamore's main street as she spoke to Terri, and as soon as she hung up, Dawn rang to tell her what she'd learned about Richard McCarthy. Seamus sat across from her cradling a mug of tea, a plate that had recently contained the largest full Irish breakfast the establishment served but was now sparklingly clean on the table in front of him. The café was a quaint, one-roomed affair with checked tablecloths and floral prints on the walls. Jessie thought it was a bit twee but kept the opinion to herself.

'Did you catch all that?' she asked after she'd hung up.

'I did,' Seamus said. 'McCarthy puts up a good front, doesn't he? I'd him written off as a harmless hippy.'

'Me too. But we were wrong. We'd best go and talk to him again.'

Jessie's phone buzzed, notifying her of a text message.

'Hold on – probably Terri again.'

It wasn't.

You draw closer to the spirit that dwells among the trees. You have a sense of what he is, this pilgrim, but you are still reluctant to make the leap of logic that will bring you right to the mouth of his lair. Remember, Jessie Boyle, that fairy tales and myths may be fiction, but that doesn't mean they're not true. Look for the kernel of reality amid the fantastic, and you will find that which you seek. And hopefully, he will find you. ∏

'What's up?' Seamus said, seeing the expression of concern on his partner's face.

'Our mutual friend from the UK,' Jessie said.

'I'd like to have a serious conversation with that guy,' Seamus said, shaking his head.

At that moment, the sound of many engines reverberated through the café from outside, and through the windows Jessie and Seamus saw a convoy of vans and battered-looking cars pulling caravans in their wake parading down the length of the town's main street. Jessie counted eight vehicles in all.

'This cannot be good,' Seamus said, standing to get a better look.

The first automobile, a blue HiAce van, stopped at the junction of main street and the Donegal Road where it idled, as if the driver, whom Jessie and Seamus couldn't see, was surveying the area. The van's engine revved for a moment, once, then twice, roaring like a beast of the forest, then the van turned sharp right and led its followers out of Ballinamore until the final caravan disappeared around the bend in the road and was gone, leaving a sense of menace in its wake.

Seamus looked at Jessie, who was chewing her lower lip with a solemn expression on her face.

'Things just got a hell of a lot more complicated, didn't they?' he asked.

'If that's who I think it is, that might be a huge understatement,' Jessie agreed. 'But it might just be the break we're looking for too.'

'The gang's all here,' Seamus said.

'Exactly,' Jessie agreed.

The Dunnes – the Traveller clan who had a price out on Joe Keenan's head – had just arrived in town.

39

It didn't take Jessie and Seamus long to catch up with the convoy, and they trailed it in the MG for seven kilometres along narrow country lanes until it pulled off the road into a large rectangular field, abutted on all sides by high hedgerows, which meant that, other than a quick glimpse passing the gate, whatever went on in the field was hidden from the road.

The vehicles parked in a loose circle, though Jessie couldn't help but notice each car and van still had its nose pointing towards the gate, as if in readiness for a hasty exit. She brought the MG to a halt right across that same gate, blocking any such egress, then she and Seamus waited to see what would happen next.

'Do you think they have permission to camp here?' Jessie asked.

Seamus considered the question. 'I'll bet they do,' he said. 'If they didn't, it'd be too easy for us to run them off.'

'And I'm going to hazard a guess that every single one of those motors is fully taxed, insured and the older ones NCTed.'

'Oh, I'd bet my house on it,' Seamus said. 'Everything will be present and correct.'

'Don't you mean your mother's house?'

'Now you're just being mean,' Seamus snorted. 'I was referring to the lease on my rental, if you must know.'

'Well I have to tell you, Seamus, if I had a mother who cooked as well as yours does, I'd never move out!'

Jessie had met Katie Keneally, Seamus's mother, and was extremely fond of her.

Seamus laughed. 'If I start thinking about my mammy's roast beef now, I'll never be able to concentrate on the task at hand, so let's focus, shall we?'

Not a single person had emerged from any of the automobiles yet. It was as if everyone was waiting to see who would make the first move.

'Do you reckon they're carrying guns, machetes and possibly even explosives in among those cars and vans and trailers?' Jessie asked.

'We could get a search warrant,' Seamus said. 'Have a look-see.'

'By the time we got it, they'd have buried them in a ditch somewhere,' Jessie said ruefully. 'We'd be wasting our time.'

'Let's just go and talk to them then,' Seamus said, pushing open the door. 'I'm fed up with the staring competition.'

As they approached, the passenger-side door of the blue HiAce that was the lead vehicle opened, and a large woman stepped out. She seemed to be as wide as she was tall: a huge, block-shaped individual dressed in a shapeless black dress, her hair a tangled bush of grey that fanned out from a face covered in fine lines and wrinkles. The eyes were dark and expressive, alive with intelligence and constantly on the move, darting here and there as if hungry to take in everything thereabouts.

'Well hello,' the woman said in a voice that seemed to belong to a much younger person. Jessie was surprised that, despite her girth, she covered the distance between them with remarkable speed, approaching with her hand extended to shake. Jessie took it and felt the force and strength of its grip.

Don't underestimate her, Jessie thought. *There's far more to this woman than meets the eye.*

'What can I do for you two nice young people?' the woman asked as she shook with Seamus.

'I'm Jessie Boyle, and this is Detective Seamus Keneally. We're from the National Bureau of Criminal Investigation, and we'd like to have a brief word with you,' Jessie said, holding out her ID. Seamus did the same.

The woman held their gaze, smiling, but did not so much as glance at the identification. 'And why do you two polis officers want to talk to the likes of me?'

'I didn't catch your name,' Jessie said.

'That's because I didn't tell you it,' the woman said, and then guffawed with laughter, as if this was a very fine joke indeed.

Jessie and Seamus exchanged glances but didn't join her in her merriment. The woman continued to giggle, though the laughter didn't seem to reach those dark eyes, which remained calm and thoughtful throughout. The whole thing was strange and disconcerting, and Jessie knew it was intended to be. The woman wanted to put the two detectives on edge.

'Are you refusing to identify yourself, ma'am?' Seamus asked after ten uncomfortable seconds had passed, with the laughter showing no signs of subsiding.

'No, no, where are my manners?' The woman wiped tears from her eyes onto the sleeve of her dress. 'I'm Maisie. Maisie Dunne. Come on up to the trailer and we'll have some tea, and you can ask me any questions you'd like to.'

'We'd like that very much,' Jessie said, and they followed her back the way she'd come.

MAISIE DUNNE

She took her role as matriarch of the most powerful Traveller clan in Ireland very seriously.

While it wasn't unusual for a female to be the spokesperson for a Travelling family, Maisie was unique in having such influence within the political landscape of her people. She was respected, for sure, but more than that she was feared. And she worked hard to earn that fear.

Her husband, Fred, had originally been the clan chieftain. He was able enough, and the asphalt-laying business that was their main source of revenue was lucrative. Yet Maisie felt they could be doing more. She suggested to her man one night that perhaps they might branch out into construction. He was dubious, at first, telling her the cost of equipment alone would make it barely worth their while. And then there was materials, insurance, not to mention the skills required to actually get the jobs done properly...

Maisie put it to him that he was overthinking the whole thing and outlined her plan.

It was then the late 1990s and the construction trade was booming in Ireland, fuelling what was the fastest-growing economy in Europe. Property developers were constantly looking for companies who could throw up housing estates and office blocks quickly, and it seemed no one really cared whether these housing developments were built to code.

'All we need to do is undercut the competition,' Maisie told Fred. 'We can charge some money up front that will cover equipment and materials. And sure, insurance certificates can be mocked up if you know how.'

Maisie's maiden name was Dunleavy, and her uncle, Joxer, was a counterfeiter of some skill.

'We still don't have people who know how to build houses,' Fred said gently. 'I mean, we could probably get the structures up, but there's a hell of a lot more to it than that. There's the electrics and the plumbing and the sewage and I don't know what else.'

'Sure the structure is the main bit, isn't it?' Maisie said, feigning innocence.

'Kind of, I suppose,' Fred said, although his tone indicated he was very unsure.

'How many construction companies leave jobs unfinished for all kinds of reasons?' his wife pressed. 'We set it up so that all mail is delivered to a post office box somewhere, so we've no offices they can trace us to. As Travellers, we can move on as soon as the heat comes down. They'll never find us, and by then they'll have hired someone to finish the job anyway. They've more money than sense, these lads. And we'll be on to the next job.'

Fred padded out the crew he used for the asphalt laying with others from his extended family and, using the solicitor who secured him jobs, tendered low prices to a number of construction contracts that were pending in the south of the country. Maisie coached Fred to ensure his bids weren't ridiculously low but tempting enough to encourage the customers to take a chance on a construction firm they'd never used before.

It worked like a dream. The money they were paid up front

was way more than any amount they'd received for even the biggest asphalt-laying job, and by working longer hours than the Builders and Allied Trades' Union allowed (they could do this because they weren't members, and had no intention of ever being), they got the shells of the houses in the fifteen-unit block built within a fortnight.

And then they disappeared.

Maisie was fully aware this scam had a short lifespan, but she had a game plan, and she needed capital to get it off the ground. Asphalt and construction were too small. The Dunleavy family had always had their toe in the waters of numerous criminal enterprises, and Maisie failed to see why the Dunnes couldn't benefit from these too: drugs, prostitution, organised theft, counterfeiting, trafficking of both people and weapons – there were few criminal endeavours Maisie didn't feel might be opportunities for profit.

While Fred and his team threw up housing development after housing development, making sure each job was a suitable distance away from the last one, and that their invoices and contracts, not to mention their vans and vehicles, all had different names emblazoned on them than they had previously used, Maisie exploited her family connections to network in the criminal underworld.

She had a former lover, a man named Beezer Muldoon, who'd acted as an enforcer and hitman for her father and uncles, and he accompanied her to meetings with various underworld bosses looking for couriers, people to transport product both inside Ireland and to locales in the UK and mainland Europe. Maisie needed an inroad into the business. Once she had it, she reckoned it would be easy to assert herself as a power player.

It was all about biding her time.

Within six months she'd secured five contracts from different gangs who needed drugs moved, and she used the introductions these facilitated to learn about supply chains for product, and about cutting that product once you had it, and about how to deal with narcotics detectives through bribes and coercion.

In the summer of 2011, Beezer Muldoon organised a team of gunmen to assassinate the heads of the five crime syndicates Maisie was working for in a Traveller version of the Night of the Long Knives. In the political vacuum these deaths left, she consolidated her position, establishing close ties with the new bosses and cementing relationships that would make the Dunnes a power to be reckoned with. Or at least she thought she did.

With their future seemingly secure, Maisie advised Fred to wind up the construction company – they no longer needed it.

'I've one job left on the books,' her husband told her. 'Let me get that done, and then I'll shut up shop.'

Maisie told him there really wasn't any need, but Fred had the unfortunate trait of taking pride in his physical work. He had started the job and wanted to finish it, at least as far as he had all the previous ones.

Fred Dunne was working late one night in that final development, putting up plasterboard in one of the last houses to be finished on the block, when he was taken. Maisie was later to learn that the men responsible were representatives of the son of one of the gang leaders whose death she had ordered.

They didn't kill Fred. That would have been too easy. Too clean.

But as the gang had been deprived of something important to them, so Fred lost something he would very much miss.

They cut out his tongue.

When he was dumped, semi-conscious, on the road outside the halting site in Limerick where the Dunnes were staying at the time, Maisie was bereft. Beezer single-handedly tracked down every single one of the men involved and killed them slowly.

Which helped Maisie to feel better.

All in all, she felt her ascension to the top of Ireland's criminal underbelly had been relatively event-free.

And she thought Fred would agree with her, if he could.

He agreed with her on most things.

He'd even stood by her when she'd been forced to kill Francis, their eldest son.

Fred saw that it was the right thing to do.

A large, gunmetal-grey mobile home was attached by a tow bar to the blue HiAce, and Maisie Dunne pushed open its door before mounting the steps, something she did with far more physical grace than her heft should have allowed.

Inside, the caravan was decorated in a surprisingly minimalist manner: the walls were a spotless, gleaming white, devoid of anything other than a simple crucifix, and the seating that lined the walls was upholstered in a muted beige that looked to be some kind of expensive felt. A table was bolted to the floor in the centre of the space, and a man of a similar vintage to Maisie, clad in a tweed waistcoat and trousers over a red-and-white checked shirt, was laying out tea things on it.

'This is my husband, Fred,' Maisie said.

Jessie and Seamus said hello, but the man barely looked up at their greeting.

'Fred doesn't say much,' Maisie explained when Jessie looked uncertain.

They sat down while Fred set a china teapot on a large coaster in front of them; milk and a bowl of sugar lumps were already in place. His task complete, Maisie's husband nodded at them again and exited the caravan without saying goodbye.

'He's a good lad is Fred,' Maisie said, smiling. 'Will I be mother?'

Without waiting for an answer, she poured tea into two cups and passed them across to Jessie and Seamus.

'I'll let you both apply milk and sugar as you please. Now – what would you like to ask me?'

'What brings you to Leitrim, Mrs Dunne?' Jessie asked, taking the cup and saucer and shaking her head at the proffered milk and sugar – she drank both tea and coffee black.

'Do you know much about the Travelling community, Jessie – is it okay if I call you Jessie?'

'That's quite all right.'

'Good. And you can call me Maisie.'

'Thank you, Maisie. You were about to tell me your reason for being in Leitrim?'

'There was a time when my people were completely nomadic,' Maisie said, adding four sugars to her cup and a liberal dash of milk. 'We never stayed in one place for long, and we had places we'd stop as we followed ancient pathways around the country. These were the same places our fathers and forefathers camped for thousands of years, and when I was a child, I thought I would carry on that tradition.'

She smiled sadly, and for perhaps the first time since meeting her, Jessie believed the emotion on display was genuine.

'But that wasn't to be. Ireland became modern. People started to be concerned about computers and iPhones, and the amount of money in their bank accounts was suddenly more important than the people in their community. The greatest curse though was that property and the pursuit of it became the bedrock of the Irish economy. There used to be something called *common land*, places owned by nobody, where you could pull up for a day or a week or a month if you wished and no one would complain about it, but as I grew from a wean to a woman, I saw all those places being snatched up, turned into petrol stations and blocks of flats and housing estates. Me and my people weren't welcome anymore.'

'I agree the way your people have been treated is shameful,' Seamus said, 'but what has it to do with your being in Leitrim this morning?'

'There are some places we're more welcome than others,' Maisie said. 'Me and my family spend part of the year in Galway, part of the year in Wexford, part of the year in Limerick and the final part in Leitrim. In those places, people are less suspicious. More welcoming. We don't get turned out of the pubs, and the shops are happy to serve us.'

'So your being here has absolutely nothing to do with Joe Keenan?' Jessie said.

Maisie Dunne smiled, and this time the expression was as much about predation as it was happiness. Jessie wasn't easily frightened, but there was something about the way Maisie's eyes flashed, and the glint of her sharp little teeth, that chilled the behaviourist to the bone.

'I'm not going to lie to you, Jessie,' the Traveller said, and her too-young voice purred as she spoke. 'Me and my family harbour no love for Joe Keenan and his brood.'

'By his brood do you mean his eleven-year-old son?' Seamus asked coldly.

'That boy is well able to fend for himself,' Maisie said, 'and is probably infected with the same illness as his father.'

'Illness?' Jessie said. 'Is Joe sick?'

'He has a sickness in his soul,' Maisie spat. 'And for that reason, I can promise you me and mine will be keeping far away from him. I want no part of that man.'

'Yet here you are,' Jessie said. 'Only a short drive away from him. You could be anywhere else in the country right now, yet you choose to be near this man you claim to want nothing to do with.'

'We always camp here at this time of year,' Maisie said. 'And we're not going to stop because Joe the big man Keenan decides to come here too.'

'An attempt was made on Joe and Finbar's lives yesterday,' Seamus said. 'The shooter was a man known to be in your employ.'

'Well now that's an outright lie,' Maisie said. 'I don't have anyone in my employ. Me and Fred are traders is all – we work for ourselves selling scrap. No one works for us.'

'From what I've been told, Beezer Muldoon is a leg-breaker, enforcer and sometime assassin who's been linked to your family for the past fifteen years,' Jessie said. 'Joe identified him as the person who tried to shoot him and his son at a childcare facility outside Ballinamore yesterday. An action that could have also endangered the lives of the other ten children and two staff members who were on the premises.'

'Beezer probably has his own differences with Joe,' Maisie said. 'He wasn't acting on my orders, I can tell you that.'

Jessie sipped her tea and put the cup back down on its saucer. 'You and your family have been visitors to this part of the world for many years, Maisie?'

'I just told you that, didn't I?'

Jessie nodded. 'You did. I just wanted to confirm it.'

'Do you know the area around Derrada Woods at all?' Seamus asked her.

'We've camped there from time to time,' Maisie said, looking puzzled at the line of questioning.

Jessie thought the woman seemed unsettled, unsure for the first time where the conversation was going.

'It's not a great spot,' Maisie continued. 'The trees are very dense, and I've never liked the feel of the place.'

'How does Beezer feel about it?' Seamus asked.

'How am I supposed to know that?' Maisie shot back.

Jessie pondered the exchange for a moment and then said, 'Maisie, I'm here to inform you that Joe and Finbar Keenan are under the protection of the Gardaí. They're helping us in our inquiries, and should any further attempt be made on their lives, I will see to it that you are immediately arrested on suspicion of conspiracy to commit murder.'

Maisie smirked. 'You can arrest me, but you won't hold me for long.'

'Oh, we'll see about that,' Jessie said. 'I think I can drum up enough evidence against you to detain you for quite a while.'

'Anything that happens to Joe Keenan will have had nothing to do with me,' Maisie said, pouring herself more tea.

'I'm glad we had this chat,' Jessie said and stood. 'I hope I've made myself clear.'

'I think we understand each other,' Maisie said.

'I believe we do,' Jessie said, and she and Seamus took their leave.

41

Waters was sitting at the reception desk of the Ballinamore police station eating a custard slice when Jessie and Seamus walked in off the street.

'It looks as if most of the Dunne clan is now camped in one of Derek Fahey's fields,' Jessie told him. 'He's given them permission, and reading between the lines, I think they're paying rent for the privilege.'

'They stay there a good bit, yeah,' Waters said.

Jessie sighed in exasperation, and Seamus let out a guffaw.

'I thought you and Glenn told us the Dunnes haven't been through here in more than a year,' he said.

'I'd say it's been that long,' the cop said. 'I don't recall. They're tinkers, like. They come and they go.'

'Joe Keenan and his family are now in really grave danger,' Jessie said. 'They need to be protected.'

'From the Dunnes?'

'Is there another clan hereabouts they're feuding with?' Jessie said tersely.

'No, but what am I supposed to do?' Waters demanded. 'I'm

meant to be on the desk today in case any calls come in. I can't abandon my post.'

'Do you have a mobile phone?' Jessie asked.

'Of course I do.'

'Well then you can have all calls forwarded to that, can't you? Which means you can head out to Derrada and be there in case the Dunnes decide to take another run at Joe.'

Waters blinked. 'I'm one man,' he said. 'What the fuck am I meant to do?'

'I'll stay with you,' Seamus said.

'You're happy to do that?' Jessie asked her partner.

'I'll call Glenn and ask him to send over some reinforcements,' Seamus said. 'But for today, I don't think we've any other choice, do you?'

'I doubt they'll make a run today anyway,' Jessie said. 'It's too soon.'

'Not sensible to take the chance though,' Seamus said. 'We can't assume that woman will be patient.'

Jessie nodded. 'I'm going to talk to McCarthy again, as planned. Keep in touch.'

42

Terri Kehoe sat in Cork City's bus station, reading Neil Gaiman's *American Gods* for the third time. So engrossed was she that she was barely aware of someone sliding into the seat beside her.

'I hope you don't mind me taking this space,' the person said, and looking up, she saw it was an elderly man wearing a tattered-looking cardigan and grey slacks, a frizz of white hair fanning out about his bald pate.

'No, not at all,' Terri said and returned to her book.

The old man sighed and stretched, seeming to relax in upon himself as he watched people milling about in the busy transport hub.

'Could I bother you to inquire what book you're reading?' he asked. 'I was a teacher once, in another life, and I love to see young people involving themselves with books and stories.'

Terri paused and held up the book so the old guy could see the cover.

'*American Gods*,' the old man said, peering at the title through squinted eyes. 'And what is wrong with *Irish* gods?

Why does everything have to be based in the New World these days?'

'Oh, there are plenty of Irish characters in this book,' Terri said. 'It's about how America is such a new country, it's had to borrow all its myths and legends from elsewhere. So in here you'll find leprechauns and selkies and the banshee alongside Odin and Thor and the jinn and lots of other characters. The idea is that they travelled to America as the people who told those tales went there fleeing famine or religious persecution or poverty.'

'I see,' the old man said. 'That does sound interesting, all right.'

'It is,' Terri agreed. 'It's really a book about the power of stories. I like that. Stories can be important.'

'That they can,' the old man agreed. 'Is the Abhartach in there at all?'

Terri froze, although anyone passing would have just seen a young woman gazing at her book while an elderly man, possibly her grandfather, sat beside her, languidly people-watching.

'No,' Terri said. 'He isn't in this book. Though I've recently read quite a few he does feature in.'

'So I believe,' the old man said. 'Can I offer you some free advice, Ms Kehoe?'

'How do you know my name?'

'It's my business to know things. I know your friends, Jessie and Seamus too. I believe they're good people, who only want to do what's right. And I think you're a good person as well. Which is why I want you all to walk away before you get hurt.'

'We can't do that,' Terri said. 'People have died. It's our job to find out who they are – and why they died.'

'What if I told you every single one of those people *deserved* the death they got? That maybe the world is a much better place without them in it? Would that make you reconsider?'

'It isn't my job to make those distinctions,' Terri said. 'If what you're saying is true, whoever did the killings should come forward and... well, they could plead their case to the proper authorities.'

'Ms Kehoe, there are some people who are not fettered by the authorities the rest of us are,' the old man said. 'You must know that.'

'Everyone answers to some kind of authority,' Terri said.

'Tell Jessie the jig is up,' the old man said. 'Tell her to come home and leave things in Leitrim as they are.'

'Even if I did, she wouldn't listen to me.'

'Make her listen. There's a storm coming, and you'll all be caught in it. When that happens, I won't be able to do anything for you.'

'What do you mean by a storm?'

When there was no answer, Terri looked up from her book only to discover the old man was gone. She stood and searched the crowd, but he was nowhere to be seen.

43

Jessie was parking outside the poacher's home when her phone buzzed.

I will tell you one more thing to aid you – I want to see what happens when you and the pilgrim come face to face! Seek out Adamant Security Solutions. They are one end of the thread that will unravel the mystery. ∩

She read the message and then jammed the phone in her pocket. She was becoming irritated by Uruz's interference.

She got out of the car just as Richard McCarthy was leaving his cottage.

'I need to speak to you for a few moments, Mr McCarthy.'

'I'm just heading out to check my traps. Would you care to join me?'

Jessie scratched her head. 'Where are these traps?'

'In the woods across the road there. It'll only take fifteen minutes or so.'

She followed him over the laneway outside his house and

then they climbed a gate and were under the cover of the trees in the hazel wood his cottage looked out onto.

'Mr McCarthy, I've just received intelligence that you may not have been exactly truthful with us about your involvement with Loyalist paramilitaries.'

'Who told you that?'

'That's not really your concern.'

'Just because I've spent time with people of a like-minded political persuasion doesn't make me guilty of burying bodies in Derrada.'

He stopped and, crouching low, moved some brush to reveal a deadfall trap, in which were the remains of a long black creature that looked like a large weasel.

'Mink,' he said. 'They escape from farms and turn feral. I'll get a few euro for the skin.'

'Can you account for your movements on the night of November the fifth?'

'I was right here. Setting some snares.'

'Can anyone corroborate that?'

'I live alone, Ms Boyle. And to be honest, I don't feel like speaking to you anymore. I've committed no crime, and you have no right to continue pestering me.'

'I think I'm going to have to ask you to accompany me to the police station, Mr McCarthy.'

At that Jessie heard a sharp snapping sound, like a very dry twig breaking, and something exploded from the bed of dry leaves and thudded into McCarthy's leg. He stopped dead for a moment, seemingly stunned, then started screaming. It took Jessie a moment to work out what had occurred: it seemed the poacher had stepped on some kind of trigger that had been buried in the undergrowth, which caused a curved branch, the end of which had been sharpened to a cruel point, to catapult upwards and impale him through the thigh.

The young man was deathly pale and would surely have collapsed if the beam that had injured him wasn't holding him upright. Jessie got her arm around him and tried to support his weight.

'Lean on me,' she said.

McCarthy, delirious with pain, nodded and did as she asked.

'I'm afraid that, if we pull it out, you'll bleed to death,' she said urgently. 'I think you may have punctured your femoral artery. Do you understand me, Mr McCarthy?'

He nodded again.

'I'm going to ring for help.'

She pulled her phone from her coat pocket but was dismayed to see she had only one bar of coverage – the trees were obviously blocking the signal. Jessie knew she had to try anyway. She dialled 999 and pressed 'send', holding the phone to her ear. Nothing happened for a moment, then she heard the call connecting, and it began to ring.

'You're through to emergency services – how can I direct your call?'

Jessie was asking for an ambulance when twenty yards ahead of them, through the trees, a strange figure emerged from the brush. As Jessie saw the shape through the gloom, she felt all the hairs on her arms and the back of her neck stand on end, and a sense of deep unease gripped her. From the distance, and in the shadow of the woods, it was hard to make out specific features, but Jessie could see it was diminutive in height and clad in a long coat of some kind, the hood of which was pulled up so she couldn't see the face. The person stood at the edge of the path for a moment, gazing at them, then vanished into the trees once again as if they'd never been there. All that remained was a cloying feel of threat and violence. And sadness.

'It's him,' McCarthy hissed. 'He did this to me.'

'Why?' Jessie asked. 'Why would be hurt you like this?'

'Because I've seen him,' he said. 'I know he's there, and now I'm talking to you.'

And then he fainted onto Jessie's shoulder.

Terri sat in the lobby of the Department of Defence. It was based in Newbridge, in County Kildare – a fact she'd only discovered when she was already on the bus for Dublin, which necessitated switching transport at Busáras, the central depot. This was a nuisance but didn't bother Terri too much. She liked travelling by bus. It gave her time to catch up on her research, and she always enjoyed seeing the countryside scrolling past.

Following up the identity of the body that appeared in the woods most recently, the one that had been buried for a time near the Burren, in County Clare, had proven somewhat more challenging than she'd expected, but Terri was nothing if not tenacious.

Her initial scans to see if there were any deaths or missing persons associated with RDF Premises had drawn a blank, which told her she needed to go deeper. Using a false identity which presented her to the world as a retired member of the engineering corps of the defence forces (Terri was aware such subterfuge was a crime in some parts of the world, but it wasn't in Ireland, and she figured such an untruth was done for honourable reasons anyway), she'd infiltrated a Facebook page

set up for army officers from Clare and began to ingratiate
herself.

Within a day she'd learned that, last June, an Irish Army
Ranger named Fiachra Boland had been reported as absent
without leave, which was unusual, as this man was a fervently
loyal member of his squad, and a highly decorated soldier to
boot. Terri had hacked into the same database she'd used to find
out about Garvey, he of the good teeth, and got the same results:
Fiachra Boland's file was heavily redacted, and she was blocked
from progressing any further. She did find a photograph of him
though: dark eyes peered at the world from a heavily lidded
brow, and his jawline showed the blue shadow of a beard. But
what had made Terri sit up was the deep scar that was evident
through the closely cropped hair. At some point, Fiachra
Boland had received a severe blow to the head. One that had
carved a groove deep into his scalp.

Which matched perfectly the details the state pathologist
had placed in her report.

It was compelling, but Terri knew she'd have to speak to one
of the gatekeepers if she wanted to get more information. And
she would only find one of those in the Department of Defence.

Jessie had asked her to get in touch with them anyway about
Emer O'Hagan, so, following her suggestion, she'd called Dawn
Wilson for assistance, and she'd soon rung her back with good
news.

'Regimental Sergeant Major Stewart O'Driscoll can see you
at four thirty this evening,' she'd said. 'He says he's familiar with
Emer O'Hagan and will speak as candidly as he can.'

'Um... what does that mean?' Terri had asked.

'Fucked if I know,' Dawn had replied. 'But he's the best
we've got.'

The building Terri was in now could have been any government office. There was nothing about it that identified it as a
military operation: no uniformed soldiers were in evidence, and

while the insignia of the Irish armed forces was resplendent over the reception desk (a star surrounded by flames with the letters FF for *Fianna Fáil,* meaning soldiers of destiny, in the centre and the words *Óglaigh na hÉireann* – the Irish volunteers – inscribed around the edge), Terri doubted most people would be able to identify what the emblem represented.

Ten minutes had passed, and Terri was starting to wonder if she was being stood up when a broad-shouldered man in a blue suit with an open-necked shirt, his shaved head still showing some dark stubble just below the skin, approached her.

She put him at about fifty, and while his face was unlined, there was something about his posture and the way he moved that spoke of confidence borne from experience.

'Ms Kehoe? I'm Sergeant Major Stewart O'Driscoll,' he said. 'Would you be so good as to come with me?'

Terri followed the man through a heavy door he opened using a key card, and then down a sequence of narrow, low-ceilinged corridors before climbing a flight of stairs, at the top of which was a door with O'Driscoll's name and rank inscribed on it.

'After you,' the sergeant major said.

The office inside wasn't what Terri had expected. The corridors and public areas of the building were utilitarian to the extreme, but O'Driscoll's inner sanctum looked like it belonged in a university, and an old one at that: a desk of burnished wood, bookshelves heaving with leather-bound volumes, a thick rug covering the floor, and on the wall facing the door, an oil painting of a Napoleonic battle scene.

O'Driscoll gestured that Terri should sit in a straight-backed plastic chair while he slid into a swivel chair that looked much more comfortable behind the desk.

'You wish to know about Emer O'Hagan,' he said as soon as they were both seated.

'I... well, I have some questions, yes,' Terri said.

'A person would need an exceptionally high security clearance if they expected answers to such questions,' O'Driscoll said.

He was lying back in the chair, almost slouching, which Terri was surprised to see in a military man.

'Why did you agree to see me then?'

'Perhaps we can help one another.'

Terri, who was getting her notebook out of her tote bag, paused. 'How do you propose we do that?'

'I contacted Commissioner Wilson a couple of days ago requesting I be kept informed of your progress on this case. She initially refused, but since you now need my assistance, she seems to have become more amenable.'

'So you'd like a report?'

'I'd like regular reports please. Whatever you learn as your investigation proceeds.'

'And in exchange, you'll tell me about Emer O'Hagan?'

'As much as I can, yes. There are still aspects of her career that are beyond my powers to share, but I'll tell you as much as I'm free to.'

'I would also like to ask you about two other former military personnel – Eugene Garvey and Fiachra Boland.'

O'Driscoll gave her a long stare. 'I'm not sure I can tell you anything about those two.'

'They're part of this, Sergeant Major. Their bodies were discovered in Derrada – Mr Boland's only within the past few days.'

O'Driscoll took a deep breath. 'This has been definitively confirmed?'

'Seeing as there is neither DNA nor fingerprints on file for Mr Boland, that's not really possible. Mr Garvey, however, was confirmed from dental records.'

'But you believe the other remains belong to Boland?'

'I do, yes.'

O'Driscoll looked at her darkly. 'Well. This is disturbing.'

'Disturbing enough to prompt an exchange of information?'

'I'll have to consider that,' the soldier said. 'For now, I've been given permission to tell you a little about Emer O'Hagan, and I'm afraid that's all I can do today.'

'Very well. Ms O'Hagan was an officer in the infantry corps?'

'To begin with,' O'Driscoll said, 'she volunteered for a couple of tours as a peacekeeper, one in Lebanon and one in the Congo. She saw action in both locations but had a particularly rough time in Central Africa – things are still very unstable there, and our forces are under constant threat of attack from various guerrilla groups. O'Hagan was on the Semuliki operating base when it was attacked in 2012. It was one of the most protracted and well-organised assaults on a UN base in decades – a large enemy force managed to get inside the compound under false pretences, so the UN team were fighting for their lives at close quarters.'

'That sounds terrifying,' Terri said, and she meant it.

'It was a nightmare,' O'Driscoll said. 'O'Hagan shouldn't have been there that day – she was on her way to Kinshasa and had stopped in to refuel her vehicle. The hostiles, who were members of the Allied Democratic Forces, planned to disable the base's communication systems. O'Hagan organised a squad to defend the radio room and held them off from destroying the equipment long enough for someone to send for reinforcements. People are alive today because of what she did, but despite her efforts there were twenty fatalities on our side, as well as fifty-three seriously wounded.'

'Ms O'Hagan is obviously a remarkable person,' Terri said.

'Oh, most certainly,' O'Driscoll agreed. 'She received a commendation for bravery, and on returning to Ireland was... well, let's just say she was invited to participate in a training programme for a rather special group of soldiers within the Irish military family.'

'Do you mean the Ranger Wing?' Terri wanted to know.

'They're associated with the Rangers. That's probably all you need to know.'

'Covert operatives?'

'I suppose you could call them that, yes.'

'Ireland is neutral though, isn't it? Why would we need a group like that?'

'Being neutral doesn't inoculate us against threats, both foreign and domestic. Our little nation doesn't exist within a bubble, and there's a need for contingencies when problems arise.'

'And Emer O'Hagan was one of these contingencies?'

'She agreed to participate in the Special Operations Force Qualification Course – usually referred to as SOFQ. The particular unit Ms O'Hagan was being considered for required her to pass a further raft of tasks and tests, a supplemental series of challenges. She passed them all with flying colours, making her the first female to successfully complete the training.'

'So she's a trailblazer,' Terri said.

'Quite. Had she been qualifying for any other part of the army, her face would have been plastered all over the newspapers. Because of the nature of her new post though, that wasn't possible. So Emer O'Hagan joined her unit without fanfare and embarked upon what should have been a stellar career.'

'She did well in her new post?'

'She was an exemplary soldier. Ms O'Hagan achieved the rank of captain within the infantry, but once you enter special operations you begin at ground zero all over again. She'd been with the unit for a year when an opportunity for promotion became available. To move up in the ranks, Ms O'Hagan needed to prove herself fit for added responsibilities.'

'How was she to do that?'

'A series of challenges were designed to test her prowess in all areas of soldiering.'

'And one of those brought her to Derrada?' Terri said.

'We used those woods sporadically for training, as their make-up and topography resembles some of the forests in Eastern Europe where personnel are occasionally sent. To be quite honest with you, the navigation and evasion exercise Ms O'Hagan was to carry out in Leitrim was the least daunting of the three pieces of work she'd been tasked with. It never occurred to anyone it would be her undoing.'

'When I spoke to Emer, she told me something attacked her in the woods.'

'Emer O'Hagan was eviscerated,' O'Driscoll said. 'Someone – who knew how to – sliced her open with a very sharp blade. I can tell you, the placing of the wound was textbook. In hand-to-hand combat training, you learn where to put a knife to disable an opponent in various ways. The injury Emer O'Hagan experienced wasn't random or accidental. The person who cut her meant to do what they did.'

'Could you say what kind of blade was used? Emer indicated it was unusual.'

'The medical reports suggested a Bowie-style knife. Or possibly even a small sword or machete. It had a partially serrated edge and, judging by the depth of the wound, was at least fifteen inches long.'

'Is that significant for a knife?'

'I would say it is much longer than the standard length for most survival knives. Many of our own operatives carry blades, but none on that scale.'

'So Ms O'Hagan's injuries were debilitating?'

'She's alive today because she kept her head. If she'd attempted to get herself out of there, she'd have bled out, or at best done even greater damage to herself. She hit the dirt and stayed where she was, holding the wound closed, until help came. But in spite of her courage and good sense, the damage had been done. The knife had carved open a good piece of her bowel, and by the time she was taken to the hospital, parts had necrotised. She needed a colostomy bag. It wasn't possible for her to continue to active fieldwork after that.'

'Which resulted in her being discharged from service?'

'Emer O'Hagan *requested* a discharge. She could have had any administrative role she wished. She was even tipped for a very prominent job in the intelligence service – I gave her a reference myself. But she wanted none of it. Asked for an honourable discharge.'

'Were you happy to grant it?'

O'Driscoll made a facial expression Terri assumed was supposed to be a smile but looked more like a brief wince.

'Had we known our former golden girl was going to draw so much attention down on herself from certain quarters, I might have been less happy to do so.'

'I presume she signed a non-disclosure agreement before leaving?'

'Of course.'

'Yet you haven't tried to quiet her? Stop her online activities?'

'Until she starts discussing official secrets, our hands are tied.'

'With respect, you've spent the last ten minutes telling me about covert operatives who are members of an organisation the general Irish populace don't know even exists. Since I've started investigating this case, my offices have been broken into and a man I don't know has accosted me at a bus station and asked me to persuade my colleagues to abandon the whole thing. So, Sergeant Major, I suspect you could bring a certain degree of pressure to bear if you really wanted to...'

O'Driscoll did that odd wincing smile again. 'Ms Kehoe, I can assure you, none of the interference you've experienced has had anything to do with me or my department. This is twenty-first-century Ireland, not Russia in the 1980s. What are you suggesting we do? Throw Emer in a gulag? I'm uncomfortable with some of the things she posts on rather dubious chat forums, but she hasn't committed a crime so is free to continue her activities until she does.'

'You must have some thoughts about why Emer was attacked?' Terri asked. 'She was almost out of the woods – wouldn't it have been simpler to just let her go?'

'I've always believed it was done to warn us off,' O'Driscoll said. 'To let us know we'd infringed on someone's territory. The bodies that have been discovered would seem to confirm that hypothesis.'

'Who controls this territory though?' Terri asked. 'Who warned you off?'

'I wish I knew,' O'Driscoll said. 'My colleagues and I have discussed it until we're hoarse, but we're still at a loss. The woods were swept in the days following the attack, but not so much as a trace of an interloper was found. Not a thread from their clothing, not a footprint on the ground. We found no sign of habitation. The woods were completely clear.'

'You're aware that Emer believes her attacker was the Abhartach, a sort of Celtic monster?'

'Yes, I'm familiar with the story.'

'Does the Department of Defence believe in vampires?'

'We do not.'

Terri nodded and consulted her notes. 'Yet a highly skilled member of a black-ops unit was catastrophically injured by someone who left not a single trace of their existence, despite the best the Irish army has to offer going in looking for him. How do you explain that?'

'There is only one explanation that makes any sense,' O'Driscoll said. 'Emer O'Hagan was attacked by a very gifted woodsman who had something to hide in those woods.'

'With respect,' Terri said, 'we'd worked that much out for ourselves.'

O'Driscoll didn't even attempt to stifle a smile. 'You did, did you?'

'My team aren't exactly amateurs. Can you offer us anything else?'

'I think you may be doing me an injustice,' the sergeant major said. 'You're not just looking for any old outdoorsman – I'm not referring to a weekend hiker, or someone who enjoys a spot of birdwatching. I am speculating a survivalist of great skill. Someone who knows how to live off the land and, more importantly, how to disappear into it.'

'Perhaps someone with military training?' Terri prompted.

O'Driscoll narrowed his eyes and seemed to think about that one. Finally he said, 'I'll tell you this much. Your killer is someone who knows how to wield a blade. That's not a skill you can learn on YouTube, and there are few places where it's taught. If you can find someone who fits that description in the vicinity of Derrada, you've found your killer.'

PART FOUR

UNDER SHADOW

9–10 November 2018

'The woods invite me into themselves so that I might be drawn out of myself.'

Craig D. Lounsbrough

45

Terri caught a bus back to Dublin, with the intention of catching a second to Leitrim. She rang Jessie when she arrived into Busáras to fill her in on what she'd learned and discovered she wouldn't be joining her friends just yet.

'How did you get on at the Department of Defence?'

Terri told her.

'A woodsman with something to hide,' Jessie said. 'I've just taken one of those to the hospital.'

'Really? What happened?'

Jessie told her.

'He's the only one locally who fits the description. I suppose he could be our killer, but if he is, there's also a second individual at large in the area, which complicates things hugely. Maybe McCarthy was hit because he'd muscled in on another predator's territory.' She paused for a moment. 'My head is spinning just thinking about it.'

'There is another possibility,' Terri said. 'Joe Keenan fits the description too. I know we have proof he wasn't responsible for all the deaths, but I've looked and looked, and I can't find evidence that puts him somewhere else for the older murders.'

'He doesn't fit the physical profile though,' Jessie said. 'The two witnesses we have are talking about someone quite small – and I can corroborate that with what I saw myself.'

'I'm wondering how small though,' Terri said. 'So far all the eyewitnesses have seen this person at night. Perspective can be a bit skewed in the dark, particularly in the woods where there are a lot of shadows.'

Jessie thought about that for a moment. 'I do hear what you're saying,' she said, 'but I wasn't *that* far away, and I can attest that I either saw a very small adult or a child. Joe Keenan is about the same height as Seamus, six feet give or take an inch. There's no way anyone is going to describe him as looking like a child, even in the dark. Anyway, he was asleep when Finbar saw the person in the woods.'

'*If* he saw him,' Terri said. 'He could be providing an alibi.'

'I don't buy it,' Jessie said. 'It doesn't make sense within the facts we have so far, such as they are.'

'I had to put it out there though,' Terri said.

'Do you think Emer O'Hagan might be involved?'

'She certainly has the skills,' Terri said. 'But she's a bit like your poacher. She was hurt by the person in the woods.'

'Or was she? What if she was injured on a mission? McCarthy's true nature was being protected by online whitewashing – maybe hers is too.'

'I hadn't thought of that,' Terri said. 'It's something to think about.'

'Well here's something else. I need you to look into a security company for me. A group called Adamant Security Solutions. I'm told they have offices in Santry.'

'Okay. Is there anything in particular I'm looking for?'

'Anything connected with the case,' Jessie said. 'It may be a long shot – this information came from Uruz, so I'm treating it as dubious. But I don't want to discount it. He knows things, probably much more than I'm comfortable with.'

'Okay. I'll see what I can learn. I wish I was there with you and Seamus.'

'I'm on my way back to Derrada now,' Jessie said. 'Things are getting interesting here, so you're well out of it, to be honest.'

'Good luck,' Terri said.

'Right back at you,' Jessie said and hung up.

46

'The afternoon has been uneventful,' Joe Keenan said when Jessie got out of the MG at the campsite – she'd parked behind Waters' patrol car, which he'd placed close to the edge of the treeline so it was clearly visible and might act as a deterrent. 'We've seen a few badgers and a fox, but other than that, there's nothing to report.'

'If the Dunnes are planning on striking again, they're obviously trying to lull us into a false sense of security,' Seamus agreed.

A fire was crackling and sizzling in the centre of a ring of stones, and a pot containing what looked to be a stew of some kind was hanging from a metal frame over it, bubbling appetisingly. Despite the fact food was obviously imminent, Seamus was leaning against a tree, a mug of tea in one hand, a sandwich in the other.

'Blood sugar low again?' Jessie asked.

'I was gettin' a bit peckish, so Finbar very kindly made me something to tide me over,' Seamus said, grinning at the boy, who was sitting cross-legged on the ground whittling a piece of wood with a red-handled penknife. 'There's rabbit meat and hawthorn leaves in the sandwich, would you believe? I've never had either before, but it's really nice.'

'Well I'm glad you're not wasting away from hunger,' Jessie said. 'Here was me worried you might be under attack, and all along you've been having a picnic!'

'I hate to interrupt, but can I go back to the station now?' Waters shouted over, looking very unhappy where he sat on the same log Seamus and Jessie had perched upon when they'd spent the previous evening with Joe and Finbar. 'I don't like these woods and I never have. There's little flies in my eyes and some of them are going up my nose.'

'I told you to sit in closer to the fire,' Joe said. 'The smoke keeps them away.'

'It also makes me cough though, and my clothes stink.'

'You're going to have to put up with the flies then,' Joe deadpanned.

'Frank, can I ask you something?' Jessie interjected, walking over to him.

'I suppose so.'

'I appreciate your enthusiasm. Are there any people hereabouts you would describe as "woodsmen"?'

'*Woodsmen?*'

'Yes. People who *really* know the woods.'

'Live in them, like?'

'Possibly. I'm looking for anyone who spends time in Derrada and would have skills that would make them very at home in the woods. And maybe someone who knows their way around a blade. Just tell me who springs to mind when you think about that. We've already spoken to Robin Tiernan and Richard McCarthy, but anyone else?'

Waters thought about it for a moment, and then, to Jessie's surprise, said, 'Sounds like Benjy O'Sullivan.'

'He lives locally?'

'On the eastern edge of the woods – all year round. Has his

own forge and everything. He's as gentle as the day is long though, so I never thought of mentioning him to you. Need to be careful how you approach him though.'

'Okay, Frank. You can head on.'

She walked back over to Seamus. 'Did you get hold of Sligo?'

'I did. They'll have a detail here tomorrow morning at six, but until then, it's just us.'

'Okay. We can take turns sleeping in the MG – the seats push back and it's comfortable enough. If one of us sleeps from ten until two and then the other rests?'

'Sounds like a plan.'

'Dinner will be ready in about half an hour,' Joe said. 'I hope you like game stew.'

'I've never had the pleasure before, but it smells divine,' Jessie said.

'That's good, because there's nothing else on the menu,' Joe said. 'Finbar, will you get the bowls and cutlery from the van?'

The lad hopped up and scuttled over to the van.

'I have some home-made elderflower wine, but I don't suppose either of you would like some?'

'Thanks, Joe, but we'd best keep our wits about us,' Jessie said. 'We don't know what the night is going to bring.'

'It would be nice if it brought just one glass of elderflower wine,' Seamus said sulkily.

'This stuff is strong, Seamus,' Joe said, winking at Jessie. 'And if I do say so myself, one glass of my wine is never enough.'

47

The stew was remarkable – pigeon, rabbit and pheasant padded out with carrots and onions bought from a nearby farmer and flavoured with herbs that grew all around them in the wood. Joe had made a huge pot of it, which was just as well, because Seamus consumed three helpings. If either of their hosts were surprised by this, they didn't show it – in fact, Joe seemed pleased.

'I love to see a man enjoy his food.'

'This is really, really good,' Seamus declared around a mouthful.

'You're more than welcome. It's been a comfort having you around today, and I'll surely sleep better knowing the two of you are keeping watch tonight.'

'Just doing our job, Joe,' Jessie said, scraping her plate of the last vestiges of the rich gravy.

'I've known a lot of Gardaí in my time,' Joe said. 'Most are decent people trying to do their best. But you two have gone over and above. I cannot thank you enough.'

'If you can find dessert anywhere in that van of yours, you can consider us quits,' Seamus said, winking.

Joe laughed. 'Oh, I always keep a supply of biscuits and cake in case we have guests. I'll make us some tea to go with them.'

When the meal was over, they sat about the fire in the quiet darkness.

'Will you give us a song, Da?' Finbar asked.

Joe smiled at the boy. 'What do you want me to sing?'

'Sing the one about Dainty Davie.'

'All right then,' Joe said, and flinging his head back, he began to sing unaccompanied in a rich tenor voice.

Jessie had never heard the song before, and found the lyrics and melody mesmerising. It told the story of a young man who arrives out of the dawn one morning and turns the lives of the people in the village upside down, until he's chased away by the local militia. Jessie assumed the anti-hero of the ballad was a Traveller, or at least a homeless wanderer, as the verses told of him sleeping in orchards and, ultimately, spending a night in the singer's bed before vanishing again.

It was in and through the rolling broads
And through the dreary weary fog
The sweetest kiss that e'er I got
Was from my Dainty Davie

He slept among by father's fields
And underneath the cherry trees.
'Twas there he kissed me as he pleased
My own dear Dainty Davie.

When he was chased by a dragoon
Into my bed he laid him down.
I thought him worthy of his ruin
For he's my own dear Dainty Davey.

Joe sang the song with genuine feeling, and Jessie wondered for a moment if he was thinking of someone as he negotiated the delicate melody.

'You sing beautifully,' she told him when he was finished.

'My own da used to perform that song,' he said. 'I always loved hearing him sing it.'

'Did he teach you many ballads?'

'I wish I'd learned more from him. Too late now.'

He paused, gazing into the flames.

'I will not let them kill me or my boy,' he said, more to himself than to anyone else. 'They've taken nearly everything, but I won't give them the little I have left.'

'They'll have to go through Seamus and me to get to you,' Jessie said.

'They might not have as much difficulty as you think.' Joe grinned, nodding at the detective, who was lying with his back against a tree, snoring quietly.

'Looks like I'm on the first watch then,' Jessie sighed. 'Brilliant. Just brilliant.'

48

The day might have been uneventful, but the night didn't pass without disturbance.

As 1.30 a.m. approached, Jessie was patrolling the treeline when she was suddenly gripped with a powerful sense of dread, as if something too horrifying to countenance was leering at her from deep in the forest.

She was reminded of the unpleasant feeling she'd had when she saw the figure through the trees when McCarthy had been injured, but now she could see nothing. It was simply a deep unease.

She took the Heckler & Koch pistol – a gun Seamus had confiscated from a gangster during a standoff in rural Kerry – and stood up, gazing through the light of the fire into the darkness surrounding her and her sleeping friends.

'You feel it too then?'

She got such a shock at the voice behind her that she came alarmingly close to shooting Joe Keenan, who'd come out of the Transit without a single sound.

'Please don't do that!'

'Sorry. I didn't mean to startle you. I didn't put me boots on, so I'm stepping lightly.'

Jessie turned her gaze back to the spaces between the trunks. 'What is it? What am I feeling?'

'I don't know. I've been livin' in places like this for a real long time, and I've only ever come across it once before.'

'And what was the cause?'

'We were in the Black Forest, on the border between Germany and the Czech Republic, camped in a clearing just off a hiking trail, but deep enough in the woods that no one could see us unless they came looking. I woke up in the middle of our second night and it felt as if every hair on my body was standing on end, like the air was full of electricity. I remember coming out of the van and standing in the forest, and I swear the darkness was looking right back at me. I had a torch and I shone it into the trees, and that was when I saw it – a long shadow with flickering eyes.'

'The Dunnes had sent someone?'

'No. This particular hunter had nothing to do with Maisie Dunne. It was a grey wolf. They've been migrating back into Germany from the Russian Steppes of late, and large tracts of the Black Forest haven't changed much in eight hundred years. It's an ideal home for a predator of that size.'

'So you *sensed* it was outside?'

'I don't believe I'm psychic or anything. I'd guess I registered movement in the woods outside that wasn't like the forest noises I was used to. I was asleep, but my unconscious picked up something that set alarm bells ringing, and I came awake fast.'

'I've heard nothing though.'

'You think you haven't. Remember, our ancestors used to live in caves and had to deal with wolves and far worse: sabretoothed tigers and feckin' woolly mammoths and I don't know what else. They had finely tuned ears and noses and eyes that must have been able to see in the dark much better than we can. But those skills aren't gone in us. Bits and pieces of them linger, buried but still present. That night, all my senses came alive when the wolf snuck into our camp.'

'What did you do?'

'Nothing. He looked at me and I looked at him, and we had a kind of conversation without words. He was on his own, and it seems to me he worked out I was going to be more trouble to deal with than I was worth. He was a long, skinny fella, and the Black Forest is full of game much easier for a wolf to take down than a man. I've thought about it a lot, and I think he was attracted to the smell of us cooking dinner. We'd not eaten until late that night, because we'd driven into the nearest village to get supplies.'

'That makes sense,' Jessie said.

'Does. So we stared each other down, that wolf and me, and then, as if he decided the exchange was over, he turned with a flick of his long tail and vanished into the shadows. Just like that. I felt him for a long time after he was gone, but I think he was probably just hanging about the area, seeing what else he could scare up to eat. I remember drifting off to sleep at around four in the morning, and when I woke, I knew he wasn't close anymore. The woods around us just seemed different.'

'You don't think there's a wolf loose in Leitrim?'

Jessie stepped forward a few paces and shone the torch from her phone into the darkness, wondering if two amber eyes would gleam back at her. None did, but the feeling of threat and unease remained.

'I do not,' Joe said. 'This isn't a wolf.'

'So what the hell is out there?'

'A hunter of a different kind, I'd say.'

'That Beezer Muldoon character?'

'He's bad, but not like this. This is something else entirely.'

Jessie switched the torch off and stowed the phone in the pocket of her coat.

'You're telling me it's whoever buried the bodies. The person Finbar saw, the one people around here call the Abhartach. Maybe... maybe the person I saw earlier today.'

'That's it. I think he's come to have a closer look.'

They heard the door to the MG opening, and Seamus got out, yawning and stretching – Jessie had considered leaving him asleep against the tree, but decided he'd be more comfortable in the car. 'What's going on?'

'Just an uneasy feeling,' Jessie said. 'I think I'll sit up with you for a bit though, just to be sure.'

'Suit yourself,' Seamus said. 'I won't complain about the company.'

'I'll make some tea,' Joe said and went to get the kettle.

The sense they were being watched didn't dissipate until after three o'clock that morning. When it did, Jessie reclined the driver's seat of the MG and dreamed about unblinking amber eyes, peering at her out of a wall of darkness.

49

The protection detail arrived twenty minutes later than it was scheduled to and consisted of two young detectives who seemed utterly disinterested in being there and sat about the camp scrolling through social media on their phones.

That said, they had handguns and wore flak jackets, and their presence made Jessie and Seamus feel better about leaving the Keenans and getting on with their investigation.

'I think the threat against me and Finbar is getting in the way of their phone time,' Joe said ruefully.

'They're here, and they've parked a brightly coloured police cruiser right in the middle of the glade,' Seamus said. 'So anyone considering taking a run at you will see it and think twice. You're as safe as you can be, under the circumstances.'

'We'll check in later,' Jessie agreed. 'And your new friends have been told to call us if anything even slightly out of the ordinary occurs.'

'I wish I had my guns back,' Joe said darkly. 'We're sitting ducks here, and I've never been one for depending on others for my welfare. You two throwin' in with us felt like friends helpin' out, but these fellas... I'm not happy about it. And to be honest, they don't look up to the job.'

'Sit tight,' Jessie said. 'Seamus and I are good at what we do. We'll get this mess sorted out.'

Joe, clearly deaf to these assurances, turned and stalked back towards the Transit, where Finbar was sitting on the step with Rufus at his feet.

'He'll cut and run if things aren't resolved quickly,' Jessie said.

'I don't blame him,' Seamus agreed. 'I'd have been gone already if I was in his shoes.'

'If he runs, there'll be nothing we can do for him. He'll look guilty as hell, and he'll go down for all this as sure as I'm standing here.'

'He will if they catch him.' Seamus opened the door to the MG. 'He's only hanging about because he wants to. I have a feeling Joe Keenan could vanish into thin air if the mood took him and never be seen again.'

'It'd be good if he didn't have to,' Jessie said, and with that they pulled out of the clearing and made for Ballinamore.

CASE NOTES ON LEITRIM BURIAL SITE – TRANSCRIBED FROM AUDIO JOURNAL KEPT BY JESSIE BOYLE

10 NOVEMBER

The bodies we can identify are from covert military operatives, and those we cannot remain enigmas.

I keep coming back to that point.

Why have none of them shown up on any of the databases? Not DNA, not fingerprints, not facial recognition from the reconstructions forensics have carried out.

How is it that a burial ground containing eleven sets of remains has failed to give us even one individual we can identify within the system? We now know who two of them are, and their identities are leading me in a direction I'm loath to pursue.

I've been wracking my brains over this, and the result I keep coming back to is that certain professions like to retain a veneer of anonymity. And these professions are the type you can't just rock up to and ask to speak to a manager.

Could this really be what we're dealing with? Buried secret service agents, covert operatives and intelligence officers?

It seems too far-fetched, but there isn't another theory that fits the facts.

I think I'll keep it under my hat until I have the chance to explore it a little further.

50

'Benjy O'Sullivan,' Jessie said. 'He's a survivalist, according to Frank, and while Richard McCarthy admitted to sometimes camping in the woods, this chap lives there the whole year around.'

'On the outskirts, you mean?' Seamus asked.

'According to Frank, he's made a camp for himself on the eastern side.'

'Is he squatting then?'

'I have no idea. Frank said we should approach with caution though.'

'What the hell does that mean?'

'I have no clue.'

'Do you reckon that might be worth clarifying before we go blundering in?'

'Seamus Keneally, I have never blundered anywhere in my life.'

She dialled Waters' number and waited for him to pick up.

'Frank, I'm putting you on speaker so Seamus can hear.'

'Hello, Frank,' Seamus said jovially. 'How's it going with you?'

'I'm okay. What do ye want?'

'Nice to speak to you too,' Jessie said breezily. 'This Benjy O'Sullivan – you mentioned we should tread carefully. What exactly do you mean?'

'Benjy used to be a schoolteacher in the St Alphonsus secondary here in town. His wife died five, maybe six years ago and he went a bit strange. Became convinced she'd been poisoned by radiation getting into his house down the water pipes and through the TV and out of their mobile phones.'

'He's not alone in thinking that,' Seamus observed.

'His family owned a few acres, and he left his house and moved out there. Lived in a tent originally and over time built himself a kind of a cabin – more of a shack really. He's holed up out there waiting for the world to end. Like I said, he's gentle, but he can be nervy. Doesn't like intruders, which in Benjy's language is anyone who arrives unannounced.'

'Is he armed?' Jessie asked.

'Has a shotgun and a permit to hold it.'

'Brilliant,' said Jessie. 'Just brilliant.'

'How do we gain access then?' Seamus asked. 'I mean, if he doesn't have a phone, how do we let him know we're coming?'

'There's an ould lad in the village – Ollie McGee. He visits Benjy every week for a chat. If you go out with him, you'll be safe enough.'

'We've met Ollie,' Jessie said. 'Nice old guy. Even if I wonder whether or not he knows more than he's telling.'

'Why do you say that?'

'Someone matching his description approached an associate of ours and tried to get her to pressure us to drop the case.'

'That doesn't sound like Ollie McGee.'

'Well there are certainly other old men but only one we've encountered so far in our investigations. What's his address? We'll go and see him right away.'

'I'll text it to you. Mind you, at this time of day he's probably in Byrne's pub having his before-lunch pint of Guinness.'

'It's only ten thirty,' Jessie said.

'That's before lunch, isn't it?' Waters said drolly.

'Text me the address, but we'll try the pub first,' Jessie said.

'All right then,' Waters said and hung up.

'Bye for now,' Seamus said to the dead line. 'Why does he never say hello or goodbye? It's a small courtesy.'

'I find it's easier to just pretend he's in a hurry and therefore not trying to be rude,' Jessie said. 'That way I'm not offended.'

'I'm already offended,' Seamus said tetchily. 'Pretending something else won't change it.'

'You're awfully sensitive for a police detective,' Jessie said.

'Yeah, well you're awfully *in*sensitive for a psychologist.'

They continued to bicker good-naturedly all the way back into the village.

51

Ollie agreed to bring them out to Benjy O'Sullivan's camp as long as they paid for his pint: they had found the old man in the pub, just as Waters suggested they would.

He finished his drink quickly though, and they followed him out onto the street.

'Benjy's a good man, but his mind has been confused since his wife passed,' he said as Jessie piloted the MG towards Derrada. 'He thinks the world is out to get him, and who are we to tell him he's wrong? To be honest with you, I'd admire him for living as he does if he didn't choose to do it in that awful damn place.'

'Yet you still visit him every week?' Seamus observed.

'Someone has to. Now don't get me wrong, Benjy isn't so unwell he can't look after himself, but there are weeks where he gets too anxious to eat – believes his food is being tampered with and whatnot. I sleep better at night knowing he's all right.'

'Frank told me he has a forge out there – makes knives and tools?' Jessie said.

'Yes. He's a talented fella.'

'Aren't you afraid the Abhartach will get him?' Jessie asked, adding a mental note that this was conditional on Benjy not being the Abhartach himself.

'Have you heard of the term "touched"?' Ollie asked.

'I have,' Seamus said. 'It means someone is touched by the hand of God.'

'That it does,' Ollie concurred. 'When I was a lad, the old people used to use that phrase to describe those who had intellectual disabilities, but it also referred to individuals with mental illness. What it meant was that they were God's special ones, people He'd shown other levels of awareness, other realities. And that meant they were *protected*.'

'You're saying it's safe for Benjy to live in Derrada because he's mentally ill?' Jessie said.

'I am. That creature won't bother him. *Can't* bother him, in fact.'

'If you say so,' Jessie said.

'I do. You can park here. We'll have to walk the rest of the way.'

As they got out of the MG, Jessie said, 'I don't suppose you took a trip to Cork recently, Ollie?'

The old man smiled mischievously at her. 'Now why would you ask a question like that?'

'A friend of mine met someone who sounds very like you at the bus station.'

Ollie cackled loudly. 'I think I just have one of those faces. Come on. The day's passing.'

For a senior citizen, Ollie McGee moved with ease down the narrow rabbit path that led through the trees. There were times the trail disappeared, and Jessie wondered if they were wandering aimlessly, but their guide appeared to know exactly where he was going and chattered about the wildlife they encountered (he had a particular loathing for grey squirrels, which he referred to as 'tree rats') and commented on various tracks and signs they came across, pointing out the hoof prints of red deer and pausing to examine both fox and badger scat.

Jessie stopped at one point to catch her breath and realised they were so deep in the forest, she could no longer see the tree-line that marked where the woods ended and the rest of the world began. The thought made her feel uncomfortable, as if the trees themselves were trying to suffocate her. Doing her best to shrug the feeling off, she hurried to catch up with the others.

Ten minutes later, the woods cleared and they found themselves in an open space, at the centre of which was a ramshackle structure that seemed to be half tent and half cabin, the walls constructed from logs that had been peeled of their bark and stacked one on top of the other, moss chinked into the cracks between them to make the dwelling airtight. The roof had been created by overlaying many branches, and then covering those with what Ollie told them was beech bark, which could be peeled in large sheets from the trees during the early autumn and made a watertight layer. A chimney made from stones cemented together with what looked like mud had been built at the rear of the shack, and it released a steady stream of smoke into the sky. A pile of neatly cut firewood sat beside it. A vegetable garden had been dug to the left of the structure, and though Jessie could make out little of what was growing there, she did spy the feathery tops of carrots.

'Hello, the house,' Ollie called. 'Benjy, I've some visitors with me, so don't shoot us, okay?'

The low door of the cabin was flung open, and a wild-looking man came out, carrying a shotgun with its barrel open across his arm. He had long, greasy hair and was dressed in a baggy woollen jumper and frayed corduroy trousers. A thin, patchy beard clung to his chin and jawline but looked as if a strong wind might blow it away.

'Who are you bringing to my home, Ollie?' he demanded. 'I'm not happy about this. Not one bit happy.'

'Mr O'Sullivan, I promise not to take up much of your time,' Jessie said, holding out her ID so he could read it. 'We'd just like to ask you a few questions, if that's okay?'

'Are you charging me with something?' Benjy asked, suddenly swooping in so he was very close to Jessie, his eyes boring into her with ferocious intensity.

'Not at all,' Jessie said, forcing herself not to take a step backwards. 'But we would be very grateful for your assistance.'

'Hmmm. My assistance, you say?'

'Yes. You live in the woods all year round, I believe?'

The man glanced about, as if he thought someone might be listening in on their conversation. 'I don't make my home in town anymore,' he said. '*Too many radio waves.*'

'That must be very distracting,' Jessie said gently. 'Do the trees help to filter them out?'

He brightened at that. 'Yes! They do. Each tree emits its own sonic signal, a biometric hum that the radio waves can't penetrate. So I'm safe here.'

His face darkened. 'They killed my Betsy. Gave her cancer. Did you know that?'

'We're very sorry to hear it,' Jessie said. 'That has to be so difficult.'

'She never hurt anyone,' Benjy said, and Jessie could sense a change in his mood – he was beginning to become agitated. 'Never harmed so much as a fly, but still they planted the carcinogenic cells inside her body. Manipulated them using their waves. Used her as a guinea pig.'

He looked from Jessie to Seamus to Ollie. 'They want to kill me too. But I won't let them.'

'Has anyone followed you out to the woods?' Jessie asked. 'Have you seen anyone else out here since you came?'

'No one comes here,' he said. 'People know to keep away.'

'And do you always stay on your few acres?' Seamus asked.

'I don't know you,' Benjy said, his eyes narrowing at the detective.

'I'm Seamus, and I'm pleased to meet you.'

'He's all right, Benjy – I give you my word,' Ollie said. 'Just tell them what you can, and I'll take them away again.'

'I sometimes go deeper in to hunt,' Benjy said. 'Sometimes I go so far in, I go to the parts where it gets dark.'

'Have you seen anyone when you were there?' Jessie asked.

Benjy's face hardened, and his agitation ratcheted up a notch. 'I've seen the Small Man,' he said. 'I see him walking in the trees.'

'Where do you see him?' Jessie asked.

'Far from here.'

'Does he live in the woods too?'

Benjy shrugged. 'I dunno.'

'Do you see him often?'

'I don't like him. He scares me.'

'Why, Benjy?' Jessie pressed. 'What is it about him that frightens you?'

'He never makes a sound when he walks,' Benjy said, his voice very low and his eyes darting all about. 'He... he has things in his bag. Bad things. Sometimes he carries a bundle over his shoulder, and it looks too big for someone his size to carry. Why doesn't he sink into the wet ground?'

'I don't know, Benjy,' Jessie said. 'I'm starting to think there's very little I *do* know anymore.'

52

Benjy insisted on making them tea, so Jessie and Seamus went into his cabin (which was surprisingly clean and orderly, reminding Jessie of the Keenans' Transit in its effective use of minimal space), while Ollie demurred and said he'd remain out of doors.

'I'll just take the air for a bit,' he said. 'You enjoy your tea, and when you're ready I'll bring ye back to the car.'

They sat at an unvarnished table made from boards cut roughly from the trees themselves, and the tea was placed in front of them with great solemnity.

'I don't have milk,' Benjy said. 'Or sugar.'

'I drink it black anyway,' Jessie said, nodding in thanks.

Seamus (who drank his tea with loads of milk and three heaped spoons of sugar) tried to keep the distaste from his face.

'My place is rough and ready, but then, I don't get many visitors except for Ollie,' the former schoolteacher said. 'He's been good to me, so he has.'

'He worries about you,' Jessie agreed. 'Wants to know you're okay.'

'I *am* okay,' Benjy said. 'I'm happy out here. I feel safe. Safer than I ever did in town.'

'That's important,' Jessie said. 'Everyone needs to feel secure.'

Benjy chewed his lower lip. 'My father was schizophrenic,' he said.

Jessie looked at him. She'd done a clinical placement as part of her postgraduate training and knew there was a time to speak and a time to listen. This was very much the latter.

'I haven't been diagnosed,' Benjy went on, 'but I know that's what's wrong with me. Schizophrenia can be brought on by trauma, and I think mine was just waiting for the right circumstances to make its appearance.'

'It's remarkable you can see yourself with such clarity,' Jessie said. 'A lot of people with your condition would struggle to do so.'

'I know the symptoms,' Benjy went on. 'Sometimes I have conversations with people I know aren't there.'

'How do you know they're not?' Jessie asked.

'Because the one I see most often is my wife,' Benjy said, and the pain was raw in his voice.

'There's medication you can get that would help to address that,' Jessie said.

'I don't want her to go away,' Benjy said. 'I like having her here.'

Jessie couldn't find an argument for that so drank her tea in silence.

'You told us you see the Small Man in the woods,' she said, after a few moments had passed. 'Have you seen him recently?'

'I don't think so,' Benjy said. 'It's hard for me to say, because I don't always know what day of the week it is, but he doesn't come near my part of the woods, and I don't go to his sections anymore.'

'Why not?'

'Ollie told me to keep away from him,' Benjy said. 'He knows the Small Man, does Ollie. Talks to him sometimes.'

'Ollie *talks* to him?' Seamus asked.

Benjy nodded vigorously. 'I've seen them, Ollie and him. Lots of times. I didn't tell Ollie I saw, but I did.'

'And they were talking?' Jessie reiterated.

Benjy nodded.

'What were they talking about?'

'I don't know. I didn't hear much of it. The last time I saw them, I think they were fighting. I'm pretty sure they were, anyway.'

'Are you're certain they were *talking* to each other?' Jessie asked. 'I mean, could it be that Ollie saw him through the trees and called out to him? Tried to scare him off maybe?'

Benjy shook his head. 'No. They were together walking along right beside one another. They *meant* to be together. I get confused, but I know that much.'

'You're telling me that Ollie and the Abhartach are *friends*?' Jessie said.

'Kind of,' Benjy said. 'I don't think Ollie likes him, but he certainly knows him well. And even though I'm scared of the Small Man, I think the Small Man is scared of Ollie.'

53

'What do we make of that?' Seamus said once they were back outside. 'Ollie knows the Abhartach? Do you think Benjy is confused?'

'He didn't seem confused,' Jessie pondered. 'I would have said he was fairly lucid when he was talking about that.'

'Maybe he's making it up then.'

'I have no idea,' Jessie said, peering around the clearing for the old man. 'But what I do know is that Ollie seems to have wandered off.'

She was right. There was no sign of Ollie McGee, and they hunted about the area, calling for him every now and again, but to no avail.

'I have to say,' Seamus said, 'Ollie disappearing at this particular moment seems too much of a coincidence. There's something weird going on here. Something very weird indeed.'

'Yes, but what?' Jessie asked.

'I'm damned if I know. But what I do know is that an elderly man braced Terri in Cork, and now we have Ollie – who warned us to keep away from the woods and just go home when we met him on our first evening here – being seen in the company of the person we're pretty certain is the killer we're hunting. We need to talk to him – and soon.'

They started to walk. The path was clear for a few hundred yards but then seemed to fade, as if it had lost interest in being a path at all, and though they peered through the gloom, they could see no sign of it continuing.

'I'm pretty certain we just walked in a straight line from the car,' Seamus said.

'I think so too, but we might have looped around a bit, or even gradually turned so we came at Benjy's camp from a different angle than it seemed we did.'

Seamus pulled out his phone and opened a compass app on it.

'We want to be going due east,' he said. 'Which is this direction.' He pointed vaguely to their left.

'Which would indicate that we really did get turned around then,' Jessie said.

Seamus shrugged.

'Well we know our direction now, so let's get back on course.'

They veered in the direction the compass indicated and trudged onwards.

'Jessie,' Seamus said after a few moments.

'Yes, Seamus?'

'I truly have not got a clue what's going on in Derrada.'

'You don't?'

'I really don't. I'm massively confused.'

Jessie gave her partner a quizzical look. 'I don't believe that for a moment. You've got a theory. I know you do.'

'Right now all I've got is that there's someone – possibly more than one person, and I'm not sure they're even working together; we may be dealing with two killers with separate agendas – using these woods for something criminal. They've been doing so for a while, because the physical description we've got is too similar.'

'What do you make of the physical description?' Jessie asked. 'It's distinctive, isn't it?'

'One of the parties involved seems to have a disability or genetic condition – so someone with medical dwarfism maybe – or else they're just plain short.'

'Yet totally lethal,' Jessie said.

'I used to work with a guy on the drugs squad who was only about five foot three in his boots,' Seamus said. 'He had such a chip on his shoulder about it – he was one of the most volatile guys I've ever met. I was on a raid with him once that went bad, ended up as a fist fight. I saw him take down four guys twice his size without breaking a sweat. This guy was a mad, mad bastard, Jessie. You would not want to take him on.'

'So that brings us back to a physically small person with wilderness and combat training, or at least experience, who's using the woods for some kind of criminal endeavour.'

'And are you ready to suggest who this person might be?'

'My money's still on Beezer Muldoon. The Dunnes have been coming here for ages, and he's their muscle. I think we should be looking at him for this.'

'Joe doesn't think so.'

'Doesn't mean he's right.'

'Still. He knows him.'

'Give me something else and I'll consider it. It just seems to me we don't *have* anything else.'

Jessie paused for a moment and then said, 'I hadn't expected Ollie to play a part in the whole thing.'

Seamus snorted. 'I'm still not sure he does. Benjy O'Sullivan is ill.'

'I have a feeling he might be the piece of the puzzle we've been missing,' Jessie said.

'You really think the old man is involved?'

'We'll have to dig into his past a little more.'

'Well,' Seamus said, 'after running out on us like that, I think Oliver McGee is at least due a thorough background check.'

And that was when the shooting started.

The shot echoed out in the still woods, the sound bouncing off tree trunks and fracturing the crystalline air. At first, neither Jessie nor Seamus actually believed they were being shot at – each thought they must have stumbled upon someone who was hunting nearby, that they were just hearing the echo of a gunshot from somewhere else in the wood.

Then a second concussion sounded, and this time the bark on an oak tree near Seamus's ear exploded in a cloud of splinters and sap, and they knew they were under fire. Without saying a word, they dived for cover, instinctively choosing individual boltholes to make it more difficult for the shooter to pin them down.

Jessie landed behind a fallen ash tree and stayed there, pressing herself into the gap between the trunk and the earth. She remained perfectly still, holding her breath.

Nothing occurred for what felt like forever, but then another shot rang out, and she heard a bullet thudding into a tree somewhere very close by.

'Seamus, are you okay?' she called out. 'Tell me you haven't been shot!'

There was no response for a long moment, and Jessie felt panic begin to well inside her, but then, from a little way off: 'Oh, you'd love that, wouldn't you, Jessie Boyle? I'm sorry to inform you that other than some sawdust in my eye and more up my nose, I'm unharmed. You're stuck with me for a while longer.'

Jessie heaved a sigh of relief and peered over the top of the trunk. In between the gunshots, it felt as if Derrada was holding its breath. 'Can you see where the shots are coming from?'

'The first came from the west, I think, but that last one seemed to be more from the south,' Seamus called back to her. 'So we've either got two shooters at separate vantage points, or one who's mobile and using the trees as cover to lay down a blanket of fire.'

As he spoke, two shots rang out in quick succession. The first hit the dead tree behind which Jessie was lying, and she felt the impact of it through the wood. She saw the muzzle flash through the trees however: as Seamus had thought, it was indeed coming from the south and looked close by, possibly less than fifty yards away.

'That one was awfully close,' Seamus said. 'He can shoot, whoever he is.'

'Or she,' Jessie said testily.

'True. Let's not assume their gender pronouns,' Seamus said. 'We can ask which they prefer when we arrest them.'

'That sounds like a plan,' Jessie said and, pulling her H&K from the holster at her back, aimed in the direction of the shooter and squeezed off a couple of return shots.

'Whoever you are,' she called out to their attacker, 'I am now informing you that we are members of a specialist task force with the National Bureau of Criminal Investigation and are therefore law enforcement professionals. I'm giving you the opportunity to give up your firearm and come with us peacefully now. If you choose not to, the consequences will be far worse for you.'

In response, a bullet exploded into the tree offering Jessie refuge, and she felt a second whizzing over her head.

'Have it your own way!' Jessie shouted. Then, a little more quietly, to Seamus: 'Can you cover me?'

'I don't have anything better to do,' he returned.

'On three then,' Jessie said. 'One. Two. *Three!*'

And she broke cover just as Seamus stepped out of conceal-ment and shot once, twice, three times at the spot where their attacker had last been. Almost immediately, fire was returned, and Jessie ran as fast as she could, veering away from the shooting but going towards where she believed the gunman was positioned.

Running in the woods was harder than she expected. She tried not to focus on the feeling of her boots sinking into the earth, almost as if the forest itself was trying to slow her down. Within seconds her lungs were burning and the muscles in her long legs ached with the effort, but finally she came to a stop behind a gnarled hawthorn close. Back the way she'd come, she heard the crack of Seamus's Glock 17. And then, only about five yards from where she was hiding, Beezer Muldoon stepped from a copse of ivy-bedecked rowan, an enormous revolver in his hands. He took aim, and as he did, Jessie made to step out of cover with her own gun trained on him, but as she was about to do so, she felt something pressing into her back.

'Don't move,' a voice hissed in her ear. 'Your buddy is to be killed right here in the wood, but Maisie wants a private word with you before you meet your maker.'

Jessie froze.

'My boss knows I'm here, and knows all about you and your people,' she said. 'Do you honestly think you'll get away with this?'

'Doesn't matter,' the voice said. 'No one will ever find your remains – I can promise you that. They might suspect, but it'll be circumstantial. Maisie won't see the inside of a courtroom.'

The voice was male – deep and assured. She could tell whoever was behind her was perhaps an inch taller than her own six feet and one half inch, and she could smell cheap cologne over the damp, woody aroma of the woods.

'Put your hands in the air and turn around nice and slowly.'

She did as she was bid. The man behind her was slim, dressed in a checked shirt and blue jeans, a woollen hat worn at a raffish angle atop his red curls. He had a friendly face, the laughter lines about his eyes and mouth making him seem on the verge of chuckling, despite the fact he had her at rifle-point, the long gun held in the crook of one arm.

'You've been following us, I take it?' Jessie asked.

'We've had an interest in your movements,' the man said, grinning as he reached over, took her H&K from her hand and stuffed it into the belt of his jeans.

Even though Jessie couldn't see what was going on, she heard Beezer fire again, and then silence broken by footsteps. She guessed now that she'd been neutralised as a threat, the enforcer would advance on Seamus and try to put him out of commission.

'Will we be buried in the wood here with all the others?' she asked.

'The others?'

'The bodies Joe's dog dug up. Your clan's burial ground.'

The man laughed. 'I don't know anything about that. But you won't need to worry about where what's left of you will be put. If I were you, I'd be more concerned about what's going to happen over the next day or so. Maisie has some plans for you and Joe Keenan and his youngster. And it isn't going to be a pleasant experience for any of you.'

He nudged her with the barrel of the rifle.

'Turn about and start walking. Maisie Dunne is not a

patient woman, and what little patience she does have has been tested sorely of late.'

Jessie turned and began to walk. More shots came from over to the left – Seamus, it seemed, was putting up a vigorous fight. Then they stopped suddenly.

Jessie felt anxiety rise in her like bile and forced herself to think about something else.

'Is someone making a run at Joe too?' she asked.

'That's none of your concern,' her captor said. 'All you need to be thinking about is that you'll be in his company soon enough.'

'Okay,' Jessie said. 'I'll take your word for it.'

'I don't really care if you do or not,' the man said and jabbed her in the small of the back with the rifle barrel. 'Now hurry up.'

Jessie accelerated her pace.

On the way into the woods, the behaviourist hadn't paid much attention to the landscape. She, Seamus and Ollie had simply been passing through trees. Now, her awareness heightened by the circumstances, she was more conscious of where she was. The forest floor hereabouts undulated, rising and falling in waves, as if someone had dug furrows between the lines of trees. Jessie wondered if this might be a sign that this part of the woods had, at some point in the past, been replanted after a fire or large-scale tree-felling – the trenches felt planned, too linear to be caused by nature. Whatever the reason, she found herself having to take long steps to move across the top of the ruts.

At one point she misstepped and almost fell. Putting her hand out to arrest her fall, she caught onto a branch which cracked slightly under her weight and started to come away from the trunk. Almost unconsciously, she tested it with her hand: it was solid enough, about as thick as her wrist – an animal, probably a red deer, had used the tree as a scratching post, and the place where the branch sprouted from the tree had weakened through repeated interference.

'Come on – we don't have all day,' the man behind her snapped.

'Just give me a second, will you?' Jessie said, feigning exhaustion, working gently on the branch, but making it look as if she was just leaning there to rest.

'You have *literally* one second. Then I'm going to shoot you in the leg, and we'll see how you do with a real reason to struggle.'

'One second is all I need,' Jessie said and, using both hands, wrenched the branch backwards, so it broke off with a loud crack.

Her captor took a step back, bringing his left foot down into the closest trench, which put him slightly off balance. Using the branch as a club, Jessie smashed the makeshift weapon into the gunman's face, and he fell backwards over the rut behind him, the rifle firing off a round that went wide of Jessie's shoulder.

Jessie Boyle didn't need any further prompting.

She took off running as fast as she could, which regrettably wasn't anywhere near as fast as she would have liked, moving awkwardly over the uneven ground deeper into Derrada Woods.

55

Seamus Keneally knew he was in serious trouble when the trunk of the tree beside him disintegrated almost completely. It was clear to him then that the person shooting had changed weapons. The initial volleys had come from a standard handgun or low-calibre rifle, but his assailant was now sporting some kind of cannon.

Seamus squatted down low and fired a shot back, but as he did there was a thunderous boom, and the oak above his head lost most of its middle section, raining twigs and leaves, and then with a crackle and a creak, the top half of the tree, no longer supported by anything, came down heavily like a jackhammer, missing him by inches. He rolled clear, shaking and panicked, and gained his feet just as Beezer Muldoon came striding out of the trees and struck him full across the face with the barrel of the biggest revolver Seamus had ever seen.

The blow was vicious, delivered with all of the Traveller's weight behind it, and along with the impact of being hit by what seemed like a metal bar, Seamus felt the flesh across his cheekbone tear as the sight at the end of the barrel ripped through it, grazing the bone beneath. He was knocked sideways, and as he landed, Muldoon delivered a kick right to his stomach, and all the wind was driven from his body.

'Now stay still till I finish you off, pig!' the enforcer said, and Seamus heard a click as the gun's hammer was thumbed back. 'I hope you've said your prayers.'

Seamus forced his eyes open and gazed up at Muldoon. He knew he should have been terrified, but somehow he wasn't. A calm settled over him, and his only thought was that he was not going to die cowering in the dirt.

'Stop talking and get it done,' he said, forcing the words out against the pain in his midsection.

The boom filled the woods – rooks and pigeons took to the sky, and a jay screamed in the canopy. Seamus's world turned into a haze of red and he waited for the pain he knew would take him to oblivion.

But it never came. The detective sat where he was in the dirt, frozen by fear and confusion, and tentatively patted himself down, seeking the wounds and injuries he knew should be there. Finding none, he wiped the blood and gore from his eyes, and suddenly understood: it wasn't *his* viscera.

Beezer Muldoon was slumped at his feet on the forest floor, a gaping hole right through his chest. And standing over him, his shotgun once again at port arms, was a very agitated-looked Benjy O'Sullivan.

'I... I had to do it,' he said.

And then he began to weep, dropping the shotgun from hands that seemed to have suddenly gone numb. Seamus dragged himself upright and, wrapping his arms around the crying man, wondered where the hell Jessie was.

56

Jessie articulated a weaving path through the undergrowth, hoping against hope that her pursuer would lose her among the trees, and she thought she'd succeeded too, until a bullet whizzed past her ear so close she felt the heat of it.

'Stop right now or the next one will go through the back of your knee!'

Jessie ignored the order and threw herself forward with even greater speed and abandon – which proved to be her undoing. Running far too fast to actually navigate the roots and branches strewn about the forest floor, her boot became entangled in a strand of bramble, and she went head over heels, walloping her head off a stump so hard she saw stars.

When she came round, the red-haired man was looming over her, gazing down the barrel of his rifle. She felt sick and giddy from where she'd banged her head, and worried for a moment she would vomit.

'I'm giving you a chance to come quietly now and not give me any more grief,' he said, and Jessie saw with some satisfaction that the man was bleeding from one of his ears where she'd struck him with the branch. 'If you so much as falter for a

second or give me any excuse to regret going easy on you, I'll
shoot you somewhere painful and carry you back to Maisie. Are
we completely clear?'

Jessie was about to answer when something black and
shapeless shot out of the trees in a burst of speed and knocked
the Traveller right off his feet. So hard and fast did the thing
come, Jessie's captor was driven almost three metres across the
forest floor, colliding with an alder tree with a sickening thump.

Jessie lay where she was on the ground, trying to process
what was happening. The thing that had flown out of the darkness of the trees was like nothing she had ever seen before:
Jessie had the impression of something surrounded by black
wings that billowed out around it, but even that didn't really
capture it.

It's him. *It's the Abhartach. And if he's here, we're both dead.*

Jessie didn't believe in vampires or demons, but despite this,
she had to admit she was terrified. She did believe in monsters
in human form, had encountered them many times in her
career, and she knew just how dangerous they could be.

Shaking her head to clear it – which caused her to see
double for a moment and sent a wave of pain and nausea
through the centre of her skull – she peered about the area,
convinced she would see him coiled to strike at her – but to her
surprise, the black shape was gone. The woods were empty
except for her and the red-haired gunman, who was clearly hurt
though was still struggling to gain his feet.

Jessie knew she had to force her advantage. The rifle had
fallen from the Traveller's grip when he'd been knocked down
and was lying not far from where Jessie was sprawled. She
scooted across, trying to keep her breathing regular and the
panic that was threatening to overwhelm her at bay, and
grabbed the firearm, coming up into a kneeling position before
pumping a shell into the chamber and levelling it on the
fallen man.

'Let's keep those movements to a minimum,' she said, hoping her voice didn't sound as frightened as she felt.

She saw that her H&K was still protruding from his belt and nodded at it. 'Toss that over to me please.'

'With the greatest of respect, you can fuck right off,' the man said.

'I'm guessing you've got a concussion and maybe some broken ribs,' Jessie said. 'I don't know what just hit you, but whatever it is, it might come back, and I don't think we want to be here when it does. So just throw me the gun, and let's get out of these awful bloody woods!'

'I don't think you get me. I can't walk out of here unless I'm bringing you back to Maisie Dunne. If I don't, I'm going to face whatever fate it is she has in store for you, only probably worse.'

'You'll be under my protection.'

'You'll pardon me if I laugh in your face at that,' the man said and did, guffawing loudly, a strange sound in the still forest. 'I'll end up in jail, and she'll have someone there and I'll be dead within the week.'

'We can discuss your options,' Jessie said. 'But I'm still taking you in.'

'No,' the red-haired man said. 'You're not.'

In a motion so fast it was only a blur, he whipped the H&K from his belt like a gunslinger from a Western movie and fired on her. Jessie threw herself sideways but still felt the burn of the bullet as it grazed her shoulder.

Ignoring the pain, she rolled onto her belly and sighted along the barrel of the rifle, but as she did there was a sound like wings beating, and something dropped onto the Traveller from the trees above him. The arm holding the H&K, pinned to the ground by the weight of the black shape, fired convulsively into the earth once, twice, three times.

Jessie froze where she was. The thing looked for all the world like a dark pelted animal – it seemed at first to be shapeless, boneless and disjointed, but as she strained her eyes to better discern what she was looking at, she realised it was black material. This was a person in a long black coat with a hood that covered the head and face.

All the material makes him seem bigger, Jessie thought, *but he's actually quite small. I think he could pass for a child if you saw him quickly, or from a distance.*

The dark shape was undulating and trembling, as if the cloth itself was alive, and it made Jessie feel even more vertiginous and sick. Her shoulder throbbed from where the bullet had grazed it, and she could feel the wetness of blood as it ran down her arm.

That was when the Traveller started screaming. From where she was kneeling Jessie saw the man's legs begin to jerk and kick, as if desperately trying to escape what was happening beneath the swathes of black cloth.

'Let him go right now!' she said, getting to her feet and advancing with the rifle held level.

Her remonstration was met with no response, so she shouted, '*I said let him go or I'll shoot!*'

Her heart was beating so fast she thought it would come wholly out of her chest, and her head had struck up a rhythmic pounding.

Do not pass out, she thought furiously. *If you keel over now, you're finished.*

The thing on top of her prisoner turned its gaze upon Jessie, and underneath the hood she saw a pale, scarred face, impossibly dark eyes and a cruel, narrow mouth. Then with a hiss and a swirl of black, it was gone into the trees, leaving the red-haired Traveller lying beneath the ash tree, his throat cut from ear to ear.

Jessie Boyle sank to her knees, dropped the rifle to the forest floor and vomited a pool of green bile onto the earth before collapsing onto her side in a dead faint.

PART FIVE
THE FINAL VERSES

10 November 2018

'Trees're always a relief – after people.'

David Mitchell

THE ABHARTACH

There were enemies in his woods.

He watched them come from his vantage point – a platform he'd constructed near the top of the highest pine. It was camouflaged from view by a thick spray of leafy branches, but he'd mounted some high-powered binoculars there and so could get a clear view of all approaches to Derrada.

He saw the sports car the policewoman drove park up to the east and three figures get out. One of them was his mentor, and he wondered what he was doing in their company.

Shortly after the trio walked into the trees, he saw a battered-looking jeep come to a stop near the MG and two men climb out. They lingered beside the vehicle and checked weapons then moved into the trees, following the detectives and the old man.

He was about to drop to the ground and investigate when he sensed movement to the west and, swinging around, saw a HiAce van arrive just outside the treeline. Four men got out, each armed – he spotted a shotgun, a crossbow, a semi-automatic rifle and what looked to be a modified handgun of substantial size.

These were not hunters. Hunters wouldn't be coming to the woods at this time of day, with those types of weapons. At least not hunters of animals. Hunters of people, he thought, would be a different story.

And he should know. Hunting people was what he did.

There was only one settlement on that side of the woods, and that was where the Travellers in their interesting van were based. He knew there were two armed guards with them, but he'd watched through the trees, and they were indolent and distracted by mobile phones and a general malaise he would never have tolerated in any man who served under him.

In a flurry of movement, he dropped to the forest floor and made his way rapidly towards the western edge of his domain.

He would deal with the four hunters first. And then double back and address the two coming in from the east.

He had sworn to protect these woods. And he had come to understand that meant those who lived there too. They were under his care, whether they knew it or not.

And no matter what his mentor said.

They had fought over it, he and his handler. But the Abhartach knew what was right.

He was beginning to think the old man had been lying to him for a very long time.

Perhaps there was an atonement coming.

But not now. Now, he had work to do.

57

Seamus and Benjy found her fifteen minutes later, semi-conscious on the forest floor.

'How badly hurt are you?' the detective asked, gingerly kneeling beside her.

Jessie's answer was little more than a moan.

'I have some water,' the former teacher said, removing a canteen from a pouch on his belt.

Jessie drank from it gratefully before seeing the state of her partner's face, the left half of which was swollen and bleeding.

'You look like crap,' she said. 'Are you okay?'

'I'll live. What happened to this guy?' Seamus motioned towards the dead Traveller.

'The Abhartach,' Jessie said. 'I... I've seen him. I don't understand what I saw yet, but he was here.'

'Did he hurt you?' Seamus tentatively pulled back a strand of Jessie's hair to reveal the spot where she'd hit her head – her scalp had been torn and was bleeding profusely. He removed his jacket and, using a penknife he took from his pocket, began to cut the lining into strips.

'No. The Abhartach didn't touch me.'

'He didn't?'

'No. I... I had the rifle. Maybe I scared him off.'

Seamus wrapped her head with one of the makeshift bandages and then eased her forward, removing her jacket to get a better look at her shoulder. 'That guy shot you?'

'With my own gun!' Jessie said, wincing as Seamus probed the area where the bullet had grazed her.

'Can I have that water, Benjy?'

He rinsed out the wound and then bound it tightly.

'I can't help but notice our deceased friend had a gun too, and it didn't seem to scare the Abhartach one bit.'

'That had occurred to me,' Jessie said.

'So why do you think you're alive and he's not?'

'I have no idea. My smouldering good looks?'

'You know I say this with love, but right now you look like you've been pulled backwards through a ditch. Of course, he *is* a violent criminal, so maybe that's what he likes...'

A thought suddenly occurred to Jessie, and she gripped Seamus's arm. 'Joe and Finbar! He told me the plan was to kill you and leave you here, but I was to be brought to Maisie Dunne, along with the Keenans, to be tortured.'

'You think they're going after the Keenans now?'

'You have to get to them, Seamus.'

'What about you? I can't leave you here.'

'You can and you will. I'll call Waters.'

Seamus scratched his head uncertainly. 'I don't know about this, Jessie. There's two armed detectives watching Joe and Finbar. What if the Abhartach comes back? What'll you do then?'

'He let me live once,' Jessie said. 'Let's hope he will again.'

Seamus looked at Benjy. 'Do you know where the Travellers are camped?'

'I do. On the western side of the woods.'

'Is there a quick way to get to them from here?'

'There's a sort of path that will take you close to them. I can show you.'

'Okay. Bring me to the start of it and then get back here and stay with Jessie.'

'Seamus!' Jessie said, annoyed.

'Don't argue with me! You're not in any fit state to fight if he comes back, and Benjy here knows how to use that shotgun. Beezer Muldoon is lying over yonder with a hole through him because this man wasn't prepared to stand back and let me be killed. You can trust him to do what has to be done. I'm sorry, Benjy, but until the cavalry show up, I need you to do this for me.'

Benjy blinked for a second but then nodded, looking a bit more resolute.

'Okay,' Jessie said. 'Go quickly.'

58

The footing was so rough Seamus couldn't sustain an all-out run and finally resorted to a jog that was just a little faster than his walking speed but was the best he could manage.

The path Benjy had guided him to was much like the one Ollie had used to bring them to the former schoolteacher's camp in that it was visible for long stretches but then disappeared completely, only to re-emerge as if by magic, usually a little bit away from where Seamus was. At one point it vanished for fifteen minutes, and he was certain he would never find it again. But just as he was beginning to wonder if he would spend the remainder of his days wandering, lost in the woods, there the path was just ahead, and he gratefully rejoined it.

He found the first of the bodies propped against a tree. It was a man Seamus was sure he recognised from the Dunnes' camp – an overweight, slovenly-looking character wearing a green parka and baggy jeans. A crossbow was lying a short distance away from him, and the front of his jacket was soaked with blood. The cause of death looked to be a crossbow bolt, which protruded from the fat man's chest. How exactly the deceased had managed to be shot with his own crossbow was a mystery Seamus realised he would probably never solve, so instead of worrying about it, he took out his phone and dropped a pin at the location so he could find it again, before jogging onwards.

Two more bodies were spread-eagled in a clearing up the path.

None of them got so much as a shot off, Seamus thought. *My God, did Joe do this? Because if he did, he's way more dangerous than I gave him credit for.*

He noted the site and ran on.

It was then that he found the final hunter.

He seemed to be relaxing against an ancient alder in a clearing a little off the path, and Seamus was almost past him before a stiff movement and a wheezing breath alerted him to the man's presence.

At first Seamus thought he was resting. It was only when he coughed and a cloud of red spray emitted from his mouth that the detective realised what was really happening.

Someone had wrapped a piece of what looked to be a tree root around the man's neck and abdomen, lashing him to the tree. By the time the detective got to him, his skin had a blue pallor. Seamus tried to cut the fibrous cord at the back of the tree with his penknife, but it was useless – the filaments were too tough. The man's struggles became more frantic, and Seamus knew he was asphyxiating. He worked furiously, his own fingers turning numb, but finally felt the prone hunter sag and knew it was over.

Cursing, he dropped the penknife from fingers he could no longer feel.

And as he did so, Joe Keenan stepped into the clearing from the other side.

59

'Jessie just called to tell me you were coming,' the Traveller said. 'What the hell happened here?'

He looked the exact same as the last time Seamus had seen him – deeply tanned and easy in his movements, dressed in muted colours of green and brown, his thick hair uncombed and his jawline stubbled.

He doesn't look like a man who just killed four people, Seamus thought, *but then, what does that sort of person look like?*

'Is that fella tied to that tree? That's rough, isn't it? I mean, Jesus, like.'

'I was about to ask you the same question,' Seamus said. 'There's three more bodies back the way I came. Whoever did it took them completely by surprise. I've never seen anything that comes close to this.'

Joe's eyes narrowed. 'Are you asking me if this is my handiwork?'

'I suppose I am, yes. Who else could it be?'

'I told the feckin' guards watching my camp that I was going to take a pish,' Joe said, 'and then I came looking for you to see if you needed help – Jessie told me which direction to expect you from. You can check with the lads – I walked out of the campsite maybe six minutes ago. And I've been there without moving since you left.'

'You decided coming to my assistance, without a gun or a weapon of any kind, when you have two armed detectives back at your van, was a good idea?'

'I needed them to keep an eye on Finbar.'

'Still, Joe…'

'I told you, I don't like anyone else doin' my work for me. I wasn't going to have you legging it through the woods to come to my aid against the Dunnes and not try to help you. I was in the camp right up to a few minutes ago.'

'I'll check, don't you worry.'

'Do. I'm gettin' used to being accused of shit I had no part in at this stage. I thought you and me had a better understanding, but it looks like I was wrong.'

Joe turned on his heel and stalked back the way he'd come.

Seamus, beginning to feel guilty, followed him.

60

The offices of Adamant Security Solutions were just off Santry's main street in a three-storey building. The ground floor was made up of the reception desk, a rack containing fliers and pamphlets outlining the various services the agency provided, and some chairs for clients to sit and wait in. The first floor – Terri had found the plans for the building online – contained offices, and the second floor was open plan, so the genealogist reckoned it was probably for filing or storage.

The receptionist was a hard-faced woman in her fifties, and she looked at Terri with an expression that suggested she found it hard to believe anyone would want to speak to her, but she asked the girl to wait and picked up the phone. Ten minutes later, a slim man with thinning blonde hair, wearing a fashion-able grey suit with a blue tie (Terri thought it was the kind of suit Seamus might wear if he could afford it) emerged from a door behind the counter.

'My name is Claude Willis,' he said. 'I believe you're a police detective?'

'Technically, no,' Terri said, 'but I am a representative of the police commissioner. Can we go somewhere private to talk?'

He brought her up a flight of stairs to a conference room on the first floor.

'My company has a very good relationship with the police,' Willis said. 'How can I be of assistance today?'

Terri gave him a brief rundown of the situation in Derrada and indicated that some of the remains might be connected with the military.

'Your company's name has come up during our investigation,' she said. 'I was wondering if you might be in some way connected with any of the deceased.'

'I won't know until you give me their names,' said Willis mildly.

'Eugene Garvey,' Terri said.

Willis shook his head.

'Fiachra Boland?'

Again, a negative response.

Terri paused for a moment. 'What about Emer O'Hagan?'

Willis perked up. 'Yes, Emer worked for us for about a year when she was discharged from the army. Quite a good worker too. I was sorry when she left to set up her own agency.'

'What did she do for you?' Terri asked.

'Emer was employed to do... well, to do specialist work.'

'What kind of specialism does she have?'

'The tasks Emer carried out required everyone involved to sign non-disclosure agreements.'

'I can get a warrant that compels you to answer.'

'I'm afraid you could not,' Willis said. 'Even if you came back here with one, I still wouldn't tell you, and the threat of sending me to prison would not compel me to talk.'

Terri made a note of that.

'Wouldn't a prison stay be something of an inconvenience?' she asked. 'I'm sure your legal team would have you out sooner or later, but you'd be a guest of the state for several weeks at least.'

'If I am to do the work I do, for the clients who employ me, I cannot simply divulge information because someone asks me politely. Confidentiality is a crucial part of the service I offer.'

'I accept that of course,' Terri said. 'But I've already spoken to a high-ranking member of the Defence Forces. My visit to your company is simply about confirming information I already know.'

Willis shrugged. 'Tell me what you think you know then, and I'll see what I can do with it.'

'Emer O'Hagan is trained in covert operations.'

'Yes. I can confirm that. She is highly skilled in both urban and wilderness survival.'

Terri paused. 'Urban?'

'Yes. Everyone assumes soldiers are only ever sent out to forests and mountains and deserts. More often than not though, your special-ops team is going to be active in a city or an industrial population centre.'

'Interesting,' Terri said thoughtfully. 'I would imagine that's a very different skillset.'

'Someone like Emer is able to infiltrate most buildings without their occupants even knowing she's there. She can work her way around security systems with only the most basic tools, and she can get in and out without leaving any trace of forensic evidence.'

'So she has tech skills?'

'She's a highly trained technical operative. Emer O'Hagan knows how to track movement of individuals online, follow their behaviour within the digital world, and can then use her physical environment to great advantage to move against them, whether that's a city or a tract of forest. She's equally at home in both.'

Terri nodded and made a note of this. It seemed Emer O'Hagan could well have been the night-time visitor to their offices. Perhaps Terri's research had inadvertently brought her to the woman's attention.

'Thank you for your time, Mr Willis.'

He showed her to reception. 'I hope you solve your mystery,' he said.

Terri shook his hand, and as she did asked, 'Before I go, could you answer me one more thing?'

'I may or I may not,' Willis said. 'But there's no harm in asking.'

'Have you ever employed an agent who is... well, who's very small in height? Who might look, at a distance at least, as if they're a child? A person who might, in less enlightened times, be classified as a dwarf?'

Claude Willis barely reacted, but Terri saw a slight flicker of something cross his face, just for a moment. It was brief, but it was there.

'No,' he said. 'We've never employed anyone like that.'

'I'm going to leave my card,' Terri said. 'If anything occurs to you, maybe you could give me a call?'

'I'm sure I will,' Willis said.

Terri didn't think he sounded sure at all.

Jessie was taken to Ballinamore's medical centre, and once she was safely there, Seamus took her MG and drove back to Derrada.

Joe did not look pleased to see him.

'What do you want to accuse me of now?' he asked tersely.

'Both myself and Jessie were nearly killed by the Dunnes,' Seamus said, trying to keep the temper from his voice. 'Now, I think we've been more than fair with you, and we've treated you more like a friend than a suspect.'

'You did up until an hour ago!' Joe said, making no effort not to sound angry.

'I'm not going to apologise for doing my job,' Seamus said. 'And I'm not going to apologise for what I'm about to ask you now.'

Joe sighed deeply and, leaning over, stoked the campfire. 'You want to know why the Dunnes want me dead.'

'And why they're prepared to kill anyone who gets in their way to do it,' Seamus said.

Joe put his head in his hands for a moment, and Seamus wondered if the man might be crying. After what felt like a long time, he sat upright again and motioned with his head at the log where Seamus had sat with Jessie so recently.

'It's a bit of a story, so you'd best sit down.'

Seamus did.

Joe called over to his son, who was playing with Rufus among the trees.

'I need to talk man to man to Seamus for a bit. Will you give us some space?'

Finbar nodded and skipped off a little, but not so far the men couldn't see him.

'When my wife died, Finbar and me, we took to the road, as you know, and lived mostly in wild places. I needed to get away from people. I think a big part of me died too, when she did, and I needed to find it again, and the empty spaces helped me to do that. In 2014, we were camped by an abandoned quarry in Connemara, and Finbar had a fall and broke his arm. I took him to the hospital, and they found a bump on his head too, and the medic wanted to keep him in for observation. I wasn't allowed to stay in the hospital car park overnight, so I parked up on a halting site in Galway city. It was there I met the Dunnes for the first time.'

'I know they spend some of the year in Galway,' Seamus said. 'Maisie told me.'

'They actually gave me a great welcome. I was invited for dinner, and Maisie offered me work, said she'd arrange a marriage for me with a niece of hers so Finbar could have a mother... they were more than hospitable.'

'You weren't persuaded though,' Seamus asked.

'No. I'd heard of Maisie Dunne. I didn't want to throw my lot in with her, and I surely didn't want Finbar associating with her.'

'Good for you,' Seamus said.

'Finbar was given a clean bill of health on the third day of our stay at the halting site in Galway.

'"If he continues to improve at this rate, we'll discharge him tomorrow," the doctor told me. "His arm is healing nicely, but one more night should allow the bones to knit sufficiently that movement won't be painful once he's out and about with you."

'I spent the afternoon on the ward before heading back to the halting site for my last evening.

'We were to visit my da in Wexford the following day, and Finbar was excited about that. I remember he wanted to know if we'd get fish and chips when we were there. We always did.'

He smiled wistfully at Seamus. 'We never got there of course. That night, Francis Dunne, Maisie and Fred's son, arrived at the Transit with a bottle of whiskey. He'd visited me on my first night at the site, and I liked him well enough. He wasn't like his mother – there was something sensitive about him. Something more gentle.

'"I hear you're leaving us tomorrow?" he said.

'"My boy's well again," I told him. "And I promised my da we'd call to see him."

'"Will we have a last drink then before you take to the road?" he wanted to know, and I told him I'd be glad of the company.'

'Nothing wrong with having a few drinks with a friend,' Seamus said. 'You'd been stressed about your wee lad. You needed to let off steam.'

'I felt at ease with Francis,' Joe said. 'We talked about how hard it is for the Travellers in Ireland – how our way of life is becoming tougher and tougher to live. Francis told me his family only travelled four times a year, moving between the same collection of halting sites where they felt welcome. We talked about times when we'd both been treated badly: refused service in shops and bars or turned off campsites by bailiffs. Francis told me how proud he was of our heritage, our history, and he actually shed tears – the Irish government had just recognised our right to ethnic status, but no real changes had happened. He told me how worried he was that, in ten years' time, there would be none of our people left travelling at all.'

'I pray that will never happen,' Seamus said.

'We were both drunk by then, and I... I kind of put my arm around his shoulder. I only meant it as friendly, like. When I... when I look back on what happened next, I suppose I'm not certain anymore what I was thinking. Maybe I wasn't thinking at all. Maybe it was pure instinct.'

Seamus had a sense of what was coming but remained quiet. Joe would tell the story in his own time.

'We'd drunk more than three quarters of the bottle of whiskey and... It would be so easy to blame the alcohol, but I try to always be honest with myself. The drink may have lowered my... um... my inhibitions, but that was all. Francis was lying up against me, and his head was resting against my shoulder. I mean, I did hug him, in the way drunken men will, and as I did, with no warning, Francis turned his head upwards and kissed me.'

Seamus still said nothing. He nodded, trying to make sure his expression stayed neutral and supportive, but he had the sense that even if he did speak now, the other man wouldn't hear him. He was somewhere else.

'I froze,' Joe went on. 'I had the urge to push him away, to say no but then... I just didn't. My wife was dead five years by then. It had been five years since I'd felt the touch of another person, and I suppose I missed it. And suddenly, I knew I wanted it to happen.'

'Sure, what harm in the world is there in that?' Seamus said. 'You were two consenting adults. More power to you.'

'Francis was gone when I awoke, and I was anxious to pick up Finbar and be on my way. I went down to the building where the old man who ran the halting site worked, to let him know I was leaving, and when I got there I found a large group of people gathered. I counted twelve men, and in the middle of them, decked out in black lace, was Maisie Dunne. And she did not look happy.

'"Are you leaving us so soon?" she said.

'"You know I am," I said, keeping it friendly. 'I told you I was making for Wexford today, as soon as I've picked up Finbar.'

'"Going to go visit your old dad," she said. "Do you think he knows what kind of a son he's reared?"

'Now that pissed me off, but I didn't rise to the bait. I noticed Francis wasn't among the group, but I figured they all knew he was what he was, and that they suspected the time he'd spent in the Transit was probably not spent playing cards.

'"My dad knows exactly who I am," I said. "Now if you'll stand aside from the door, I'd like to take my leave."

'"We're not done talking yet," Maisie said, and by then she was screaming. "You were welcomed as a friend and invited into our home. We offered you food and we offered you work, and in return you betrayed us and defiled our family's honour."

'"I have nothing to say to you," I replied, and I tried to push past a sweaty-looking man in a frayed Aran jumper who was leaning against the door jamb of the caretaker's hut.

'And that move proved to be a mistake. I was grabbed and they laid in to me. I knew it was useless to fight back, so I rolled into a ball, wrapped my arms around my knees and tried to make myself as small as possible. They kicked and beat me every which way, and I was just passing out when I heard sirens in the distance. The caretaker must have called the police.

'I heard them, and I remember thinking they were too far away, that they'd never make it in time. Then I did pass out.'

'You're lucky they didn't beat you to death,' Seamus said. 'I have a lot of time for the Travellers, but their attitude to LGBTI culture leaves something to be desired.'

'I know I'm not gay,' Joe said. 'I loved my wife.'

'I'm not doubting that,' Seamus said. 'But I take it your experience with Francis wasn't unpleasant for you.'

The other man gazed into the fire. 'No. It wasn't.'

'Feck it, Joe, I'm no expert, but all I do know is that these days, you can be pretty much what you want to be, and no one can argue the point. It happened, and you don't regret that it did. What you regret is the response from Francis's family.'

'That's it,' Joe said. 'I woke up to find a big country guard looking down on me. He drove me to the same hospital Finbar was in in the Transit, and I was patched up in A&E. I stayed in the hospital overnight, then me and Finbar drove to Wexford. When we got to my father's small house in Maudlintown, Paddy Keenan, instead of inviting us in, stepped outside and closed the door behind him. I'd never known him to do that, and I knew right away they'd got to him.

'"I hear tell you've taken to lying with men now," he said in a whisper, and the hurt and shame in the old man's voice cut me to my core.

'"It's not like you to listen to gossip, Da," I said, but my eyes must have told the old man the truth.

'"A friend of the family who has dealings with the Dunnes' called to the house an hour ago," he said. "He wanted to warn me. They're coming after you, and when they get you, they're going to kill you. The lad, too."

'I asked him if I could count on the protection of the clan, and he said they couldn't stand against the Dunnes. They had too many men, and a lot of my people are terrified of them.

'"They don't fight with honour, Joe. They're bad. You're going to have to run."

'I asked him where I could run to.

'"Get out of Ireland," he said to me. "You've been living in wild places here, but there are bigger and wilder places in England and beyond where you can hide and never be found. Find them and lose yourself."

'Now I'd never been outside Ireland in my life, and here I was, faced with the idea of leaving everything I knew and loved. But I reminded myself that Finbar's life depended on it, and that was that really.

'My da gave me a wad of euros with an elastic band wrapped about it, and he said to me: "Go tonight. They're already after you. There's a ferry leaving for Fishguard at half past seven. From there you can go anywhere."'

'You must have been terrified,' Seamus said.

'I never saw my father again,' Joe said, his voice little more than a whisper. 'He died of a heart attack ten months later, and by the time news reached me, he was long buried. But that wasn't enough for Maisie Dunne. She sent people after me, and she's never stopped.'

'I promise you this, Joe,' Seamus said. 'We're going to make her stop. It's happening as we speak.'

Seamus would rue those words before the evening was out.

Terri Kehoe sat with Dawn Wilson in her office in the Phoenix Park. Dawn was drinking tea from her Batman mug – Terri had the insignia of the Green Lantern Corps on hers.

'I haven't read many comics set in the DC universe,' she said to the commissioner.

'You're a Marvel girl?'

'I suppose I am. I liked X-Men when I was a teenager.'

'Nothing wrong with X-Men.'

'Stories are powerful,' Terri said. 'I'm learning that more and more every day.'

'No argument here,' Dawn said. 'So what story brings you here today?'

'You know Jessie received a message from Uruz telling her to look into a security firm called Adamant Solutions?'

'I do.'

'I looked. Emer O'Hagan worked for them, and the manager there divulged that she's specially trained to infiltrate buildings, just like the Elysian.'

'You think she's the intruder?'

'It makes sense. But when I asked if they'd ever employed

someone who fit the description of the Abhartach, he gave me a funny look too.'

'Maybe he thought it was an odd question.'

'I did ponder that,' Terri agreed. 'I was on the bus on my way here when I received a call on my mobile from Adamant's offices. It was the receptionist. She informed me that she'd overheard my asking Willis – that's the managing director's name – about an operative of... of small stature, and she said that, while she'd worked for the company for two decades and had never seen him, she'd heard of a man who'd been recruited from some obscure wing of the Irish Ranger Corps and who became one of their most sought-after employees.'

'What services do Adamant provide?'

'They do all the standard things like guarding building sites and office blocks at night, but they're also private military contractors.'

'Propping up dictatorships and providing all kinds of mayhem if the price is right,' Dawn said.

'That's about it, yes,' Terri agreed.

'Did she give you a name?'

'She said he operated under aliases. She mostly heard him called Lautrec, after the French painter.'

'Charming,' Dawn said. 'And not much help.'

'Actually, it was some,' Terri said. 'I ran some searches, and I found some mentions on the deep web of a... well, an assassin, for want of a better word, who operated under that name from 2007 until 2013.'

'Any background on him?'

'They suggested he was a former Ranger. But I don't see how that could be the case. Not with a physical disability.'

'Is being short a disability?'

'I think once you go below a certain height, it technically is.'

Dawn sat back and stretched. 'It all keeps coming back to

the army, doesn't it?' she said. 'The victims seem to be military operatives, and now the killer or killers are too.'

'Can we say that for sure about all of the remains though?' Terri asked. 'We've only successfully identified two.'

'I wonder,' Dawn said. 'Or if they're not, they're people whose deaths the military at the highest level want to remain a secret. Possibly because they're involved.'

'You're suggesting state-sanctioned assassinations,' Terri said. 'That's... well, it's alarming, isn't it?'

Dawn nodded. 'The Irish army is always seen as too small and insignificant to ever be involved in activities of that nature. The truth is, though, we have one of the most effective intelligence services in the world – the fact no one really knows it exists is a testament to that – and our special forces can stand shoulder to shoulder with any other in the world. So while the concept seems to be right off the pages of a John le Carré novel, that doesn't mean we should discount it.'

'Sergeant Major O'Driscoll more or less told me not to be so silly when I suggested something similar,' Terri said.

'Hardly surprising,' Dawn said. 'Seeing as he never wanted us involved in the first place. I have to tell you, there have been rumours of this kind of thing for years, but I always discounted them as too fantastical. But I don't think we can come to any other conclusion.'

'What do you think he's trying to keep us from finding out about?' Terri asked. 'Do you think it's the deaths, or the person – or it seems we're talking about two people – who brought about the deaths?'

'Maybe both,' Dawn said. 'I think we're overdue another chat with Sergeant Major Stewart O'Driscoll.'

63

Emer O'Hagan booked into a B&B just outside Ballinamore on the Donegal Road at the exact same time Dawn Wilson was dialling Regimental Sergeant Major Stewart O'Driscoll.

Emer had a bag slung over her shoulder. It contained clothes, antiseptic tablets to facilitate cleaning her stoma bag (as well as a spare just in case), and a Glock 19 handgun with load. In another bag she had a laptop with 3D satellite maps of the woods, including all known trails and paths, downloaded onto the hard drive.

She didn't know whether or not she would come away from this, her final job, alive.

And she didn't really care.

———

Elsewhere in town, Jessie Boyle lay in a narrow bed in the town's small health centre, really just a GP's office with a couple of beds for emergency cases that required overnight care, having antibiotics pumped into her system via an intravenous drip. She'd just finished eating a bowl of chicken noodle soup and was considering switching on the TV but decided against it, instead putting on the *Folklore* album by the Americana band 16 Horsepower which she listened to on her earphones. She couldn't kick the feeling that something bad was coming and hoped the meditative quality of the music might soothe her anxiety somewhat.

———

While Jessie lay back and tried to lose herself in the acoustic soundscape, Seamus was tucking into an enormous mixed grill at the café. The laceration across his cheekbone had required three stitches and still stung every time he moved, and his ribs had been bandaged. The staff at the medical centre had advised him to stay overnight, but he refused, informing them he had a mountain of paperwork to get through that evening as a result of the six bodies the medical examiner had taken out of Derrada Woods that afternoon, and that such work would not require any physical strain. The nurse had tried to persuade him, but Jessie had informed the medic that her partner was a 'macho eejit' and that she was wasting her breath.

The nurse shrugged and went back to her station muttering something about men never really getting beyond their adolescence, and the young detective made good his escape.

Seamus reckoned he and Waters would be at it until well after midnight, so getting a hearty meal in now seemed a sensible thing to do.

He felt bad about how things had ended with Joe Keenan – the Traveller had completed his story and then asked the detective to leave, refusing to take his hand when Seamus had offered it. The detective wondered if he'd been wrong to ask if Joe was behind the deaths, and knew that forcing him to recount his history with the Dunnes was upsetting, but finally decided he was just doing his job, and Joe would have to like it or lump it.

Which meant that continuing to beat himself up served no purpose.

Joe Keenan would come around or he wouldn't, and no amount of fretting would change that truth.

———

For his own part, Joe sat brooding over the fire in his camp in Derrada, still hurt over Seamus's behaviour. Yet as he thought about things, the ice at his centre began to thaw. When he'd come upon the young detective that afternoon, Joe could see he'd been desperately trying to free a dying man from the roots that held him to a tree, cords designed to choke him. Of course Seamus was upset at having failed to do so, and the man had died horribly right in front of him. Seamus had also been sporting a cut to his face that was bleeding profusely, and Joe had later learned he'd only narrowly escaped being shot by Beezer Muldoon. All in all, Seamus Keneally had not had a great afternoon – it was hardly surprising he'd not been in the best of moods and might have behaved in ways he normally wouldn't. As Finbar whittled a piece of wood and Rufus slept beside the fire, Joe decided he would bury the hatchet with the detective the next time he saw him.

———

Ten yards away from the Keenans' camp, two armed detectives napped in their police cruiser. These were a different two to the ones Jessie and Seamus had met earlier that day, those having completed their shift and gone home. But these fresh guards were no more concerned about the risk to the Keenans than their predecessors had (so incorrectly) been. The fact that someone had foiled an attack on the family only that afternoon made them believe another assault was unlikely.

———

Another reason such an attack seemed less than probable was that, at that very moment, the Dunnes' halting site was being turned over by a team of police officers from Sligo, led by Josh Glenn. Maisie Dunne stood on the steps to her mobile home and watched the policemen coming and going with a cold eye.

'Ye won't find anything illegal here,' she insisted. 'We're a law-abiding people, so we are.'

'How does that explain the six men, all of whom are known associates of yours, who met their ends in Derrada today?' Glenn, who was standing nearby, shot back.

'Woods are dangerous places,' Maisie said. 'It sounds like a terrible hunting accident to me.'

'One of the deceased *told* Jessie Boyle he was there under your orders.'

'Did Ms Boyle get a recording of that allegation?'

'She did not.'

'Did the man who said it sign an affidavit confirming that was the information he wished to impart?'

'You know he didn't.'

'Well then, isn't it an awful shame no one who heard him speak those words is alive to tell about it, other than Jessie Boyle, who's been coordinating a vendetta against me from the moment I arrived in town. I'm sorry to say, but I think she has some prejudices towards the Travelling people.'

'You're not going to play that old card, Maisie,' Glenn said. 'We might not have any material evidence, but you and me both know what happened here. You made a mistake. It might be one that costs you.'

Maisie waved the possibility off and continued to watch her camp being searched with seething annoyance.

———

While Maisie gave the police filthy looks, Frank Waters was, despite his better judgement, making a start on the paperwork regarding the bodies found in Derrada – bodies of men who may or may not have gone to their deaths under Maisie Dunne's instruction. Seamus and Jessie had already given statements, and he now had to cross-reference the facts those documents contained with the details relating to each of the bodies and the manner in which they had died. Seamus would be joining him soon, but he thought he'd make a start on it.

Looking at the volume of work, Waters reckoned he and Seamus would be there most of the night.

———

And atop the canopy, on a platform of boards he'd attached there, the Abhartach slept. He had a busy night ahead of him too, although he didn't know it yet.

There were people to kill.

64

'Sergeant Major O'Driscoll, this is Commissioner Dawn Wilson.'

At the end of the line, Dawn could hear what sounded like a car engine. Then: 'I've been awaiting your call, Commissioner,' O'Driscoll said.

'Really?'

'Yes. I am, in fact, parked outside. Will you please instruct the men on the gate to let me in?'

'Hold for a moment then,' Dawn said and pressed the button on her desk phone that put her through to the gate. 'That's done. I'll see you in five minutes. Terri Kehoe is with me. Anything you can say to me, you can say to her.'

'Excellent. I'd hoped I might see Ms Kehoe again before this was over.'

'Well you have your wish.'

He was dressed in a plain grey suit and white shirt this time, and accepted tea when it was offered. Dawn gave it to him in a mug with the image of the Joker, Batman's nemesis, on it.

O'Driscoll looked at it quizzically. 'Are you making a point, Commissioner?'

Dawn pantomimed looking askance. 'Oh, did you get the Joker mug? It was the first one that came to hand is all.'

'Very well. You know why I'm here?'

'Is it something to do with Eugene Garvey?' Dawn asked.

'It is indeed. And Fiachra Boland. And Emer O'Hagan. Terri's investigation triggered alarms within the department, and while I was prepared to let that go, just a few hours ago an attempt was made to hack into the department's mainframe.'

'That's scandalous,' Dawn said. 'Was this attempt successful, Sergeant Major?'

'Partially. Ms Kehoe, do you know anything about this matter?'

Terri threw Dawn a look. The commissioner nodded.

'Yes, that was me. The firewalls stopped me when I got to a certain point though. Your system didn't exactly tell me the information I was trying to access was top secret, but it certainly gave the impression.'

O'Driscoll had some tea and looked at the two women. 'Eugene Garvey worked for us,' he said. 'You know Fiachra Boland did too. And I've been quite candid about Emer O'Hagan. They all worked at a level that precludes me from saying any more than that.'

'I think we'd reached that conclusion on our own,' Dawn sighed. 'The bit we're unsure about is why their mutilated remains ended up in Derrada Woods. Why *them*? And are the other bodies recovered there of people with a similar background and... um... work status?'

'You know I'm limited in what I can tell you.'

'Sergeant Major, we have two dead government operatives in the lab in Galway. We have eleven other bodies and sundry remains, and imaging shows what we believe to be countless more in the surrounding area. I'm not sure if you're aware, there was a massacre in the woods today, and six people died. One of my team is currently in hospital, and we have reports of a very strange figure, who seems to be behind a lot of this mayhem. And then there's your involvement. And Emer O'Hagan is mixed up in it all too.'

O'Driscoll listened with a genial expression on his angular face.

'What the fuck is going on?' Dawn asked. 'I mean, what the sweet fuck are we dealing with here?'

'I'm not sure what you want me to say, Commissioner.'

'Is this another one of your people doing the killing?' Dawn pressed. 'Has one of your projects got out of control?'

'I can't tell you, Commissioner,' O'Driscoll said. 'But I am going to do you a favour.'

He reached into the inside pocket of his jacket and took out a sheet of paper.

'This is an order, signed by the Taoiseach, instructing you to stand your team down, effective immediately.'

Dawn took the letter from him and read it, passing it to Terri.

'That's it?' Dawn said. 'You're pulling the rug out from under us?'

O'Driscoll sat forward and placed his mug on the edge of Dawn's desk. 'You are an intelligent and capable woman, Commissioner,' he said. 'So I know full well you can grasp that I might just have done you a very great favour.'

'I must not be as smart as you think I am, because I don't see it like that at all.'

'I've saved the lives of your people on the ground,' O'Driscoll said. 'Thank you for the tea. Please call them immediately and tell them to come in. Time is very much of the essence.'

He stood, smoothing the material of his suit down as he did so. 'There is a clean-up operation required in Leitrim that is long overdue,' he said. 'Believe me, you don't want your team mucking about in the woods while it's happening.'

As soon as he was gone, Dawn grabbed her coat. 'Get hold of Jessie and Seamus and tell them to lie low – and not to go anywhere near Derrada Woods,' she said.

'Where are you going?'

'To see if I can't get us some transport to Leitrim.'

Terri blinked. 'I thought we'd just been ordered to stand down.'

'Jessie is currently in hospital. Seamus is determined not to abandon Joe Keenan. They can't or won't leave the area, despite whatever shitstorm is coming. I might be standing down, but I'm not leaving my team in jeopardy. And there *is* a murderer still on the loose out there. It doesn't seem right to walk away with that still outstanding.'

'Isn't travelling to Leitrim the opposite of standing down though?'

'I don't know what you mean. Now, you make those calls and I'll be back as soon as I can. Be ready to go right away, because I don't think there's much time.'

'I'll be ready,' Terri said and dialled Jessie Boyle on her mobile.

CASE NOTES ON LEITRIM BURIAL
SITE – TRANSCRIBED FROM AUDIO
JOURNAL KEPT BY JESSIE BOYLE

10 NOVEMBER

My old chief inspector, Giles Dunwoody-Taft, is a former SAS officer.

Giles is as warm and caring a man as you could hope to meet. I never really knew my dad, and my stepfather, well, he wasn't a good person, so when I went to London to find work in law enforcement, Giles became a sort of adoptive father. It wasn't something I was expecting, and it wasn't something I sought out, but he, in a very kind and gentle way, let me know he'd be there for me if I needed someone.

And when I did, he didn't let me down.

So what I'm about to say, which is based on things Giles shared with me, is all said under the proviso you understand I have nothing but love and respect for the man of whom I speak.

Giles doesn't talk about his time with the Special Air Service very much. In fact, he can't talk about it, as the majority of the missions he carried out were highly secret and confidential. But when he'd had a few glasses of Scotch, Giles would sometimes make reference to being in that elite unit.

One of the things he impressed upon me is the process of dehumanisation that goes on as part of the training. The opera-

tive's individual personality is stripped down to its essential components. You're trained to see yourself no longer as a single, unique organism but instead as existing only within the context of the unit.

Decisions going forward are not based upon what serves the person but rather the group. And violence and aggression are part and parcel of every facet of communication. Giles told me that beatings, sleep deprivation, psychological torture, isolation, starvation, being left in stress positions for hours – these were all normal and accepted parts of the training process. And successfully negotiating this training, succeeding through endurance, was seen as a great achievement.

By the time you graduated, you were no longer the person you'd been when you started. They'd rebuilt you. You now belonged to them.

Being in the special forces was all about your capacity to follow orders, even if those orders went against everything you held dear in your previous life. Giles told me he'd done some things he wasn't proud of, things he would take to his grave. And he also shared with me that he didn't think he'd have made it back to the world outside the military unless he'd met his wife.

When he was demobbed, he didn't know how to be a normal person anymore. He struggled with anger, with intrusive thoughts and broken sleep. With guilt.

'I'd have ended up dead or in a military prison if it wasn't for Bessie,' he told me. 'She saw something in me, and with patience and kindness helped me find my way back. If she hadn't, I'm pretty certain I wouldn't be sitting here, talking to you now.'

I remember asking him about his comrades, the ones who didn't have a Bessie. What happened to them?

'The lucky ones found something to do using the skills they'd developed with the SAS. So some, like me, went into the police or the fire department, which has the same feeling of community you'd had in the service, and it gives you something to cling to.'

I asked him about the unlucky ones.

'They took to a bottle, or crawled down the point of a needle, or took to hurting themselves just to feel alive. I saw one or two on the news, from time to time, who'd gone mental and killed someone in a bar fight or in an act of road rage. It was heartbreaking, but I learned to block it out. If you dwelt on that stuff, the guilt became too great. Survivor guilt – why them and not me? And that was something I didn't have an answer for.'

On another occasion he told me he'd run into an old comrade, who approached him with a job offer. This friend was working for a mercenary unit, carrying out some sort of private war in Central America, and was looking for people to take on command positions.

'I barely recognised him,' Giles told me. 'When I knew him, he was tough as old boots, definitely someone you didn't want to cross, but he still had a smile that told you of the lad he once was. There was a decency in there.'

'I take it he'd changed,' I said.

'It was like he'd lost his soul somewhere along the line,' Giles said. 'I looked into his eyes and I knew he'd done some things I couldn't even dream of. There would never be any coming back for him. He hinted at the fact that the people he worked for didn't just provide private armies. They did other things too. Assassinations. Espionage. Staged coups. Propped up dictators of all creeds and political affiliations. I remember thinking that, regardless of where we were sent with the SAS, at least we could tell ourselves we were doing it for queen and country, even if we didn't really believe it deep down. We had a cause. But these guys, these soldiers of fortune... they were only in it for the money.'

I pointed out that everyone works for money. Did he think the people who served his food in McDonalds believed in what they were doing?

'That's true,' he told me. 'But it doesn't matter how much money these guys are paid. It's never going to be enough. Because *every time they get sent out into another war zone or to kill some industrialist or to stoke political unrest in a poverty-stricken backwater, something is taken from them. They* lose *something of themselves. Something they can never get back.'*

That conversation made me think.

How many young men and women went to war and never really came home, even when they physically did? How many are still lost?

How many are still fighting a battle with an enemy they can never beat?

Terri told me that Emer O'Hagan described the Abhartach as 'death'. I think she was right. I think something in him died a long time ago.

He just doesn't realise he's dead.

65

10 P.M.

Jessie had just finished recording her audio diary, which she made using the voice recorder app on her phone, when her handset buzzed, indicating a text message. She spotted the UK international code and immediately knew who the sender was, even though she was certain the number, when traced, would be for a recently bought pay-as-you-go SIM card.

Jessie Boyle, I am torn. While the idea of you being in peril gives me a great deal of satisfaction, I fear that in this instance, the end you would meet would be far too quick and uninteresting. I have misjudged my friend the Abhartach, and I kick myself when I realise there are machinations at play involving parties and interests of myriad ethical and political persuasions that are about to reach crisis point. You and your little group of conspirators are but trivialities among the greater schemes unfolding, and I must urge you to use discretion and exit the stage. A war is coming, Jessie Boyle, and it will crush you in its wake. You and I will have further dealings. I see what I am doing here as tantamount to a hunter releasing a game animal so he has the pleasure of hunting it

*again. Please do not make me regret my decision. Run while
you can.* Ո

Jessie read and reread the message and was still none the
wiser. Was this some kind of game the killer was playing? An
attempt at reverse psychology? It didn't matter how many times
she tried to analyse the words, she could discern no subtext.

Finally, she dialled Seamus, gazing out the window at the
dark night sky as she listened to it ringing.

'Where are you?'

'In the station with Frank, writing up the paperwork for
today's adventures. We'll be here for a while.'

'Wrap up as soon as you can. I just got a message from Uruz
advising us to get out of town.'

'You what now?'

'I agree it's weird, but from what I know of him, I think he's
being genuine. He thinks we're going to get caught in the cross-
fire of something big.'

'What though? We're no longer on the clock. I'm only doing
this bloody paperwork because they all died on our watch. I
mean, you and me didn't actually shoot any of these guys, when
you think about it.'

'I'd still feel happier if you were somewhere safe.'

Seamus snorted. 'I'm in a police station, Jessie. What could
be safer than that?'

Those words would come back to haunt him too.

66

10.12 P.M.

A convoy of military vehicles wound its way through boggy countryside, using backroads and rural laneways as they travelled to Leitrim through the darkness. The cluster contained three jeeps and a truck carrying weaponry and explosives.

Regimental Sergeant Major Stewart O'Driscoll sat in the passenger seat of the lead vehicle dressed in camouflage fatigues and a khaki-coloured cloth cap, his face mottled with green and brown paint. His second in command, Commandant Peter Mulcahy, was driving.

'This is not a mission I relish,' Mulcahy said as he piloted the jeep.

'Me neither, but you know as well as I do that it's not our call to make.'

'You served with him too. You know what he's like. How good he is.'

'It makes no difference. He's not superhuman. If we have to burn the woods to the ground to get to him, we will. He's been permitted to lie low for long enough, but the fact is, he's drawing too much attention to himself.'

'So in a way, he's given us no choice.'

'Precisely, Commandant. Precisely.'

'ETA is at approximately 2330 hours, Sarge.'

O'Driscoll nodded. 'We go in hard and we go in fast.'

'Do we have a pin in his location? Those woods cover a wide area.'

'We don't need one,' O'Driscoll said, gazing out the window at the night-time bogland as they passed through it. 'He'll come to us. Of that you can be sure.'

Maisie Dunne stood on the steps of the police station in Sligo. Detective Josh Glenn was beside her.

'You're being released on your own cognisance,' he said. 'Do you know what that means, Maisie?'

'It means I'm to be a good little tinker and not cause any more problems.'

'That's it in a nutshell.'

'You're letting me go because I've done nothing wrong, so I don't know what all these warnings and conditions are about.'

Glenn sighed a deep sigh. 'You're being released because you have an excellent lawyer and we haven't enough material evidence to keep you. That's very different from your being innocent. Are we clear on that, Maisie?'

She gave that simpering look that was supposed to be a smile and skulked down the steps to where Fred and another man, Henry, was waiting beside their blue HiAce van. Fred embraced his wife, and Maisie turned, gave Glenn a wave, and got into the van.

'Did ye retrieve the weapons?' she asked as soon as the doors were closed.

'We did,' Henry said.

Two of the clan's soldiers, Terry and Bernard, had, in fact, gone to a nearby quarry and dug them up an hour ago. The cache of arms had been deposited there when the convoy was on its way into Ballinamore.

Fred handed his wife a burner phone, which she flipped open.

'Bernard, we'll be with you in an hour, but I'm going to be honest and say I don't want to wait. Move on Joe Keenan *now*. I want him dead, and I don't care who else has to die to get it done.'

She paused, listening to the response at the other end.

'Yes, I'd still like those polis officers to be done away with too. That Jessie Boyle insulted me and my family. Let's clean this whole thing up, kill the lot of them, and then I think we'll get out of Ireland for a while. Get things in motion, and we'll be with you soon.'

Maisie Dunne hung up and, laying her head back on the seat, went to sleep. She always found being interrogated by the police tiring.

And she knew Fred would wake her when they got back to Ballinamore and the fun was about to begin.

10.20 P.M.

Seamus thought that if he had to fill out the standard Garda Síochána incident report form one more time, he would go insane.

He glanced over at Frank Waters, who was perched on his usual stool at the reception desk, doing the same job as him but seemingly with much more grace.

'Frank, am I wrong, or are you actually enjoying this?'

The older guard looked over at him and grinned. 'I kinda like the paperwork. It's relaxing.'

Seamus shook his head incredulously. 'Well I have to say I find it about as relaxing as I would putting my balls in the mouth of an angry Rottweiler.'

'I haven't had the pleasure, but I'll take your word for it,' Waters sniffed and returned to what he was doing.

Seamus stretched expansively, wishing he was just about anywhere other than in this police station at that precise moment doing this particular job when his phone rang. Delighted to have any distraction, he grabbed it.

'Seamus, this is Josh Glenn. I know Jessie is in hospital, so I'm assuming you're acting team leader?'

'You assume correctly. What can I do for you?'

There was a brief pause at the end of the line.

'Josh, I'm up to my neck in paperwork here, so is there something you need?'

Glenn took a few deep breaths, then said, 'Look, Seamus, I know you and me have had our differences over how to run this case, but I need to tell you, I've just been forced to release Maisie Dunne.'

The younger detective laughed without humour. 'I could have guessed that would happen. Not enough evidence?'

'Everyone involved in the massacre in the woods is dead except you, Jessie and that mental fella who shot Beezer Muldoon. Maisie claims Jessie has flouted her human rights and waged a hate campaign against her from day one. And on top of that, she's got a top-of-the-line solicitor from Limerick, a guy who represents a lot of the hoodlums around that neck of the woods, acting for her. He had us tied up in legal knots. We had no option but to let her go.'

'Thanks for the heads-up,' Seamus said. 'I'm going to bet she left with her tail between her legs though.'

'I wish she did,' Glenn said. 'I've known that woman a long time, and I'm telling you she was livid when she walked out of here. She isn't going to take it lying down.'

'How do you mean?'

'If I were you, I'd go and get Joe Keenan and his lad and get them out of harm's way. They're going to need to be locked up for their own safety for quite a while, after which I'd be inclined to put them in witness protection or something.'

'You don't think she'll make another run at them so soon?'

'Maisie Dunne is an extremely dangerous woman,' Glenn said. 'She believes herself to be above any of the laws the rest of us live by, and for as long as I've had dealings with her, people who piss her off end up dead. It's a miracle Joe Keenan's survived as long as he has, but I'm telling you now, he will not see tomorrow's sunrise unless you give him direct protection. She *will* try and have him killed tonight.'

'Thanks for the heads-up,' Seamus said again. 'I do appreciate it, Josh.'

'I should probably also tell you she's furious with you and Jessie. Jessie in particular, as it happens.'

'Jessie has a knack for annoying dangerous people. It's on her CV under special skills.'

'She's already tried to kill you both once,' Glenn said. 'She'll try harder next time. Don't say I didn't warn you.'

'Message received,' Seamus said. 'I'll pick up Joe and get him and the lad into the station here, and we'll see where we are after that.'

'If things get hairy, call me, okay?'

Seamus hung up and pushed his chair back.

'We've been rescued,' he said to Waters.

'How's that?'

'A gang of desperadoes is threatening the safety of an innocent family, and only you and me stand in the way of their demise.'

Waters shook his head sadly. 'We're going to Derrada again, aren't we?'

'What gave you that idea?' Seamus asked. 'But yeah, we are.'

10.50 P.M.

Before she left her B&B to drive to Derrada, Emer O'Hagan sent an email to the Minister for Defence. Regimental Sergeant Major Stewart O'Driscoll made sure it ended up in a specially encrypted file in the department database, and as he (by then) understood that such things would not keep the likes of Terri Kehoe out, he later permitted Jessie and her team to read its contents before it was buried for the next seventy-five years.

Minister,

I am sending this to you because you are, effectively, the dark heart of the Irish armed forces, though I'm aware you've never worn a uniform nor served anyone other than yourself nor been inspired by a cause greater than your party's political interests. However, you are at the top of the chain of command, which I am trained to observe, so this missive goes to you. It strikes me that you may not understand it or have any sense of the real weight of its import. Should this be the case, which I fear it will, I'm sure at least one of your advisors will be able to furnish you with the information you require to grasp what I'm saying.

So here it is: Five years ago, I was sent on a mission which I believed was a test of my abilities, a task to determine whether or not I was fit for a command post. I now understand that while it was a test, it was not of my skills. I was, to all intents and purposes, a sacrificial lamb, an experiment to see what would happen if military personnel crossed into the territory of a volatile and dangerous former operative who was entrenched in some woods in Leitrim. My superiors wanted to see how he would react – what he would do if threatened. They wished to understand how dangerous he'd become.

I was sent because I was considered skilled but expendable.

My contact with this individual ended my military career, and it seems clear the Abhartach, which is what the locals call my attacker, was permitted to continue living hand-to-mouth among the trees, scaring children and running off gunrunners and meth-heads.

Well, Minister, I've had enough. I'm going to finish what you should have five years ago. I don't expect to survive, but I promise you this: neither will he.

Before I die, I want you to know that both our deaths are on your hands.

Sincerely,

Lieutenant Emer O'Hagan

Late of the Irish Army Ranger Corps

10.55 P.M.

Jessie sat on her bed, brooding.

Something about the whole thing just seemed wrong to her. And she'd never been one to just sit idly by and wait for things to happen around her. Reaching for her mobile, she dialled Seamus but just got an out-of-service tone. She tried Waters but with the same results.

Sitting on the side of the bed, she looked at the IV bag. It was almost empty, and Jessie reckoned whatever good she was going to get from it had mostly been delivered. Wincing, she removed the cannula from her arm and took her clothes from the locker beside the bed.

The nurse on the desk was busy in another room and didn't notice as she slipped out the front door. Seamus had left the MG parked right out front, and she got in, turned the key in the ignition and turned for Derrada.

She had a theory she wanted to test.

10.53 P.M.

Dawn Wilson drove the unmarked SUV she'd requisitioned from Garda HQ's vehicle pool towards the town of Ballinamore, and while she did, Terri worked on her laptop. The dark countryside rolled past her unnoticed as her fingers danced across the keys.

'How are you getting on?' Dawn asked, a smouldering cigarette dangling from her lower lip.

'Jessie asked me to run a check on a man named Oliver McGee,' she said. 'He's a senior citizen who lives in Ballinamore. And I... I know him.'

'How's that then?'

'Remember I told you an old man approached me in the bus station in Cork and advised that the team should pull out? He said all the people who were buried in the woods had got the deaths they deserved.'

'And he was this guy?'

'He was. And what's more, the trail I've followed leads me right back to the Armed Forces database and an identical firewall to the one I hit with Eugene Garvey.'

'So you're stuck then.'

'Not at all. I restrained myself the last time, but seeing as we're not following orders this evening, I think I'll hack my way around it if you don't mind.'

'Knock yourself out,' Dawn said.

'I will, thank you.'

They drove on. Leitrim was twenty minutes away.

72

11 P.M.

Joe Keenan wasn't happy.

'You're telling me that after everything we've been through, all the effort you've made on my and Finbar's behalf – after all of that, you want me to go back to jail?'

'No one's arresting you, Joe,' Seamus said. 'This is just a safety precaution. Maisie had to be released, and the lads in Sligo reckon she's pretty angry.'

They were standing in the shadowy clearing outside the Transit, Waters waiting in the driving seat of a police cruiser just beyond the treeline. Seamus could see Finbar sitting on one of the beds in the van, Rufus perched on his knee, gazing out at him, wide-eyed. He could see how scared the boy was and feel the anger radiating off his father, his frustration palpable in the air.

'She's always angry! I'm not going back into that cell. If you're that worried, let me run! I've been going crazy stuck here anyway.'

'This business with the bodies is nearly over,' Seamus said. 'I wouldn't say we know exactly what's going on yet, but what we do know is that you didn't do it. So as soon as we're certain it's safe for you to go, you can go.'

'I'd like to take my chances now, if you don't mind.'

'I would love to say I'm okay with that,' Seamus responded. 'But—'

At that moment, the dirt less than six inches from their feet was ploughed up by a line of automatic weapon fire. The bullets hit before they heard the gunshots, so Seamus knew they were being fired on from some distance away. Both men froze for a second, but the second flurry, which caused both rear tyres on the Transit to deflate with a pop and a hiss, shook them into action.

'Finbar, come on!' Joe called. 'Time to go.'

The lad was already out of the van and running. Waters, to his credit, had brought the car around as soon as the first shots were fired and had the doors open. The three of them and the small dog piled in – Seamus in the front, Joe and Finbar in the back – and the cruiser was moving before the doors were even closed.

'Frank, get us the feck out of here,' Seamus shouted, pulling his Glock from its holster and firing blindly into the trees before pulling the door shut as the guard piloted the cruiser onto the road, accelerating rapidly.

'I should have stayed doing the paperwork,' Waters moaned as they turned a corner, only to find a red HiAce van parked right across the road, blocking their way.

The guard didn't slow but turned hard left, ploughing into the ditch, which caused the cruiser to lean precariously, and Seamus was convinced they would topple over and end up stuck on their side in the roadside dyke. The speed and momentum Waters had built up carried them through though, and they skidded past the blockade. The side of their car ground along the van's bumper, but then they were through.

The van, not to be perturbed, roared into life, articulated a

U-turn and gave chase. Peering into the rear-view mirror, Waters saw the passenger-side window roll down, and a thickly bearded man leaned out holding what looked to be a Kalashnikov rifle. Bullets thudded into the rear of the cruiser. Finbar made a squealing sound and put his hands over his head.

'Everyone down!' Seamus shouted and leaned out of the speeding car to shoot.

Joe wrapped his arms around his son and pulled him low in the seat.

As the automatic fire rained down upon them, Waters swerved hard right then left, weaving in and out on the road, making them a harder target to hit but making it almost impossible for Seamus to aim effectively.

The detective fired anyway. His first two shots went wide, but more by luck than design, his third hit the windscreen dead centre, shattering it in a filigree of cracks and fractures.

The van slowed as the driver's visibility was diminished, and Waters didn't need to be told to capitalise on the advantage. He pushed the cruiser to the limit of its speed, which was just as well, because as he did so, first one, then two, and finally a third car swooped around the dwindling HiAce and careered after them.

'That is really not good,' Waters observed.

Seamus noted the guard had become deathly pale, his face shiny with sweat.

He's scared out his wits, Seamus thought, *but he's still functioning. I have to keep him focused. We're all going to need him before this is over.*

'Just get us home,' Seamus said, squeezing the guard's shoulder. 'Forget about them and drive.'

Waters nodded and, grim-faced, kept his foot pressed to the floor.

Someone in the middle car opened fire, but the cruiser was

just out of range, and the bullets pinged and ricocheted off the road.

'Do not slow down, Frank, do you hear me?' Seamus said urgently. 'You're doing great, and let's hope they don't have it in the tank to narrow the gap.'

As he said it, the middle car, some kind of souped-up Ford, zoomed forward just a touch, and they all heard the staccato report of a machine gun. Three rounds burrowed into the rear of the cruiser, and then they all heard what sounded like a sigh and the car lurched to the left.

'They've hit one of the tyres,' Waters said. 'We're screwed, Seamus.'

'Only if you believe we are,' the detective said. 'The car can run on the rims if it has to. We're almost at the town boundary.'

He was right. They tore past the *Welcome to Ballinamore* sign and less than one minute later screeched to a halt outside the station. They rushed inside just in time to see the three cars and van skid to a stop outside in a loose semicircle. No one got out, but they didn't leave either.

Waters locked and bolted the front door, and then they all peered out at the unwelcome visitors outside.

'What do they want?' the fat guard asked.

'They want Joe,' Seamus said, deciding not to point out that Finbar was equally under threat, as the boy seemed scared enough already. 'And from what Glenn told me earlier, they want me as well.'

'But we're in here and they're out there,' Waters observed. 'So we're safe, right?'

'It's called a siege,' Joe said wearily.

'Surely backup will arrive before they come in and get us,' Waters said, his tone becoming very high-pitched.

'We'd better hope so,' Seamus said.

He pulled out his mobile and dialled Glenn's number.

Nothing happened for a moment, then a lilting sing-song

tone sounded, telling him there was a failure to connect. He tried again. And a third time. He attempted to dial Jessie but got the same tone.

'Frank, can you check the landline?'

Waters picked it up, listened. 'It's dead.'

'And I'm going to assume the Internet is down too,' Seamus said.

'How?' Waters demanded, starting to look deeply distressed.

'Best way to knock out the mobile network is to feck about with the masts,' Seamus said. 'I presume somewhere like this is served by one, maybe two phone pylons. If you disable them, you'll knock out the data connection too. The Wi-Fi in the station is piped in through a cable that runs up the outside of the front door. Cut it, and you cut off access to the web in here.'

'Are there any Wi-Fi hotspots nearby?' Joe asked.

'I thought you were a wild man with no use for such things,' Seamus said, looking at the Traveller with a raised eyebrow.

'I don't use it, but that doesn't mean I don't know anything about it,' Joe said.

'It'd be great if there was,' Seamus said, checking his phone for available networks. 'Unfortunately, we're in Ballinamore, not Dublin city centre. So no. We're trapped in here with no channels to the outside world.'

'What can we do then?' Waters said, sweat running down his face in rivulets.

'We wait and see what they do next,' Seamus said.

11.05 P.M.

'I'm in,' Terri Kehoe said as Dawn Wilson lit a cigarette from the butt of her previous one, tossing the finished smoke out the window as she drove.

'And?'

'Oliver McGee is a former Irish Army Ranger who served with honours in more than thirty campaigns all over the world. He was taken off active service in the early 1970s and worked as a trainer before leaving the armed forces... it says he left without unit support. Do you know what that means?'

'My guess would be he did something to forfeit his pension,' Dawn said.

'Yes, that makes sense. There are several pages that outline his involvement with various private security companies. But it doesn't seem he was doing security work, per se.'

'No?'

'No. He was stationed in a lot of out-of-the way places. Rwanda. Nicaragua. Cuba. Colombia.'

'He was a mercenary,' Dawn said.

'Um... it says here his specialism is tactical analysis, covert operations and the psychological aspects of warfare.'

'Charming,' Dawn said.

'There's also a note that he's suspected as being a handler for a number of special operatives.'

Dawn blew a stream of smoke out of her nose and nodded. 'Now I'm starting to understand how this all fits together,' she said. 'That all makes a lot of sense.'

'Could you explain it to me then?' Terri asked.

'If Oliver McGee is a handler,' Dawn said, 'that means he's the psycho who keeps the really dangerous psychos under control.'

'If that's the case,' Terri said, 'he hasn't been doing a very good job.'

'Or maybe he has,' Dawn said. 'Maybe it's all gone to hell because the police got involved and drew all kinds of bad people to the town.'

'You're saying he was right?' Terri asked. 'We should have walked away?'

'It's too late for that now,' Dawn said. 'I suppose we'll never know.'

And they could see the lights of the small town in the distance.

Now that he no longer worked for the old man, the Abhartach was free to spend all his time watching the family in the woods – and to keep them safe.

He'd watched the six men approaching the Keenans' camp and observed them taking up positions in the trees. He kept to the shadows and came upon the closest man, who was leaning against a stump, using it to steady his rifle. With one sweep of his blade, the Abhartach severed the man's windpipe. He fell without so much as a sound.

By then the shooting had already begun, but the police had arrived for some reason, and the man and his son and their little dog managed to get away. Before he could reach the second shooter, the group were running, and he pounced on another man and put his knife between his ribs before they reached their cars and gave chase.

The Abhartach stood in the darkness, his blade still wet with blood, feeling something he hadn't in a long time: uncertainty. He'd driven them away from his home, but something told him the Traveller family were at serious risk. The attackers would not give up.

And he wasn't sure the police had the skills to vanquish them.

He took off at speed through the trees, running at a full sprint, his body low to the ground as he'd been taught by the tribal people when he'd been sent to fight... somewhere. He could no longer remember where.

He reached what looked to be a pile of deadfall branches and with a couple of deft movements pulled some of the detritus away, revealing an ancient-looking jeep. The old man, as well as bringing him jobs and whatever food he couldn't provide for himself by hunting and foraging, kept the vehicle in diesel and oil. The jeep was registered under the old man's name, and he paid the tax and insurance on it, and brought it to be NCTed. The Abhartach used it to travel to jobs but rarely had use for it outside of that.

He didn't like leaving the woods.

But now it seemed he must. If he didn't confront these people, they would keep coming back. And his peace had been disturbed enough. Ever since the bodies had been found and the police started sniffing about, his dreams had been troubled and he could find no rest.

He climbed into the jeep, the seats of which had been modified to facilitate his size, and took the keys from their place atop the sun visor. The engine came alive at the first turn of the key.

The Abhartach was going into town.

75

11.12 P.M.

Not a single person had emerged from the semicircle of vehicles arrayed outside the police station, and Ballinamore's main street was deathly quiet when the blue HiAce carrying Maisie and Fred Dunne and the red-haired man called Harry pulled up right behind them. Maisie did not stand on ceremony and was out and on the street in a moment, which elicited a similar response from her crew, all twelve of whom clambered out too, awaiting instruction.

'They're all in there,' the bearded shooter from the van said.

'Who, exactly?'

'The Keenans, Waters and that young fella – Keneally.'

'What about the woman? Jessie Boyle?'

Jessie's name was said as if the words left a bitter taste in Maisie's mouth.

'I can't say for sure. I didn't see her in the woods. But she might have been waiting in the car.'

Maisie lowered her head as if she was thinking for a moment, and then, without any warning, drew back her fist and punched the bearded man directly on the nose. She may have been a short woman, but she was broad with a low centre of gravity, and the blow had all of her weight behind it. The punch landed with a popping sound, and the man, more than a head taller than his boss, staggered back a step, blood flowing freely from his nostrils and down his hairy chin.

'How long have you been working for me, Andy?'

Andy was breathing heavily. He pulled a rag from his back pocket and tried to staunch the flow from his injured face. 'I... I don't know.'

'Fifteen years. A decade and a half.'

'Yes... I suppose it would be that long.'

'It is. Now, in all that time have I ever seemed to you like a woman who wants to leave things to chance?'

Andy knew this was a rhetorical question, but for all that, he felt he should answer. At the same time, he suspected a response might earn him another punch – or perhaps something worse. Yet silence was never a good idea around Maisie Dunne. Gaps in the conversation could always be filled with violence.

'You don't, Maisie. You surely don't.'

Maisie, wild-eyed and florid-faced, even in the darkness, looked around at her men. 'Burn them out. Blast them out. I don't care how you do it, but I want them dead. All except for Joe Keenan. Him I want alive. Are we clear? And if that woman is in there...'

She paused for a second, considering Jessie's fate.

'I want to kill her myself. Make sure I get the chance before we leave Ballinamore.'

Nodding at Fred, she walked back to the van, and he opened the door and waited for her to climb in before closing it. Harry remained with the others.

'All right, lads,' Andy said to the assembled men. 'You heard Maisie. Let's get it done.'

And without further ado, they opened fire on the police station.

76

11.13 P.M.

Seamus, Joe and Frank Waters watched Maisie Dunne arrive outside.

'There's no way she's come to call off the hounds, is there?' Waters asked.

'She's here to blood them before the hunt,' Joe said.

He turned to his son. 'Right, Finbar, I want you to take Rufus and get into the cell out back. There's going to be more shooting, and I want you both safe, all right?'

'Can't I stay with you, Da?' the boy asked, and for the first time since he'd known them, Seamus heard genuine fear in the child's voice – Finbar was teetering on the brink of tears.

'I know you do, son, and there are very few things I wouldn't want to go through without you by my side. But Seamus and Frank and me, we need to do some hard things, and it will be easier for us if we know you're safe. Safer than you would be out here anyway.'

'Okay, Da,' Finbar said, and the tears came then for both of them, and they embraced quickly, with Rufus held between them, lapping at their tear-stained faces.

'Go on now,' Joe said, and the boy picked up the dog and walked quickly out the door to the cells.

Waters took some keys from a drawer and opened a cabinet behind the reception desk.

'I trust you're going to give me one of those,' Joe said, wiping his eyes on his sleeve.

The open door of the storage locker revealed four shotguns and several boxes of cartridges, as well as five Glock 19 handguns.

'You're not a guard, Joe,' Waters said, tossing a shotgun to Seamus.

'Oh for God's sake will you deputise him or something,' the detective said in irritation. 'We need all the help we can get!'

Waters gave Joe a hard look. 'It's just a loan then, okay?' he said. 'I think I have a form around here somewhere you can sign to say I've given you leave to use police equipment on a temporary basis—'

And at that moment the window behind Seamus shattered and the heavy wooden door rattled in its frame as the first flurry of bullets hit.

It had begun.

77

11.13 P.M.

Jessie moved through the woods, following the trail she and Seamus had taken when they'd fallen foul of Beezer Muldoon and his friend. The hours on the drip in the medical centre had given her time to think, and she remembered tripping over a shallow trail that intercut the larger one she'd been using. It was smaller, and she wouldn't have noticed it at all if the ground had been more passable. In fact, she'd really only discerned it with her feet.

It was almost invisible to the eye.

Using the torch on her phone, she finally picked it out and set out along it, delving into the undergrowth quickly, but finding, if she crouched low, that the way was clear. As if it were regularly used by someone of small size.

She'd gone about twenty yards when she came across a patch of loose earth. Using her pocketknife as a makeshift spade, she dug down into it, and just inches below the surface found a body – an old man, the fringe of white hair that ringed his head darkened by the brown soil. She knew who he was – this was Oliver McGee. The man whom, it seemed, had a relationship with the Abhartach. One that was now concluded.

Jessie looked at the pale corpse coldly.

And as she did, she heard movement ahead of her, up the wilderness corridor.

She took her Heckler & Koch pistol from her pocket, sat stock-still and waited.

78

11.13 P.M.

Emer O'Hagan picked her way through the woods by torch-light, following subtle signs only a trained military tracker would know to look for.

The Abhartach was careful, of that there was no doubt. He didn't use the same routes through the woods with any regularity, so there was no well-worn trail to follow. Yet no one, not even the most skilled and articulate woodsman, could move through an environment without leaving some trace of their passing, and it wasn't long before she spied a bent frond here, a disturbed patch of earth there, a branch pushed back to allow quicker passage through.

She knew he would shun the clearer parts of Derrada. His height would make using overgrown and less hospitable parts less of an encumbrance, so using a machete, she cut her way into one of these, making no effort to be quiet. In fact, she hoped her purposely clumsy activities would bring him to her.

To Emer's surprise, though, the terrifying little man didn't come.

After what felt like an age of battling her way through the densest of foliage, she came to what seemed like a tunnel among banks of briars. Following it, Emer arrived at a large mature pine tree, which blocked her from continuing through the brambles any further. Shining the beam of her torch upon its trunk, she saw the bark had been worn almost clean at various points, each just above a branch or an outcropping.

Someone had climbed the tree – and often.

Placing her torch between her teeth, Emer planted her booted foot on the lowest branch and began to climb.

The pine was taller than she'd expected. Emer wasn't exactly phobic of heights, but neither was she an experienced climber, and at one point she had to fight a crushing bout of vertigo that had her clinging to the branch above in a white-knuckle panic.

What am I doing? she asked herself. *I don't need to be here. I rebuilt my life and could have forgotten all about him. Let bygones be bygones.*

Then she felt the soft weight of the stoma bag at her waist, and the slight pull of the plastic ring that connected it to her stomach, and she knew that was never going to be possible. In that instant, she saw herself lying in the dirt in this very wood, her guts exposed to the night sky as that poisonous being leered at her, uncaring, hate-filled.

Gritting her teeth, Emer O'Hagan continued to climb.

She almost banged her head on the platform. Using the heel of her hand, she pushed and tested the base of it, and finally found a trapdoor, which opened with very little effort, swinging upwards on well-oiled hinges. Climbing through the gap, she found herself on a series of rough boards that had been lashed together using rope and attached to the trunk of the tree with what looked to be a notch and groove system. She'd heard of a tribe in New Guinea, the Kolufo people, who lived in similar dwellings. The whole structure was constructed so that weight and gravity kept it in place. It was simple yet ingenious.

The branches of the pine itself provided camouflage,

protecting the platform from being seen by anyone below, and in so doing created a roof and walls, which the owner had augmented by attaching a green tarpaulin underneath to keep the rain off. A set of high-powered binoculars had been mounted atop a tripod made of three straight sticks, and Emer saw that the tree was the perfect vantage point. From here, you could see every approach to the woods.

But this was more than just a tactical position. It was a home.

Shining her torch around the space, Emer picked out a filthy sleeping bag, a small cooking stove, some candles sitting on pieces of slate, a few books and a selection of tools. Stacked against the trunk of the tree were some cans: tomatoes, fruit and beans.

He's been living here for a while. But right now, he's not home.

She sat cross-legged for a moment, trying to sense the dread the thought of him always elicited in her. But she couldn't get it from this crude living area. All she could detect on this dark night in the forest was a feeling of deep, paralysing loneliness.

Feeling like an intruder somehow, Emer climbed back down, which proved much more difficult than getting up had been. In the dark, she could barely see the branches and found herself waving her foot about blindly into space until she found one.

It took her almost fifteen minutes to get back to the safety of the forest floor, by which time she was soaked in sweat and her arms were almost numb from holding on. Sitting for a moment to get her breath back, she spied another pathway that had been cut around the back of the pine. The opening was low down, so she wouldn't have seen it at all had she not sat down.

She continued down the trail and almost crawled into a woman who was crouched in the darkness, a handgun extended in a shooter's stance. Emer was so surprised she didn't have time to draw her own weapon.

'Emer O'Hagan, I presume,' the woman said.

'Who the hell are you?'

'I work for the police force, and I'm here to take you in.'

'I'm here to bring down the Abhartach. He owes me a debt. You won't stop me from collecting.'

Jessie paused. 'So you're not working together?'

'I hate him,' Emer said. 'With every cell in my body, I hate him.'

Jessie nodded slowly and put her gun back in the pocket of her jacket. 'Maybe we can help one another then,' she said.

Emer O'Hagan didn't wait for any further conversation. 'Come on,' she said.

Continuing down the trail, they came to a large pile of deadfall branches, some of which seemed to have been tossed aside. And leading from the pile, to her great surprise, was a set of tyre tracks.

'He's on the move,' Emer said. 'Let's see where he's going.'

The tracks led them through the trees until they met a laneway that crossed a farmer's field. As luck would have it, the field was wet and muddy from recent rainfall, which meant the tyres left a mark briefly on the road when they met it. It wasn't much, but it was enough to show that the Abhartach had driven in the direction of Ballinamore.

And that was all she and Jessie needed to know.

11.15 P.M.

Dawn Wilson and Terri Kehoe arrived in Ballinamore just as the shooting started.

Dawn brought their car to a halt a little up the street from the conflagration, killing the lights quickly to avoid detection. She needn't have bothered: the men who were blasting the police station were so busy with what they were doing, they didn't notice the dark SUV and its two occupants.

'I have to believe where there's this level of chaos going on, Jessie and Seamus are involved in it somewhere,' Dawn said.

'I think you're probably right,' Terri agreed.

'I can't help thinking they might be just a tad outnumbered though. I'm counting twelve shooters, and two sitting in the van behind. Doesn't seem fair.'

Terri peered nervously at her superior. 'What are you suggesting, Commissioner?'

Dawn switched on the engine again and, reaching across Terri, popped open the glove compartment to reveal a Sig Sauer P226 handgun, which she took out and shoved in the pocket of her uniform trousers.

'Hold tight,' she said to Terri, 'and when I tell you to, get down and stay down.'

Terri knew there was no point in arguing. Dawn Wilson had a look on her face that suggested she was absolutely committed to whatever course of action she'd decided upon, and no amount of discussion was going to dissuade her from seeing it through.

She gunned the engine once, twice, spinning the tyres in place to build torque, then roared down Ballinamore's main street, accelerating rapidly as she went. With all the gunfire, the Travellers didn't realise she was coming until it was too late.

11.16 P.M.

The front door of the police station was made of heavy teak and more than a hundred years old. Teak is hard wood, meant to withstand weather of all kinds, not to mention the usual stresses and abuses of human contact. If the Dunnes had never come into its sphere of experience, that door would probably still be standing, just as solid as it had been the day it was fitted by a journeyman carpenter while Ireland was still under British rule and its police force were called the Royal Irish Constabulary.

But the Dunnes *did* have a role to play in that door's history. A terminal one, in fact.

The first bursts of gunfire caused it to bang and rattle in its frame, but no bullets came through, and Seamus actually thought they might be okay, that the structure would hold. There was only one window to the front of the building, and someone'd had the good sense to fit it with safety glass, the kind with a metal mesh embedded to prevent it from exploding when hit.

This meant no one was going to be sprayed by glass splinters, but as a barrier to entry, Seamus was painfully aware the window would take perhaps two or three more bursts before it would simply fall into the room in one piece.

'Help me get a filing cabinet in front of this,' he said to Waters. 'It won't keep them out, but it'll make it harder for them to get in.'

They dragged a large metal cabinet over and put it in place. It wasn't tall enough to completely block the area, but only a very skinny man could get in over it.

'Is there another door to this place?' Joe asked.

'No. Just the front. These stations were built with a view someone might have to hole up in them in case of a rebellion,' Waters said.

'Lucky for us,' Seamus agreed.

There was a thud and a crack, and the door, as if it somehow knew they were talking about it, cracked down the middle. This was followed by three small explosions, each of which created holes, and bullets and shot peppered the reception desk. As if encouraged by this success, the men outside redoubled their efforts, and within minutes the door looked like it was made of Swiss cheese. Seamus, Joe and Waters crouched in the corner, trying to stay low.

'Okay,' Seamus said. 'That isn't going to hold much longer. We need to take up positions. They have to come in that door, so that gives us an advantage.'

'How?' Waters asked.

'They've no choice but to use that entrance, and the most they'll manage is two at a time,' the detective said. 'If they stick so much as a nose inside, we shoot it.'

Waters looked as if he was about to be ill.

'We'd better just hope they run out of people before we run out of cartridges,' Joe said and turned one of the desks on its side to create cover. 'There's fourteen out there at the moment, but if more arrive, we might have a really serious problem on our hands.'

As he spoke, something that sounded like a rocket launcher hit the door and it imploded, showering the room in splinters and sawdust. Joe and Waters jumped behind the desk, but Seamus remained where he was, his shotgun trained on what used to be the door. The atmosphere in the room was cloudy with dust and cordite, and for a moment the now-empty door frame was obscured. Then a dark shape loomed in it for a moment, and Seamus fired.

The shape disappeared instantly, and the detective followed his comrades behind their makeshift bunker.

'That'll give them something to think about,' he said.

Outside, they heard engines revving, and then the sound of metal grinding against metal, and something smashed into the front of the building, causing the entire wall to shake.

'Tell me they're not trying to widen the door!' Waters moaned.

Seamus ignored him, leaning his shotgun on the top of the desk, his eyes focused on the narrow gap in their defences.

But no one came through.

11.17 P.M.

Dawn Wilson watched as the speedometer on the unmarked police SUV hit eighty kilometres per hour. As it did, she pressed her foot even harder on the accelerator and turned the nose of the vehicle so it was pointed right at Maisie Dunne's blue HiAce van.

The SUV hit it front and centre with the deafening sound of screeching metal. Dawn and Terri were whipped forward as the van stopped the forward trajectory of their car and then lashed back as their seat belts prevented them from going through the windscreen. It felt like being picked up by a giant hand and shaken back and forth, and then the airbags were activated, and Terri actually passed out for a couple of seconds. The side panel of the van buckled inwards as the HiAce was pushed into the vehicles behind it, knocking them like dominoes in four different directions. The shooters scattered, but one – a tall thin man with a skinhead, wearing denim dungarees – was crushed as his VW Golf tipped over on top of him.

Dawn quickly unlocked her and Terri's seat belts and pushed the historian down on her side out of harm's way, then stepped out of the car, her Sig in hand.

The world outside looked like a war zone. The police station was riddled with more bullet and buckshot holes than she could count, and the door was missing. A man was lying flat on his back on the ground outside the station, clearly dead. Dawn assumed he'd tried to gain access but had met with some resistance.

The blue HiAce looked as if its chassis had been broken and was sitting at an odd angle, and as she watched, the driver's-side door, which had buckled, was kicked open (it took two attempts) and a well-dressed man with a neatly trimmed beard almost fell out, a cut in his forehead spilling blood down his face. Dawn could see he had a pistol of some kind in his hand.

'Sir, I am a police officer, and I am instructing you to put that weapon down. If you do not, I am authorised to use force – lethal if necessary.'

The man looked at Dawn as if he found focusing difficult and aimed the handgun at her.

'I'm asking you one more time to lower your weapon.'

The man squeezed off a round, which went right over her shoulder, and Dawn, swearing under her breath, shot him through his shoulder in turn, causing him to slam back against the door of the van. To her surprise, this seemed to only stall him for a moment, and he redirected the gun at her.

'You fucking *idiot*,' she said and put one between his eyes.

This time he went down.

Dawn saw there was another person in the van, an elderly-looking woman who seemed to be unconscious. Deciding she was no threat, the commissioner gingerly looked around the bonnet of the HiAce.

There were four vehicles behind it: another van, which had spun fully around and was now facing her, a Ford Fiesta that had been modified to look like a miniature sports car, the tipped-over VW Golf she'd noticed earlier, and a Citroën hatchback that had smashed into the wall of the station and whose bonnet had accordioned upwards. Smoke was seeping from the engine, and Dawn could smell petrol.

'I am informing the rest of you boys that I'm an officer of the Garda Síochána, and you can consider yourselves under arrest,' she called. 'I advise you to throw down your weapons right now before things get really bad for you.'

In response, the boom of a shotgun sounded in the night air.

'Have it your own way,' Dawn said and stepped out of cover, walking calmly in the direction of the shooting.

This was a trick Dawn had learned early in her career. Most gangsters aren't in gunfights very often and labour under the impression that their simply holding a gun will frighten an opponent so much they'll be unable to put up any real resistance. Meeting someone who is *not* terrified at the sight of a firearm tends to render the average criminal so confused, he's unable to shoot straight.

The man who'd fired was hiding behind the second van, and as he saw Dawn strolling towards him, calm as you like, he blinked, completely perplexed, and fired at her again, the shots kicking up dirt several feet to her left. He'd stepped out from behind the van to shoot, and Dawn, without slowing her stride, unhurriedly sighted along the barrel of the Sig and gently squeezed the trigger. The man's kneecap exploded in a red cloud.

Bellowing, he fell backwards, his weapon dropping from his limp hands and sliding across the tarmac. Dawn, still showing no sense of urgency, scooped up the shotgun and, grabbing the fallen man by the collar, dragged him back behind the van whence he'd come.

'You're a very stupid man,' she said. 'I didn't want to shoot you, but here we are.'

'You're a... you're a dead woman,' the man said through clenched teeth.

Dawn noticed there was a lot of dried blood on his face, and his nose was swollen – possibly broken.

'Now that is a silly thing to say, in that I am very obviously alive. Now please be quiet. I'm busy, if you hadn't noticed.'

'Boss, is that you?'

It was Seamus, calling from inside the police station.

'Hello, Seamus. I hoped I might find you alive and well.'

Any further conversation was drowned out by the sound of gunfire as the nine remaining Travellers made their presence felt. Dawn sat where she was, waiting for a gap to return fire. Distracted, she missed two important things.

The first was Maisie Dunne regaining consciousness and slipping out of the van where the commissioner had left her.

The second was a vintage jeep pulling into town, and a small, dark-clad figure disembarking.

11.17 P.M.

Emer O'Hagan stopped her car just up the street from where the gunfight was taking place and got out without saying a word to Jessie.

'Where are you going?' Jessie asked, but the woman struck off at a run up the main street and disappeared down a side road.

Jessie considered going after her but figured there were more pressing matters afoot. She began to move with deliberate speed towards the regular percussion of gunfire that could be heard.

She was almost upon the scene of the battle when something caught her eye in the shadows of the porch of a drapery shop. A small shape. Hooded. Hunkered down. She stopped dead and looked into the darkness.

And it looked back.

11.20 P.M.

Terri Kehoe was aware someone was shaking her.

For a moment, she thought she was back in the residential unit where she'd grown up, being woken for school, but then she was struck by a terrible pain in her neck and remembered where she was. Opening her eyes, she saw that a broad, wrinkled old woman was reaching into the SUV and had her by the shoulder.

'I need you to wake up, girlie,' the woman said. 'Time for us to go now.'

'I think I'm hurt,' Terri said. 'There was a crash...'

'Well it's been that kind of night,' the old woman said, and then Terri saw she had a small revolver in her hand, one of those ones made so women can carry them in their handbags.

'Who... who are you?' Terri asked, pushing herself back against the passenger door in a bid to get away from the strange woman.

'My name is Maisie, and if you don't come right now, I will shoot you in your right tit. How would you like that?'

Terri had a can of pepper spray in her bag, but it was on the ground at her feet, and she knew she would never reach it in time.

'I don't think I can walk,' she lied.

'Oh, I expect you'll find the strength,' Maisie said. 'I'm going to count to three, and after that I'm not giving you any more warnings. You'll be one boob lighter, and that'll be that.'

Terri looked into the little black eyes of the woman and knew she wasn't lying.

She pushed herself across the driver's seat and climbed out.

11.22 P.M.

Seamus and Joe took up positions just inside the door of the besieged station and Waters stood on a chair, placing the barrel of his gun across the filing cabinet so he could fire out the window.

'Boss, are you okay?' the detective called out.

'I'm hemmed in,' Dawn shouted back. 'There's a shooter by the Ford there, and he's got me pinned down.'

Seamus could see she was right. A young man who looked to be little more than twenty-one was lying across the roof of the red Fiesta, firing bursts with a machine gun. The detective was just taking aim at him when a shot rang out, louder and more insistent than the others, and the kid fell suddenly still.

Confused, Seamus looked about, wondering where the shot had come from, but then another rang out, and a man who'd taken up a position behind the toppled VW Golf cried out loudly and fell forward. Seconds later, two shots came close together, and the men behind the Citroën were taken.

'I can't see where it's coming from,' Joe said.

'Someone's firing from above, whoever they are,' Seamus said.

Three more shots came in quick succession.

'I think that leaves one,' Seamus said.

Joe grinned. 'Let's go and get him then.'

They both lunged away from the door but were only in time to see a fat man in an anorak running away from the cluster of vehicles, his bowed legs desperately trying to propel him from the danger. He managed to put ten yards between himself and the fracas when he was hit right in the middle of his back.

Joe and Seamus stood, their shotguns cradled in their hands, and looked about them at the devastation.

'What in the name of God just happened?' Joe Keenan asked.

'I seem to have been asking that question a lot this past week,' Seamus said.

Maisie Dunne was dragging Terri away from the SUV when the sniper on the roof began to take out her men. It happened so quickly and with such vicious precision, she barely had time to utter more than a sob of dismay, which turned to a roar of anguish when Joe Keenan emerged from the decimated station with Seamus. Maisie froze for a moment, apoplectic with anger, then screamed, '*Joe Keenan! I see you, Joe Keenan!*'

Joe, who was surveying the devastation, turned quickly, bringing his gun up, but stopped dead when he saw the woman was using Terri as a shield.

'That's my friend she's got,' Seamus whispered to Joe. 'Mine and Jessie's.'

Joe nodded and called to Maisie, 'It's over. You've lost. Now let that woman go and walk away from this while you still can. Leave this town and trouble me and mine no more.'

Maisie laughed, a loud, ugly sound on the now silent street. 'You don't get away that easily, boy. Do you see this girl?' She shook Terri viciously as she spoke.

'Are you okay there, little sis?' Seamus asked Terri.

'*Iontach*, Seamus,' Terri called back – *excellent* – though the tremble in her voice suggested otherwise.

'If you don't come with me,' Maisie said, ignoring Seamus and Terri's exchange, 'I'm going to take her instead. Everything I was going to do to you, I'll do to her, only worse. She'll be *pleading* to die before I'm finished with her.'

Seamus looked over at where Dawn Wilson was still crouched behind the second van. His boss was sighting down the barrel of her Sig at Maisie. The detective knew the commissioner to be a crack shot and that his job now was to keep the clan leader talking until Dawn could take her without harming Terri.

'You're not in a position to bargain, Maisie,' he said. 'All your men are dead. Your clan is finished. You're going to be hunted by the police no matter where you go in the world. Give it up now and maybe we can negotiate a more comfortable end to all this for you.'

'You don't seem to understand me,' Maisie Dunne said. 'I don't care about any of that. All I care about is seeing *that* man dead. None of the rest of it matters.'

The Traveller pressed the derringer into Terri's forehead so hard it grazed her skin. '*I'm not messing, you fucking pig. Now give me Joe Keenan or I will shoot her right in front of you.*'

'I thought you wanted me too,' a familiar voice called out.

Seamus suddenly saw that Jessie Boyle was standing in the shadows on the other side of the street. She had her hands raised and took a couple of steps forward, so they could see her. Maisie and Terri were now on one side of the road, Jessie opposite them on the other. Right behind Jessie was the porch of a drapery shop, wreathed in shadows. It seemed she'd been hiding in it, biding her time.

'Let her go and you can have me,' Jessie said. 'Maybe we can go somewhere and have a talk.'

Maisie turned ever so slightly to look at the behaviourist, and at that moment two things happened at once.

Dawn Wilson took her shot: as Maisie turned, she angled her body just enough so that her left shoulder was exposed, and the commissioner put a bullet in it, causing her to spin sideways, releasing Terri, the small gun flying from her hand. Knocked off balance, Maisie staggered backwards a few steps.

And as she fell away from Terri, something black and very fast sprang from where it had been crouched in the porch behind Jessie. It seemed to rise up like a cloud of rippling shadow and then descended on the Traveller woman, wrapping itself around her upper body as if consuming her. Maisie made a keening, wailing sound, which suddenly turned into a gurgle as a blade went to work on her throat, and then she collapsed onto the street, the quivering darkness still on top of her.

Maisie's fat little legs skittered and kicked for several painful moments and then became still. As the life ebbed out of her, the dark shape seemed to take form and they could see the small frame in its long black coat, the hood drawn up over the pale visage. He was holding a long-bladed knife, red now with Maisie's blood.

This close it was possible to see he was a little over five feet in height and not a young man, though how old was impossible to discern – he could have been anything from fifty to seventy. The face, marked by what Jessie took to be tribal tattoos, which made the flesh look like it was covered in ripples and waves, spoke of years of hardship and sadness.

The Abhartach rose and looked at the small group.

'It's okay,' Jessie said, slowly approaching him. 'You don't have to run.'

The scarred face seemed puzzled for a moment, then a look of something almost like relief spread across it.

'What's your name?' Jessie asked, extending her hand. 'I'm

Jessie. This is Seamus, and I think you know Joe. And that's Dawn – and Terri.'

Small dark eyes surveyed them all nervously. Then a voice, hoarse and halting from underuse said, 'I think I was once called Dominic.'

'Dominic. It's very nice to meet you.'

The Abhartach – who was also a man called Dominic – reached out to take Jessie Boyle's hand, and at that moment another shot rang out, and a hole appeared in his forehead, just above his right eyebrow. The small man released a short sob and then crumpled, as if whatever energy had possessed him was released.

Jessie gave a wail of frustration and sadness and turned to see Emer O'Hagan – the sniper on the roof – gun in hand, standing among the ruination of Ballinamore.

'Now it's over,' Emer said and spun on her heel, walking back the way she'd come.

The army arrived when it was finished.

As the locals began to creep out of their homes, where they'd been taking cover, and formed a curious cluster on the periphery of the battleground, kept at bay by the military, Regimental Sergeant Major Stewart O'Driscoll looked at the black-swathed body on the ground.

'We'll put an all-points-bulletin out on Emer O'Hagan,' he said to Dawn.

'Why? Weren't you coming to do exactly what she did?'

'You know I can't tell you that.'

'Oh fuck off, Sergeant Major. Me and my people deserve some kind of an explanation. We'll sign whatever papers you need us to promising not to divulge what we know, but you should probably be aware, we've worked out quite a bit of it already.'

The soldier pondered this for a moment, and then said, 'Is there somewhere we can get a cup of tea?'

'The health centre up the street,' Jessie said. 'The night nurse will let us in, I'm sure.'

'As good a place as any,' O'Driscoll said. 'Let me radio your people in Sligo, and then my boys can secure the site until they arrive.'

'His name is... was Dominic Boswell,' O'Driscoll said when they were seated and all had tea, except for Finbar, whom the night nurse had provided with orange squash. 'He was originally part of the Corps of Engineers. You don't need me to tell you his... his disability initially prevented him being placed on active service, but he put himself forward for whatever tasks he could, and when the guidelines changed in 1975, he was able to ship out as part of a peacekeeping mission to Ghana.'

'He didn't seem very disabled to me,' Jessie said. 'Quite the opposite.'

'I don't make the rules,' O'Driscoll said. 'At any rate, he passed the medical in '75 and was deemed fit to work with the clearance boys – they're the ones who would be sent out ahead of troop deployment to clear pathways for vehicles. Boswell proved to have a knack for that. There didn't seem to be any terrain he didn't have a feel for, and he was excellent at striking up a rapport with native populations wherever he went. His... well, his small stature seemed to make him appear less of a threat.'

'The tattoos,' Jessie observed.

'He picked them up everywhere he was stationed,' O'Driscoll said. 'He always maintained that if people were looking at those, they weren't looking at him. He called them his camouflage.'

'And he was partly right,' Jessie observed. 'No one knew what they were seeing when they spotted him in the woods.'

'It was Oliver McGee who saw the potential in him,' O'Driscoll continued. 'McGee was a training office for the Rangers by then, but he'd been moonlighting with a private security company and was recruiting personnel from right out of the ranks. It earned him a dishonourable discharge, which meant he was removed from the ranks without a pension.'

'But not before he took Dominic with him,' Seamus said.

'Took him and trained him,' O'Driscoll confirmed. 'And warped him beyond all recognition. Turned a good man into a killer of the worst kind. Boswell augmented the training he received from McGee with a lot of woodcraft and survival skills he picked up from native communities all over the world. It made him a uniquely skilled operative.'

'Ollie is dead, by the way,' Jessie said. 'I found him in a shallow grave in the woods.'

'I'll send someone in to get his remains,' O'Driscoll said. 'His family will want them.'

'How did Dominic end up in Ballinamore?' Jessie asked.

'Things all got a bit strange for Boswell in the late 1980s,' O'Driscoll told them. 'His marriage fell apart, very probably because of the impact his work was having on him emotionally and psychologically. He had a small child too, and back then fathers were rarely given anything but the most cursory access visitation. When you add the fact he was disabled, the judge refused custody and granted only a couple of hours' supervised access a month. I think that broke Boswell completely.'

'He went to ground?' Jessie asked.

'We thought he'd been killed, if I'm honest,' O'Driscoll said. 'He went completely off the radar. It was the late 1990s before we cottoned on to the fact that a spate of killings of certain individuals we had an interest in bore the hallmarks of his style. And it took us a few more years to track him to Derrada.'

'And you left him there?' Jessie said. 'I don't get that.'

'By then it was clear Oliver McGee was acting as his agent, but he was only doing a few jobs a year, and he usually took out people we weren't sorry to see the back of, so it seemed a mutually beneficial relationship.'

'So why send Emer O'Hagan in?' Terri asked.

'That was a mistake,' O'Driscoll admitted. 'My superiors wished to bring Boswell back into the fold, so to speak. There was a job we needed done that suited his skills, and we wondered how approachable he might be.'

'Not approachable at all,' Jessie said. 'Which you learned at Emer's cost.'

'I regret it,' O'Driscoll said, 'but hindsight is twenty/twenty as they say.'

'So when we were drawn to Derrada, you tried to keep us away, because you didn't want us learning the truth,' Dawn said.

'I thought one of two things would happen,' O'Driscoll admitted. 'Either you'd discover the reality of who was living in Derrada, which would be uncomfortable and embarrassing, or your people would find Boswell and he'd kill them. Neither seemed desirable. So I tried to dissuade you. And when that didn't work, I fed you tactically inaccurate misinformation. I hoped you would be distracted just long enough for us to send someone in to extract Boswell. But then Ms Kehoe got too close to the facts, and I decided to dispense with subtlety. Of course, by then the situation between Mr Keenan and the Dunnes had escalated wholesale, and there was no way I could have predicted Boswell would involve himself in that. It was a wholly unforeseen circumstance.'

'Why do you think he protected us?' Joe asked. 'I mean, I never laid eyes on that man before this evening. Finbar saw him once, but even then they never spoke.'

'I have no idea,' O'Driscoll said. 'But if I had to hazard a guess, I'd say you were the family he thought he might have had. By protecting you, he was protecting that part of himself.'

And they all sat and thought about that for a while.

EPILOGUE

THE DUST SETTLES

17 November 2018

'In the backwoods of nature's soul, I left my wild true heart.'

Angie Weiland-Crosby

Dawn Wilson came to visit them in their offices in Cork a week later. They sat around the table in the small meeting room, happy to all be together again after what felt like far too long.

'Emer O'Hagan handed herself in at a police station in Wicklow three days ago,' Dawn said. 'The Gardaí there turned her over to the military police, so I doubt we'll hear anything further about it.'

'I don't know how I feel about that woman,' Jessie said.

'I think she was as much a victim as Dominic Boswell,' Dawn retorted. 'She deserves to serve some prison time, but I think she's been serving a sentence these past five years. So I hope they go easy on her.'

'How's Richard McCarthy doing?' Jessie inquired.

'I hear he'll be walking with a limp for the foreseeable future,' Dawn said. 'Which will probably make his hunting and foraging a bit more difficult than it was before. But it'll also slow down his paramilitary activities. So I suppose every cloud has a silver lining.'

'Oliver McGee was buried yesterday in the church in Ballinamore,' Seamus said.

'It was him who was in these offices that night, not Emer,' Terri said. 'I've turned it over in my head, and the figure I saw was just the wrong shape to have been her, and the steps I heard in the bathroom – I know I didn't *see* him, but I'm sure he moved differently. And of course, there he was in the bus station the next day.'

'I hear Joe Keenan has been cleared of all wrong-doing,' Seamus said.

'More than that,' Dawn told him, 'he was offered a medal for his part in defending the station in Ballinamore, but sure, he wouldn't have any part of it.'

'At least he's safe from the Dunnes now,' Terri said.

'He's not so sure he is,' Dawn said. 'Last time I spoke to him, he reminded me Travellers have very large and very complicated family structures. He fears others will take up the baton now Maisie is dead.'

'All he did was return the affection one of the Dunnes offered to him,' Seamus said. 'Most people would see it as a compliment.'

'If only everyone saw things so simply,' Dawn said. 'Frank Waters tells me Joe and Finbar slipped away during the night two days ago, as is their God-given right. I wish them well, and I know you do too.'

'It would have been nice if they'd taken the time to say goodbye,' Seamus said, looking more than a little hurt.

'That's obviously not Joe's way,' Jessie said. 'I'm just glad he and Finbar made it out of that whole mess alive and unharmed.'

'Amen to that,' Seamus said, and Terri muttered her agreement too.

'So are you all ready for your next assignment?' Dawn asked.

'You've got one lined up for us already?' Seamus asked.

'Criminals don't stop being criminal just because you three need a holiday,' the commissioner chided.

'Brilliant,' Jessie Boyle said. 'Just brilliant.'

A NOTE FROM THE AUTHOR

Jessie, Seamus, Terri and Dawn have become like family to me. I know the sounds of their voices, how they would respond in most situations, what they like to eat and what music they enjoy listening to. Which is good, seeing as fate has tasked me with recounting their adventures. What makes that job such a pleasant one, however, is that sometimes they surprise me. And that happened a lot during the writing of this book. I like that. It's wonderful when characters take the reins and steer a story where they feel it needs to go. That's when writing becomes a kind of magic, an alchemy wrought with words.

I had no idea Terri was going to spend so much time away from the team, doing a lot of the really important investigating on her own; nor did I know she and Dawn were going to strike up a partnership. Dawn and Jessie are like sisters, but Dawn sees Terri maternally, I think, which is perhaps what Terri really needs.

Jessie and Seamus have settled into an easy friendship that is simply a joy to observe. Their conversations are so easy to write, as they've reached the point where they can say almost anything to one another and feel safe doing so. Somehow, it felt natural for these two very different people to rapidly develop a relationship of remarkable depth and understanding. A lot of what they express is non-verbal, things communicated with a look or a gesture, and I hope I capture that a little.

The other major characters in this story, Joe and Finbar Keenan, have featured in one of my previous novels, *If She*

Returned, and I knew I wanted to spend more time with them. I have long had a fascination and fondness for the culture and history of the Irish Travelling people, and I had a feeling Seamus and Jessie would get on quite well with Joe.

And in *Lost Graves* I was once again able to weave a strand of folk horror – the story of the Abhartach is a genuine piece of ancient Irish lore, and many scholars believe it was a major inspiration for Bram Stoker's massively influential horror novel *Dracula*. Some historians suggest the events the myth recounts originally took place around Derry, in the North of Ireland, but there are versions that situate the action in both Leitrim and Kerry. I loved the idea of placing the terrifying figure of the ancient vampire in the real-life environs of Derrada Woods, one of the oldest forests in Ireland, deep in the least populated part of the country. The best way to get to know more about all of these locations is to visit them. The people are friendly, the landscape is breathtaking, and I can assure you there are no vampires, serial killers or dangerous gangs lurking about. Those dwell only in crime novels. Do yourself a favour and spend some time there – you'll be glad you did.

Everyone loves a vampire story, and it gave me a chance to explore the idea of the outsider a bit more. After all, Jessie, Seamus, Terri, Dawn and even the Keenans are outsiders too. And as frightening as the Abhartach turned out to be, we learn that he's the ultimate outsider – and a victim of society's prejudices in his own right. I think he's a scary yet also very sympathetic figure. And I very much wanted my antagonist to be more than just a cardboard cut-out monster.

I hope you enjoyed meeting him.

A LETTER FROM S. A. DUNPHY

Dear reader,

I want to say a huge thank you for choosing to read *Lost Graves*. If you did enjoy it and want to keep up to date with all my latest releases and all other news, just sign up at the following link. Your email address will never be shared and you can unsubscribe at any time.

www.bookouture.com/s.a.dunphy

I hope you loved *Lost Graves*, and if you did I would be extremely grateful if you could write a review. I'd love to hear what you think, and it makes such a difference helping new readers to discover one of my books for the first time.

I love hearing from my readers. I wouldn't be able to do what I do without you. If you'd like to, you can get in touch on my Facebook page, through Twitter, Instagram or through my website. I'm pretty active on social media, and value each and every interaction with my readers.

So thanks again, and I look forward to sharing more stories with you very soon.

Very best,

Shane (S. A. Dunphy)

https://shanedunphyauthor.org

 facebook.com/shanewritesbooks

twitter.com/dunphyshane1

instagram.com/shanewritesbooks

ACKNOWLEDGEMENTS

This book could not have been written without the help of a few people, whom I must thank. My literary agent, Ivan Mulcahy, and his team at MMB Creative, are a constant source of friendship and support. I simply could not do what I do without Ivan's input and guidance, and he is, at this stage, very much a member of my family. Thank you, Ivan.

Therese Keating has been my editor for the first two books in the Boyle and Keneally series and working with her has been a pleasure and a privilege. Therese has a deep understanding of how the crime genre works, and her innate grasp of character development, pace and humour have made collaborating with her a unique experience. Thank you, Therese, for everything.

In fact, the entire team at Bookouture are simply remarkable. Kim, Sarah, Melanie, Peta, Alex, Radhika, Rhianna and all the others have made me feel truly valued and appreciated as an author. That *Bring Her Home*, book one in the Boyle and Keneally series, topped the Amazon charts in the Folklore listings and hit the Top 10 in several of the crime lists is in no small part due to their remarkable dedication to producing the best product imaginable, constantly testing, researching and fine-tuning until we got it right. It has been a massively enjoyable learning curve to be a part of the process.

This book is dedicated to my dear friend Emily Clarke, and I want to mention her here too. Emily gave generously of her time during its writing, reading some early chapters, giving me some pointers on pace and she also, during the writing of the second draft, spent an hour talking me through the Aristotelian Plot Structure, which actually proved invaluable in some pretty major restructuring I knew needed to be done. Emily is one of those rare things: a hugely talented person who puts on no airs and graces but simply tells it as she sees it. That she is also one of the most gifted writers I know is an added bonus. Thank you, Emily, for being such an amazing friend.

If you want to know more about the legend of the Abhartach, there are lots of places you can look. There are plenty of books (Patrick Joyce's *The Origin and History of Ireland's Names and Places* was published in 1875, but my local library has a copy and I learned lots about Leitrim and its legends and stories in that fine old book – it has a great retelling of the Abhartach legend) but you'll also discover many interesting things online. Check out *https://www.theirishroadtrip.com/the-abhartach/* for a fascinating breakdown of the various different versions of the tale, which I found really enlightening.

Paul O'Brien and Wayne Fitzgerald's *Shadow Warriors: The Irish Army Ranger Wing* (2020, Mercier Press) was a huge resource for me when writing this book, and I highly recommend it to anyone interested in discovering more about Ireland's special forces, who really are considered some of the best in the world.

Finally, I would like to thank you, dear reader. Launching a new series is always scary, but it felt like Boyle and Keneally arrived to a very warm welcome. The comments, messages of support and glowing reviews *Bring Her Home* received were hugely heartening and meant I could throw myself into writing *Lost Graves* with a real sense of optimism.

And there are so many more stories to be told. I know you'll enjoy sharing them with me.

Printed in Great Britain
by Amazon